# ROCK REVIVAL

# ROCK REVIVAL

NATANIA BARRON

*For Llana Barron, my bandmate from day one.*

# CHAPTER ONE

WE WERE RIGHT in the middle of laying down Kurt's bass track on "Eleven Melodies" when everything went to shit. I mean, we'd seen it coming for weeks. As usual, Tom had been showing up less and less to studio practice sessions, letting us set the stage for most of the songs before gracing us with his presence, always with a knowing smirk and his infallible pitch. He'd seemed distracted, even more than when he was using regularly, but we'd come to accept it. Having Tom in the studio always meant more griping anyway, so we didn't really argue with his irregular schedule. At least he was singing.

Our focus was on finishing the album. So when Tom burst in with his announcement, I think we all expected he was leaving or getting married or going solo or something.

I know what you're thinking, but I knew he was not talking drugs. God, we'd been through that enough over the years for me to know what it looked like. Tom and his addictions, man. Checking in and out of rehab like it was a frigging Foursquare spot.

But honestly, I'd have taken coke and weed and whisky over what happened next any damned day of the week.

People think they know Tom Chesley. He's got the gait and swagger and charm only the most rare of British imports manage (see:

Robert Plant), and yes, he's always eclipsed the rest of us in the band without so much as half a thought. Being so effing handsome has a lot to do with it—his mane of corkscrew blond hair, those piercing green eyes, those abs. Even I'm not immune, as you know. Having lived with him (the longest relationship I've ever had, and it wasn't quite a year) and slept with him (fourteen times—not sure why I counted) and dragged him drunk and stoned and bleeding out of gutters (more times than I slept with him), well, my awe of him never really went away. He's intoxicating to be around. Intense and childlike and talented, but fragile, sentimental, and surprisingly hard on himself. And of course, he's always had that need, that predisposition, toward addiction. Maybe that's why we were so drawn to each other for a while.

Yeah, I'm not doing a good job of starting this thing off. Let me try again.

So, Kurt and I had been in the studio for like fourteen hours before Tom came in, and we were starting to get drunk and testy, which is never a good combination. James was dealing with his girl of the moment, and Kurt was struggling to pay attention let alone produce anything worth keeping on the track. It was up to me to prevent Kurt from going all Prog-Rock on us and finding some musical tangent James was inevitably going to hate.

"This riff is boring," Kurt said, reaching for his drink in between takes. Jeff, our intrepid engineer, had sent me in to give Kurt a pep talk. "I mean, it needs something more. I can just—"

"Boring is good. This part of the song builds, remember?" I tweaked his chin. He'd dribbled the remnants of his drink, a now watered-down gin and tonic. "Just take it slow, and save the excitement for the chorus."

"I fucking hate taking it slow."

Kurt was quickly approaching the point where he just didn't care anymore. Dangerous territory. I was starting to worry we were never going to get the bass part done tonight, which would give James reason to go on a tirade when he got back. Our last album, *Lester Hotel*, Kurt and James had gotten into it so badly (proof of James's crush on him, Kurt had insisted) we'd used a session bassist for two songs in order to make the deadline for the album. No one wanted to repeat that again.

"Yeah, so your boyfriends tell me," I said.

"Katie..." he warned.

"You guys figure it out?" Jeff asked over the intercom. "It's one a.m."

As if I needed the reminder. The last joint had lost its effect hours ago, and I knew more liquor was going to put me over the edge into sleepyland. I'd had enough of sleeping on studio couches over the years, not to mention roach-ridden motels. Knowing my own Tempurpedic bed was waiting for me one cab ride away was becoming dangerously tempting.

"Can you play back the last take?" I asked Jeff over my shoulder. "From 'when I fell into the weeds' and stop it just before the bridge."

We sat back and listened, and sure enough, Kurt started going off on a musical spiral about six bars in. It wasn't that the bass line was bad. Quality was never Kurt's problem. It just didn't fit, which was typical. Making music with Kurt was a thrill-ride, but sometimes reining him in was tough. And nowhere was it more obvious than recording with October Revival. Like an Impressionist playing with a bunch of Cubists. It wasn't his fault—he wasn't in the original lineup and had spent years in jazz bands while I was playing coffee shops. But we made it work. When Sara left, we had to.

"Hear that?" I asked. "That run you do in E flat. It's pretty, but it sounds like it's from another song. It's pulling away from Tom's vocals."

Kurt rolled his eyes. "You told me you wanted something different there. It's different. And Tom's vocals aren't even final. We're still using the same fucking take he laid down in April, and he doesn't even get the lyrics right."

He leveled me with his mismatched stare from under his black curls. A journalist once implied that his heterochromia proved his crazy tendencies, an old-world superstition brought into the twenty-first century. I don't think Kurt Bastian is crazy. I think he's madly gifted. I think his intensity is off-putting, and it makes people uncomfortable. Watch any interview with him and you see it. He's playing a game. He's always playing games. Hell, sometimes I think he's been playing a game with me for years, and he's my best friend.

That night while we attempted to record "Eleven Melodies," I was pretty sure he wasn't going to relent. I could sense we were approaching the point where we were going to argue well past sunrise unless he just decided to play nice. But Kurt's bouts of stubbornness are legend; no one knows it more than me.

I gave him my most earnest smile, adding doe eyes for effect. It was all I had left.

"Aw, hell," he said and started fiddling with what would eventually be the final take. I didn't have time to celebrate, though, because Tom Chesley showed up.

As usual, Tom was with his entourage. Though this group was smaller, more buttoned up. I don't even know the names of half of the people he hung around with, as they changed so frequently, but there were a few you could usually expect. Tom's cousin Dougie was a pervasive presence most days, especially if drinking was involved. Oh, and we could sometimes expect a woman named Annisse who, on top of spelling her name in a gloriously stupid way, was some sort of fortune teller or palmist or something. She also fucked Tom whenever he wanted.

Dougie and Annisse, however, were both missing from the group. There were two young women with long, braided black hair, wearing saris but clearly not of any Asian persuasion. Maybe sisters though. Pretty but not the kind of knockouts that Tom typically preferred (me being a wild exception to his big boobs and butt rule). There were also two men, one with dreadlocks and a pasty complexion wearing lazy hippie clothes, and another portly guy in a button-down carrying a briefcase.

I exchanged looks with Kurt, who looked even more perplexed than me. The intercom was off, but Tom was talking with Jeff animatedly. He was clean, which was a plus, and had his hair tied back. A striped polo shirt and some dark jeans completed his look, and I didn't have to see to know he'd be wearing his favorite flip-flops. You had to bribe him to wear anything else. Dusty had, rather famously, bribed him with heroin once to wear a pair of custom sneakers on stage during Bonnaroo during our darkest years.

"What are they doing?" Kurt asked me.

Jeff and Tom embraced, clapping each other on the back, heads buried in shoulders.

Then everyone went to their knees, and their hands went up in the air.

"Holy shit, Kurt," I said. "I think they're *praying.*"

---

**Rolling Stone: Tell us about your relationship with Tom. How did it shape your music?**

*Kate Styx:* There's not much to say that hasn't already been said. I mean, I'm pretty transparent in what I write, and you don't have to listen to much of our catalog to hear what I have to say on the matter. I don't usually talk too much about it, y'know? To me, it's a short story. We were together a while, it didn't work out, but we've both moved on. He's a dear friend, one of the best things in my life.

**RS: You've said "Lost and Loving" best reflects your relationship. Why is that?**

*KS: [laughs]* I was really mad when I wrote that. We'd just broken up for good, and he was so calm about the whole damned thing. Me? I was a mess. But that song just sort of fell in my lap one night when I was feeling really stupidly sorry for myself. I had a working demo in two hours and woke James up at four a.m. to get his take on it. He loved it, tweaked it a bit, and we laid down the track two weeks later. Tom really is like a river, as hackneyed as that reference might be. I could tell he was sorry we'd broken up, but he just kept moving on. I wasn't so good at it. I don't like to talk too many details, but I still feel the same way in the song. I probably always will.

**RS: That was your second number one hit. Do you feel**

**strange having to revisit such raw emotion every time you play live?**

*KS:* After a while, it just becomes a song. Sure, I bet if the band broke up and didn't play for twenty years and got together again, it'd have some meaning again. You know, like the way Stevie Nicks and Lindsay Buckingham did with "The Chain" during their reunion special. The air was charged, man. The way they look at each other. I think it's part of going through something like this with someone and then having to continue working with them. Time is weird. Distance is important. Perspective changes. But I don't think you ever stop loving someone entirely. You share something special with them on stage. And sometimes, even when they're not singing with you any longer, you remember. It sort of gets under your skin that way.

**RS: You famously ousted Sara Plummer and brought aboard your childhood friend Kurt Bastian to replace her. There's been a lot of speculation around the change in lineup. Care to set the record straight?**

*KS:* There's nothing to be set straight. Listen, all my music life I've been collaborating with bassists. Before Sara, there was Kurt. When Sara left—and she did leave on her own, I didn't "oust" her —I needed someone I could trust, musically and personally. Kurt's been playing music all his life, and he's solid. After all the drama of the last few years, we really wanted someone strong to root us through the last album and tour. It wasn't a hard decision to make. But he's with us for the long haul, and we're excited to see where we go.

**RS: He's said some unflattering things about James Vayne in the press. How do you respond to that as his friend?**

*KS: [pauses to think]* Listen, I'm not here to gossip about my bandmates or apologize for what they say or pick apart their motivations. They are who they are. No, we don't always get along. Yes, sometimes we say stuff we don't mean. But in the end, it's the music that matters. And right now, we're as good as we've been in years. Ever, really. I think our earlier dysfunction was keeping us from our potential. Now we've moved on, and we're making progress. We're growing.

**RS: Tell us something about the new album.**

*KS:* Well, we're taking a much slower pace, for one. The first two were sort of done at the speed of light. We had crazy schedules and all these big early successes. Not to say we're not thankful for the fans or the support, but it's been taxing on all of us. So, we wanted to really take the time with this album this time around to do something to represent a return to our roots. I'm really happy with where we're at right now.

**RS: Has October Revival settled down? You and your bandmate Tom have made some intriguing headlines in the past, especially Tom's battle with drugs.**

*KS:* Tom's doing better. He really is. I've had my wild moments, but it's nothing I can't handle. It is rock and roll, after all.

# CHAPTER TWO

I WOKE up the next morning with a headache that started in my back molars and ended somewhere around my pinkie toes. My first thought had nothing to do with the previous night's religious antics. It had to do with finding coffee and some eggs and wondering why the hell Kurt was playing his bass in my living room. The pulse of his Warwick was a thudding counterpoint to my own heartbeat, and as I staggered out of my bedroom, still fumbling for my robe, I almost fell over.

Still a little drunk I guess. Yes, there had been some bourbon. We'd gotten the track right after that bizarre prayer session and gone out to Stolcie's Pub and… I don't remember anything after. Typical me.

Kurt was bright-eyed, though. He even looked rested. He never drank to excess, not since I'd met him in college, and he seemed to live on a constant infusion of green tea.

"What time is it?" I asked.

He put down the bass and gave me a once-over. "Does it matter?" he asked. "You need a beauty rest reboot. The last application didn't work."

"Fuck you, Kurt. I already feel like shit," I said, rubbing the side of my face. It was inexplicably sticky. My hair smelled like cigarettes and was crusty. Apparently, I'd gone to that point. Again.

I swear. I used to be able to manage my alcohol. I could drink and function the next day. But since Sara left the band and I broke up with Tom, my confidence in my own drinking tolerance was starting to wane. I was blacking out. Making headlines, as people noted. I was accused of stealing a scarf from a department store in New York a few months ago, and even though we settled (it was a fucking thousand-dollar scarf), the worst part about the whole thing was I didn't remember a second of any of it. There were plenty of surveillance tapes though.

When I started to say something about Tom, Kurt put his fingers to his lips and gestured behind him. That's when I heard someone rattling around in the kitchen and noticed the smell of eggs and bacon for the first time.

I only needed to look at the kitchen archway for Kurt to answer my unsaid question.

"Oh. And Tom's here," he said lightly, suppressing his smile by turning and pretending to tune his bass. The little amp he was using crackled, and he kicked it with his foot.

"Tom. Why is Tom here?" I asked.

"He followed us home from the pub last night. Which, in hindsight, was kind of helpful. You were a mess. You were singing 'Amazing Grace' at the top of your lungs by the time we wrestled you into the cab."

I could feel myself blushing, and I pulled at my matted hair. Knowing Tom was seeing me this messed up was doubly uncomfortable. To say I never quite got over him would be a good way of putting it. I let him move on, but part of me never did. Love is like that sometimes. But the thought of having to deal with a whole religious judgment thing along with all our other baggage? Christ, I grew up with that kind of religion, and it almost killed me. Once upon a time, I'd lived just outside Atlanta as Katherine-Anne Mendenhall Marshall, and the stink of the church still lingered around me sometimes. It made me think of picnics and pulpits and my father and my drunk, self-medicating mother. And worse things.

Hence the bourbon. Nothing chases away the blues like straight Kentucky bourbon. My mom's family is from Kentucky. It might be why I've always been so partial to the stuff. Straight from the source.

Tom walked into the living room, kicking away some refuse on the floor. It'd been a week since the maid had been by, and with all the studio time, the whole apartment was a real wreck, but Tom's eyes were kind when he saw me. Like a kid seeing a puppy in a box with a "Free" sign. Poor soul. Poor lost Katie. If only she could accept Jesus Christ as her lord and savior and run away with me to happy land, everything would be fine…

"Hi, Tom," I said.

The clouds shifted just right outside, sending yellow light through the windows and shooting across Tom's hair. He stood there, haloed, carrying my breakfast, and smiling like I hadn't seen him do in five years. I was going to say something, but my voice vanished.

"Oh, Katie," Tom said. "Sit down and eat, darling. I made you eggs and toast, sprinkled it with Bacos. You didn't have anything else."

I had such a weird sense of *déjà vu*. I'd done the same thing for Tom dozens of times. In his heyday, he made my taste for weed and booze look Spartan in comparison. I'd be the one in his crappy motel room scrounging food together from the convenience store down the street or ordering in if the venue was better. I'd wash his hair and kiss his cheeks and promise him he'd feel better, making sure he stayed hydrated and conscious. He'd OD'd on me twice during the Dark Years ('05–'09), and I'm quite sure I saved his life at least once.

The Bacos had already swollen from the moisture and were perched on top of the omelet like rat poop, but I took the plate anyway. He came back from the kitchen with coffee, and in the space between, I just stared at Kurt. He was enjoying the whole thing. Bastard.

"Thanks, Tom," I managed. I'd downed half the coffee but was having a difficult time with the eggs. I didn't know I'd had Bacos in my kitchen, so the likelihood they were eons past their expiration date was pretty damned high. Not that it matters with Bacos, necessarily.

Tom sat down next to me. I cringed inwardly, feeling the heat of his body so near. I couldn't remember the last time he'd been so close, and all that could come to mind were inappropriate thoughts and memories of what had happened between us in bed. Half of the time he was too drunk or stoned to be anything to write home about, but there had been moments during our time together I wouldn't ever be able to forget.

"Did you get enough sleep?" he asked. "You look..."

"Like shit."

"A bit." Tom smiled. "Your hair looks good, though."

Kurt rolled his eyes and put down his bass. His phone was ringing, and he excused himself, but it was good enough timing to be suspect. Kurt was acting cool, of course, even though I knew he was writhing inside due to this whole new Jesus thing.

"I wanted to talk to you," Tom said. He linked his long fingers together and stared at his hands. Which was good. Because I was useless while he stared into my eyes.

The bit of egg I'd put in my mouth tasted like bacon-flavored soap. I swallowed hard and went for more coffee, hoping to delay things. I knew what Tom was going to say. It'd happened a few years back when he'd entered AA, though this was before we'd technically started dating. He'd apologized for his behavior and begged forgiveness and all that, and even asked me to go to a meeting with him. Which didn't happen. But like AA, I wasn't expecting this to stick.

This time was different though. This time there was more baggage between us than our tour bus could carry. Things he should have apologized for and hadn't. It's not that I minded being apologized to. It's that I hated it took Jesus for him to do it. Tom's always been a good kid, just one with way too much of an addictive personality. Typical lead singer, you know? Full of charisma, but always trying to fill the void with stuff that makes him feel something more than everyday existence. For a while, I was that drug. Then I wasn't. And we still had to work together. I loved his simplicity, his ebullience—he really has always been the sunniest person among us, even during his blitzes.

"There's the bit in the 'Last Time We Talked'—y'know, the line about pretending to forget. That after a while it becomes true," he said.

"James wrote that line, I didn't," I replied. Was Tom Chesley quoting our own song lyrics in his apology? Good God.

He laughed. "Well, the sentiment's right. I've spent the last year pretending that I don't remember any of the things we went through. Any of the hurt I did to you. Telling myself that you're strong enough and wise enough to get on with your life and what I did…somehow doesn't matter."

I didn't have anything to say. I couldn't eat any more, so I put the food down and curled up on the opposite side of the couch from Tom, cradling my coffee protectively.

"Uh, go ahead," I said, feeling continually more sheepish.

"I just need to ask you to forgive me," he said, looking at me again.

I pretended to pick something out of the coffee cup to avoid the long green-eyed stare. "Tom…"

"No. Some things were downright magical about the two of us together. Just…" I could tell he was searching for a swearword, but avoiding it. "Really amazing. And I…messed it up. It wasn't that I chose other women over you, though it's sort of what it looked like— it's that I chose drugs over you. And you chose…"

"I, um, I really don't want to talk about this right now. My head hurts." What an understatement. Most of my skin felt as if it'd been poached in oil the night before. Dehydration, for the win.

"I don't expect you to forgive me right now. But I'd like to ask you to go to church with me on Sunday and—"

"Tom."

He was being so fucking earnest. He had tears in his eyes. "It's just… I think you could benefit from some peace—"

"*Tom.*" I said it a little louder.

In typical Tom fashion, he was plowing over me. I guess a religious experience didn't get rid of every irritating quirk. He touched my knee. "Katie, darling, you need this as much as I do…"

I was on the verge of slapping his hand away. Church. Fucking *church*! My skin wasn't just on fire, it was crawling now, and I stood up out of the chair, ready to lay down to law. To remind him why I would never go to church again, that I'd already been through this. About the years of hypocrisy, my dad's affairs, my mother's alcoholism, the lying and politics and bullshit. The whole homosexuality thing. The whole teenage pregnancy thing I had never told any of my bandmates because I'd buried that shit so deep down inside of me it had crystallized and turned into some creepy bezoar. The whole life I'd kept wrapped up and separate and secret—it was all threatening to come out and spill all over the floor like a dish of upturned communion wafers.

Then Kurt walked in, smirking.

"Tom," he said, diplomatic and smooth, "you're wanted at the studio for some vocals. Just heard from Dusty. You're going to be late."

Kurt. My beloved gay angel.

Tom winced and rubbed his forehead. He'd gone a bit pale.

"Yeah. You should go," I said. Even my voice sounded flat and bitter in my own ears. I should have told him to get the fuck out of the apartment, but I gave him a fake smile that said I didn't care if he got hit by a car on his way out.

"We'll talk later," Tom finally said, as if I'd agreed and Kurt was not part of the deal. While I doubted he'd try, I would have *paid* to see Tom talk to Kurt about religion. He was even more scarred than I was, and he wasn't even a rehabilitated Evangelical like me. His mother was part of some fringe sect of Christianity that believed the Rapture was about to happen every few years. She had enough food, provisions, and guns in her basement to militarize a small island nation. And shoot Kurt if he ever showed up at the house again.

All things considered, I think Kurt and I tied in the religious cuckoo department.

Kurt and I were due in the studio in an hour, so I went back to the bedroom to get ready. I had to wash the puke out of my hair and look somewhat presentable, but I just wanted to bury myself in a sweatshirt and be done with it. Some journalists from *Spin* were going to be there in the evening to talk about the album, and, oh God, I just couldn't imagine what sort of field day they were going to have with Tom and his new religious experience.

Jesus.

I found my phone smeared with something sticky—I figured I must have used it after it'd gotten soiled, hence the sticky spot on my face—and found a series of texts from James. The last was from two minutes previous, and he responded quickly.

**James:** Someone needs to commit him. Dear God, I'm so furious right now.

…

**James:** Kate. Katie. Wake up.

…

**James:** Drunkard. Cunt!

…

…

**Kate:** Good day, sunshine.

**James:** He called me last night. Told me.

Tell me this is a dream.

This is a dream.

Kate.

Cakes.

**Kate:** It is a dream. Full of Jesus monsters.

Let me go back to bed.

**James:** Dusty's furious. Kyle's furious. No one wants to talk about it.

**Kate:** He's your friend. Your fellow countryman.

Can't you talk sense to him?

**James:** Sense? You're still talking about our Tom?

**Kate:** Haha. He asked me to go to church with him.

**James:** Did you smack him round the head?
**Kate:** Kurt arrived just in time to prevent me.
He means well.
I think.
My dad would approve. Always said Tom needed Christ in his life.
**James:** I want to vomit.
**Kate:** I did that plenty, for the both of us. Goddamn bourbon.
**James:** gtg — omw to the studio
**Kate:** What are we going to do, J?
**James:** Fuck if I know, mate. My people don't talk about religion. This is not something I'm prepared for.

---

**SPIN: Tell us about how you met Tom Chesley.**

*James Vayne:* Well, I'd been doing the songwriting thing a while in a band called Marlowe's. That's where I met Tom again. I knew him from school. We'd been mates in school, but he was a few years younger than me. He started out sort of half stalking us, showing up at gigs all over Cambridge. He was afraid to talk to me, apparently, and one day my mate Rob tells me this kid says he can sing better than our current lead singer, Jim. We all have a laugh and then let this kid do some singing and he fucking blows it out of the water. Literally, my knees went weak hearing that voice. Part choir boy, part I don't know what. Like nothing I'd heard before. Like Freddy Mercury married Paul McCartney and had a darling little boy. I mean, I knew Tom before. He was this scrawny, posh kid who got all the girls. I just had no idea he had that sort of talent in him.

**SPIN: And the rest is history?**

*Vayne:* Pretty much. There really wasn't much discussion. We wanted to be a better band, and Tom was the key to that. Up until that point, we'd been middling. Two years later, all that was left of Marlowe's was Tom and me, and we were crumbling in that incarnation, so we packed it up to New York. Which is where we met Kate and Sara.

**SPIN: Why "October Revival"?**

*Vayne:* Our first time in the States we came across some signs in Boston for a revival meeting, a concept that was utterly foreign to me. It was entitled "July Revival!" with all these bad fonts and a picture of Jesus with an electric guitar. We were baffled by it, but I liked the sound of the word. We settled on October Revival as a bit of a joke, since October is when everything starts to die, right? That and the name wasn't taken.

**SPIN: And how did you meet Kate Styx and Sara Plummer?**

*Vayne:* We met at a coffee house gig. Our lineup was pretty horrible at the time. We had this practically homeless bass player, with Tom playing tambourine and bongos and whatnot because the drummer was all over God's creation most nights. Truly abysmal. Anyway, we saw Kate and Sara playing with Blue Trixies, and I was blown away by their original material. The two of them had solid vocals, but it was really the words and melodies that spoke to me. I went up after and asked Sara who wrote their songs, and she directed me to Kate. It took a month or so to woo them both away, but it happened eventually.

Writing with Kate isn't really work. We're friends, and we don't have any of that baggage that, y'know, Kate and Tom or me and Sara have. There's just this open, trusting relationship there in which each of us can express what we're thinking musically. It's really one of the most amazing connections I've ever had with another person. We don't always agree, of course. I'm sounding like fucking Pollyanna. But really, I can't say enough about how thankful I am for what we have.

**SPIN: You've been described as a yin and yang songwriting duo. Do you feel like your strengths complement one another?**

*Vayne:* Oh, absolutely. It's not entirely spot on, that yin/yang thing. But I'd say in general Kate is a very organic writer. She sort of meanders into a song, pulls up her sleeves, and mines it out. I help her sometimes, but that initial phase she usually works on by herself. Then it's a matter of chiseling away what works and doesn't work. That first idea, too, it's not always hers. We have these sessions where we talk about what kind of songs we want to "find" and usually her process stems from that. I'd say, when it comes to the studio, I spend a lot more time on the ground than she does. I love getting in and working to crystallize a song, to really get it to where it's honed and perfect.

**SPIN: How have the band's relationships affected the music?**

*Vayne:* A fuck-ton, obviously. [Laughs] I mean, we're lucky that we've kept together so long going through as much as we have. Letting Sara go was one of the hardest things I ever had to do, but it had to be. In the end, our relationship couldn't withstand that. The band couldn't withstand that stress. With Tom and Kate, it's different. They seem to move in different circles, now, like their time together sort of existed and now it doesn't. In some ways, I envy them. But obviously, if you listen to the music, I don't think that relationship is exactly resolved. Kate's an intense person, and after she experiences things, they resonate with her for a long time.

**SPIN: October Revival has been called the Fleetwood Mac of alternative piano rock. Do you agree with that?**

*Vayne:* Well, no, not really. I mean, I guess people like to make comparisons. For a while we were the whole English/American thing, the girls and the boys. But, vocally, Fleetwood Mac always had a varied front—Stevie, Christine, Lindsay, all singing, all creating, all sort of driving against each other until the whole thing imploded. For us, the girls aren't the pretty faces—which they are, I assure you—but they're part of the collaborative force. The personalities aren't driving against each other. Kate and I are writing songs for Tom to sing and, of course, sometimes our own lives bleed into that as well. And sure, I think there are some instances where the intensity is obvious. But it's far more about the music than the cult of personality.

**SPIN: You've never made headlines for drug abuse or**

**alcoholism or infidelity like your bandmates have. What's different about you?**

*Vayne:* Hell, that's a loaded question. Look, I'm not going to comment on Tom or Kate's struggles. That's just not fair of me. They're my bandmates. I love them like family, y'know? I just find my drive in the music. I've never felt the draw to excess. Sure, I had my wild days, but I guess it's never been part of my creative process. I do my best to stay strong and hope that, as time continues and they keep working at it, they'll come to this side too.

# CHAPTER THREE

I COULD HEAR the yelling before I even entered the studio. Kurt was a few paces behind me, looking scandalized and enjoying the whole drama-rama considerably more than any person ought to. That's probably because he hadn't had to deal with this as long as I did. He was still, and likely always would be, an outsider.

No, I couldn't see the humor in it. We didn't have to ask what the problem was. Jesus had entered October Revival, and things were heating up already. James had endured Tom's antics longer than anyone, and there was no way he was taking this sitting down.

Opening the door as slowly as I could, trying not to make too much noise, I saw the scene unfolding. Jeff—who was the one who had introduced Tom to the whole Christian scene a few months back —was standing protectively by Tom near the mixers. Tom looked placid, but he was keeping something in. I could tell he was furious but doing his best to stay in control, which, all things considered, wasn't one of his strong points. Especially when he and James got into it, which was slightly less often than when Kurt and James did.

The other tech, Ian, gave me a terrified look. Like a crazed cat put into a corner by a bulldog.

I felt Kurt squeeze my shoulder before I could even open my

mouth. I've always had a habit of walking into their arguments. I'm grateful Kurt has my back sometimes and prevents me from getting overinvolved. It was a lot harder when Kurt wasn't part of the band. Sara was always a catalyst, a lightning rod for disagreements. And typically it had to do with my relationship with James. She was jealous. Even when nothing was going on.

"This is bullshit, Tom. You know it is," James was shouting. "It's not any different than anything else you've pumped into your bloodstream. I keep thinking you're just fucking with me, mate. *Are* you fucking with me?"

"I'm full on serious, James. One hundred percent. This is not easy for me," Tom said, looking genuinely hurt. "I thought you'd be happy for me."

"I've put up with your shit for a long time, mate. But fuck if I'm going to turn our tour bus into a prayer wagon."

"I'm not asking you to change anything. I'm just asking you to think about forgiving me. I'm forgiving you—"

It was not the right thing to say to James Vayne.

James took a threatening step forward, chin jutted out. "Oh, you can take your forgiveness and—"

"Hey, hey," Jeff said, holding a protective arm across Tom as if James was going to strike him (which, in his defense, had totally happened before on multiple occasions). "This is a personal choice."

"Personal choice? Are you fucking serious, Jeff?" James asked. He raked his hand through his hair, messing up his curls so they stuck up in the front. "When you're in a band, you don't get to make *personal* choices. Everything affects everyone. *Everything.* Jesus!"

It got worse. Much worse. James is passionate. But the other side of that is a temper that doesn't turn off. You wind him up and he explodes, and it takes hours—sometimes days—for him to get himself back together.

Kurt and I sat down on the leather couch, exchanging uncomfortable looks and texts.

**Kurt:** It's almost hot.
**Kate:** Oh, FFS.
**Kurt:** I mean, not my type. But sometimes I wish they'd just kiss and get it over with.
**Kate:** In your dreams.
**Kurt:** Like it's not in yours?
**Kate:** Not usually. Unless I'm all out of fantasies with you and Paul.
**Kurt:** That is low, even for you.
**Kate:** He would be a little low for you, you're right. But I'm sure you could figure out the height disparity just fine.

KURT PUNCHED MY SHOULDER, and we giggled inappropriately. We were planning to leave altogether when Dusty Brown, our manager, came in a flurry of fringe and sequins. Almost six feet tall and built like a Valkyrie, her natural blond hair fell to the middle of her back and made the ubiquitous designer sunglasses that much darker. She doused herself in a variety of perfumes, but most often Shalimar. The scent preceded her.

She didn't have to say anything to get James to shut up, she just sent him a withering glance (presumably, since she kept her sunglasses on) and he snapped his mouth shut and flared his nostrils, a sign he was letting her have the floor. I wouldn't say the two of them had a particularly good relationship, but they did respect each other. I never knew what to make of Dusty, honestly. She was just on the opposite side of the woman spectrum from me: bossy, loud, flamboyant, social. In all our business dealings, James has always taken responsibility. I can hardly keep track of the various agents and managers and PR folks, but he's got the talent for it. Not to mention he's the only reliable member of the band.

"Now listen up. This is what's going to happen," Dusty began, tossing back her hair and claiming Ian's swivel chair for her own. She delivered a smirk in Tom's direction. "Tom. Honey. I'm happy for you. Really, I am. But if you want this to work, you're going to keep your thoughts and beliefs to yourself right now. We're entering the final phases of the album, and I'm up to my neck in journalist requests. It's already big news that this is your first sober recording in six years; let's not get the 500 Club involved."

Dusty swiveled in her appropriated throne, pointing to James. "And that means we all keep quiet. All I want to hear from you—all of you—is album talk. Let's get *Something Else* out the door before we do anything to alienate an already strained fan relationship. Religion is even harder to cover up than an overdose."

"That's one way of putting it," Kurt muttered.

"I'm not going to candy coat," said Dusty, squaring her shoulders. It's part of a speech she's given us a thousand times, and I tried to prevent myself from visibly rolling my eyes. "And of course, that includes anything added to the current lineup. No lyrical emoting, you two. No Gospel redirection. You've got half an album to write already, but it's going to be straight, typical, understated. What people expect out of October Revival, okay?" She waggled her fingers at James and then at me.

James sighed. "Of course."

I nodded.

She continued, apparently satisfied we will follow her commandments for the most part. "When it comes to my part in this whole business venture, it has nothing to do with feelings or faith or religion. I'm here to manage your asses so you get this album done and make money. Unless you've changed your mind about wanting money."

"I still like money," Kurt responded.

"Me too," I said.

"Good. Listen, I've heard the work you're all doing, and it's great. All the synthesizer shit from the last album is done. This is back to the heart of what people want from you. People are going to *love* this. The critics are going to love this. The whole social mediasphere is buzzing with anticipation," Dusty said, standing again. "So keep going. Heads down. Focus. No crazy shit."

We all muttered assent.

Yup. Six minutes. Which was slightly longer than she usually stuck around—my guess was that the severity of the situation called for the extra minute.

Dusty clapped her perfectly manicured hands together like a contented Kardashian. "There. All understood now?"

She got nods from most of us, and even a reluctant sigh and thumbs up from Tom. He was holding out. First week out as a new shiny Christian, and he was already cracking. Or, at least, figuring out the world was a far scarier place than it was the day before.

Before she left, she turned around and offered her last word of warning. "Just focus on the music."

The room erupted again when Dusty left. It wasn't as if I expected her to get the boys to behave. So, yeah, I did intervene by grasping James by the elbow and half wrestling him out of the door and down the hallway before he realized Tom wasn't in striking distance. I knew Kurt would start working with Tom right away—the one thing that always got Tom out of a funk was singing. It's just he forgot that half the time. Considering we managed to get him to the studio, it was a good start.

I almost laughed as I walked with James, arm in arm like brother and sister. He was cooling down and didn't say a word as we descended the staircase at the studio and toward our favorite coffee shop on Edgehill.

"I hate this fucking town," James said, as if on cue, as we rounded the corner from 16th. "I hate this fucking country. I hate everything."

"Don't mince words, James. It isn't good to keep it all in."

"I almost hate you. But you're too dear." He almost cracked a smile, then he shook his head. "It's because we're *here* that this happened."

He had a point. When we were based in New York, it was highly unlikely Tom would have stumbled upon the kind of religious zealots Nashville spawns. But we'd relocated for Tom's sake in the first place. LA and New York, they're amazing music cities. You can practically hear the songs moving around you as you walk, but there's too much temptation for someone like Tom. Nashville was beautiful and hot and Southern. We were a handful musicians in a huge sea of them.

Being part of music was expected, and with it came a surprisingly nice amount of anonymity.

"It started with AA," I reminded him. "Even though AA didn't work out, I think the seeds were planted then, y'know?"

"No. I don't know. My parents are fucking Hindus, Katie, English Hindus. We don't talk about Jesus, or Shiva, or Buddha, or whatever. Religion isn't spoken aloud. Why is everyone over here so obsessed with proclaiming every damn conviction to the whole world? And why is everything about biscuits? A biscuit goes with tea. Not with gravy."

"Welcome to the South, brother. Our biscuits and gravy are the stuff of legend." Kurt and I had done a good job since arriving in Nashville of devouring every bit of soul food we could find. James, our vegetarian, was far from pleased. At the time, I think that inconvenience was on par with Tom's newfound spirituality.

"The sheer volume of pork consumption here is staggering." He almost laughed, but then the reminder of the Holy Ghost came back. "Cakes, this stuff Tom's into is fucking bullshit. Have you seen his Twitter feed? It's all, 'The Light is so beautiful' and… ugh," James said, stopping mid-stride. He started laughing, looking up to the sky. "He asked me to *forgive* him. For things I haven't thought about in years. Is that what these Angelicals go on about all the time?"

"Evangelicals," I corrected. "And yes. Sometimes."

"Know what the stupid thing is?"

"There's a lot of stupid things going on right now," I sighed. "It's hard to pick one out of the lineup."

"I don't want our Tom to go away. I don't want that broken, vulnerable Tom to get all perfected and righteous. We had a thing going. This is… I can't even imagine what it's like for you."

"I've managed years of good old religion with only minor scars," I replied, which was not the truth. I wanted to comfort him. All I could think of to say was, "Maybe this won't last. Maybe this is like the time he tried Hare Krishna. I mean, how long could he go without meat? I think it was six hours."

"So you're saying we should hope Tom fucks up everything good in his life, just like always, for the betterment of the band?" James asked. The look he gave me was chilling, reflecting just how horrible my own words were.

I sighed. "It sounds a lot more reprehensible when you put it that way, but yes."

Yeah, I was hoping Tom would break down. I didn't want to deal with a curveball in our routine. This was not part of the contract. Jesus didn't belong in my band.

We're all really messed up.

---

*2:20 A.M. Later that night.*

**James:** I need to apologize to Tom.
**Kate:** Oh?
**James:** I was a dick. I am a dick. You're a dick too.
**Kate:** Technically, I can't be a dick. But that's irrelevant.
**James:** Your lacking a dick has never been irrelevant. It's part of your charm.
**Kate:** Uh, thanks. I think. Anyway—apologies?
**James:** It probably would have been better for all of us if I'd just have shut my mouth and got him in the booth to record the damn final vocals.
**Kate:** Probably.
**James:** Now he knows just how much this all bothers me. Why can't I be like you? You were impenetrable out there.
**Kate:** It's all a grand act, buddy. It's still better than him coming into the studio high off his ass. I'm just not ready for all that this shit entails.
**James:** You ran away from home to leave this stuff behind, eh?
**Kate:** Yup. Remember who was the most against moving to N-ville?
**James:** That'd be you. After Kurt, who threatened to kill himself if we moved. And yet he still persists.

**Kate:** He sure does. He's a persistent motherfucker. You've got to give that to him.

**James:** We're mixing down "Alight" from today. Tom sounds like an electric angel. His voice hasn't been this strong in a long time. And I almost hate him for it.

**Kate:** We could always warble together. Damnit. I'm tired AF, man.

**James:** Why don't you come down to the studio? I could use your opinion on this riff.

**Kate:** Nah. Need more bourbon. Send barrels.

**James:** Maybe you should try some tea. And coffee. You know, loads of people get by without…

I tossed the phone on the bed. Tea was not an option. I had an open bottle. It was go time.

I didn't expect James to make a one-eighty on Tom so fast, but I knew it was inevitable. Funny thing about working with bandmates as long as you do, you get to know their quirks. James runs really hot. His temper is off the charts. But so is his passion for music. And if Tom was really performing as well as it sounded—and James was one of his biggest critics—then it was enough to make up for the ugliness before.

But James was right. He was English and really didn't have any baseline for understanding Evangelicals to the extent I did. He hadn't grown up in it. He didn't understand the nuances, the culture, the pressure of it.

And maybe James was moving on, but I wasn't ready to stop being angry. Tom's stunt brought back a hundred memories from childhood, dragging up years of crap I thought I'd buried deep enough. But that's the thing, I guess. You can bury things deep in the sand, but eventually the waves erode it away.

It didn't help that it wasn't just the Jesus stuff but the Tom stuff too. The thing is, I pretended for a long time Tom was just someone I fell for off the cuff—like he was someone who just happened to be there, and we hooked up while it was convenient. At least, that's how I talked about it to myself. But it's bullshit.

Listen. I'm not a romantic at heart; what romanticism I possess is clothed in cynicism and pessimism. The gushy stuff in our lyrics, it's almost never from me even though everyone assumes the girl must be the one with the heart. That's usually stuff James insists on adding. "Lost and Loving" was originally "Lost and *Losing*" because, well, that's how I think about things. I want to love people. I want to fall in love and be happy. But I'm always so focused on how it's going to end I fuck everything up on my way toward the goal like Godzilla walking to the sea. I'd already broken up with Tom before we'd been dating a week. In my head, anyway. Which might as well be my heart.

I fell in love with Tom the first time I saw him, which is cliché and pathetic and totally unsustainable. Back in our early New York days, when I was with The Blue Trixies, we played the same circuits as the original lineup for October Revival. I'd heard their name a thousand times it felt like before I actually saw them perform the first time. I think some article I read once misquoted me saying they were rubbish —but that's not what I meant. I'm not even sure they quoted me correctly. Rubbish sounds a lot more like what James would say.

The original band was rough, really rough. But it was less about technical skill and more about a sense of things being really off balance. Fred and Kent, the original bassist and drummer, came from a metal background, and you could feel it behind every thrum. They were holding back so much that the entire rhythm section was strained, like the musical equivalent of blowing through a closed straw. From the first few chords of "Move My Way," you could sense an underlying current of offness. And for someone like me, it made it almost painful to listen to.

Until Tom Chesley started singing.

I wasn't really paying much attention that night at the Bar Five in Baltimore—I mean, other than being a critical ass about every set. I'd started drinking steadily since we were following October Revival, so I was sitting at the bar trying to hear Sara's whining at me above the band. I noticed Sara's face first, since she was facing the stage. She just closed her mouth and her eyes got wide. Getting her to shut up is no easy task.

Then I heard the voice. Those telltale chills began before I could even turn around to see him, starting at the top of my head and shivering down my arms to my fingers. Only the best music did that to me. And his voice set the PA on fire.

Rail thin, Tom was barely twenty at the time, with this crazy mane of corkscrew curls, honey blond. The meager house lights were blue and green, flicking on and off around him. Handsome, beyond handsome. He eclipsed the guitarist, a pudgy Indian kid, James something.

"Who the fucking hell is he?" Sara shouted in my ear. "Damn."

We weren't the only ones enraptured by Tom's voice. I'd never heard Bar Five so attentive. Even the waitresses stopped to listen. The magic with Tom's voice was a combination of the smokier lower register and the ethereal upper range. I've always been able to carry a tune; I can write melodies and fake it along with the best. I'm not a bad singer, but my voice isn't an instrument. Tom's is.

Listening to him sing and watching him move on the stage, I felt like a giddy teenager. My face flushed; my stomach fluttered. I immediately started worrying about what I would say to him if we had a chance to talk, but I mentally threw the thought aside figuring the likelihood of me gathering enough courage was zip to zero. Chances were he didn't have a thing for stubby little Gothy girls.

By the time we were ready to go on stage, I was so nervous I messed up the intro to "Blue Sky Falling" rather astonishingly. Sara goggled at me, since it was not the sort of thing I ever did, and I gave her a stupid grin before we finally got our footing. I kept looking for Tom in the audience, but I could only see the Indian kid, sitting very attentively a few seats down from where I'd been at the bar.

While we were breaking down, the guitarist—James—came up to Sara and started chatting her up. Story of my life. (It took lots of Dusty's interference to get me remotely glam, but back then there was no hope for me. I was a sartorial nightmare. Skinny, short black hair, vaguely punk-meets-hippie vibe. Not a good look, and therefore most often passed over for Sara who, despite playing bass and singing backup vocals, appeared as though she walked out of Tori Amos's entourage: flowing natural red hair, effortless style, delicate features.

I'm not sure who got more ass in the early days, honestly, Tom or Sara.)

Sara pointed toward me, and the Indian kid's eyes lit up. Most men's eyes don't do that when they spot me, and I must have scowled at him because he sort of flinched when we made eye contact.

"You're Kate, then?" he said with a flawless Cambridge accent. "The songwriter for Blue Pixies?"

"The Blue *Trixies*," I corrected. "And, um, yeah."

"You're amazing." He was nervous, blinking a lot. "I just...we're not used to hearing that quality of lyrics."

"Um, thanks? I enjoyed your set too." I sounded as uncomfortable as I looked, I'm sure. Later James reported I looked like "a stunned toad." Leave it to him for the charming simile.

He laughed nervously. I spotted Tom over his shoulder, picking his way across the stage with his arm around some blond chick. Figured.

"I'm James. James Venkatesan. I'm the songwriter and guitarist for October Revival. I just wanted—I mean, are you and Sara based here?" he asked.

"New York, actually. But we come down here when we can," I replied.

"No shit. We're in New York as well."

I nodded. Sara was watching me, grinning. Edging me along with that manic, brilliant stare of hers.

James looked relieved. "I know this is a long shot. But—when we get back to the city, would you have coffee with me or something? I'd love to know more about what you do. Musically."

Reluctantly, I agreed.

I stood him up the first time, calling him a half hour after we were supposed to meet, claiming I was sick. I was just depressed over whatever flavor of the week it was, and Sara was out visiting her family in Alabama. No, I'm not a social person. Why do you ask?

When we met again, it was three months after our initial meeting, even though we'd seen each other now and again at gigs. I'd done a very good job of ignoring James and quietly stalking Tom. When it came to Tom, I hadn't managed the courage to talk to him or anything remotely brave, but I knew his hangouts in the city and learned a surprising amount of information about him just based on the people he hung out with. At the time, he wasn't known for any sort of hard drugs, but he had a penchant for pot and gin and women. I could roll with that.

James had been waiting twenty minutes when I caught up with him at the coffee shop, and I was hung over and irritable. But things weren't good for me in the music department—we'd been dropped from our indie label because we just weren't marketable enough—and Sara was being pressured by her parents to go back to school.

He was handsomer than I'd initially thought. He wasn't pudgy; he just had a baby face.

"Sunglasses. Hat. Scarf askew," James observed as I sat down across from him with my chai. "Rough night?"

"Yeah," I replied, charmless as usual.

He cleared his throat. "Listen. I initially wanted to speak to you about music, but the situation's changed a bit for us."

"Oh?" I asked. "You guys sounded great last Friday, by the way. Especially the second set."

"Odd, considering we self-imploded shortly after," James said, far too coolly for the actual statement.

"You what?"

"Okay, not precisely broken up. But entirely lacking a rhythm section. I fired Fred, and Kent is leaving in the aftermath because he's always hated my guts anyway. Finding a drummer isn't hard, I've already got a guy in mind…but the bassist is tricky…"

I had no idea why he felt the need to explain the details about his band, and I was really regretting taking him up in the first place. He'd appealed to my ego, all the talk about my magical songwriting capabilities, and I'd been a sucker.

"Sorry to hear?" I made an attempt at not sounding like an uncaring ass, but it was unconvincing. There's only so much I can cover up.

He must have noticed my look of "don't give a shit" because he laughed a little self-consciously. "Okay, so I need a bass player."

I bit down on my tongue and dug my nails into my jeans. He wanted Sara. Of course! Everyone always wanted Sara. She was the marketable one.

"And?" was the best response I could think of.

"Well, Sara's good…"

"Listen, you're not taking my fucking bass player," I said, standing up. I almost lost my footing and had to steady myself on the rickety table. "In case you didn't notice, we're a two-person band. It'd kill us."

He blushed and put his hand to his face. "Shit, no. That's…that's not what I was proposing. I mean… Please don't leave yet. I'm a bit of a mess."

Well, he was being as honest as possible, and I wasn't being particularly kind. I thought I almost caught tears in his eyes.

"Go ahead," I said.

"October Revival, we're on the brink of something really big. Our manager, this bird named Dusty, she's got us in with some really important people next week. Big wigs. Producers. A real record deal, y'know? But now I'm lacking a bassist, I have to break in a new drummer, and I have absolutely no confidence in the material I've written. It's all like a soft-boiled egg…it just doesn't hold up when you get to the center."

A soft-boiled egg, huh?

"And?"

"I'm proposing you and Sara join us. I know it's unconventional, but you're strongest where we're weakest. We need a solid songwriter collaboration; I feel like I write in a vacuum and could really use you to help work on some of the demos we've got. And we need someone who can learn Fred's parts quickly."

"I think Sara can handle the constant quarter notes." I shrugged. "But…we're a duo. It's sort of our thing."

James laughed. "Well, I won't beg. But if you change your mind, just give me a call."

In the end, I didn't even wait to ask Sara. I called James that evening. It had nothing to do with his offer of being part of something about to hit it big. It had to do with one thing: Tom Chesley. Yes, I'll admit it: I wanted to be near him. But more than anything, I wanted to write songs for him.

---

Kate Styx

*From Wikipedia, the free encyclopedia*

**Kate "Katie" Styx** (Katherine-Anne Marshall Mendenhall) (b. July 17, 1979). Kate Styx is an American singer-songwriter and musician. She currently plays keyboards for the British/American band, **October Revival**. Styx joined October Revival in 2003, along with **Sara Plummer**, who were part of the band **The Blue Trixies. James Vayne** of October Revival had long admired Styx's songwriting skills and, as the relationship between Fred McMyre and Kent Silver deteriorated, Vayne asked Styx to join the band. Plummer was brought on board shortly after. Styx dated October Revival lead singer, **Tom Chesley**, briefly, and she has confirmed many of their songs reflect this relationship.

The Styx/Vayne songwriting team went on to cowrite the next three albums for October Revival, including their most successful album to date, *Blindside*. Vayne credits Styx with the majority of the lyrics on the band's albums, insisting he's more involved from a conceptual and organizational standpoint, as well as studio production. Styx and Vayne won three Ivor Novello awards combined for their work on *Blindside*. The song "Lost and Loving" was featured in the motion picture *Three Times Too Many* starring **Joseph Gordon-Levitt** and **Sadie Clapton** and is the group's most successful song to date, hitting #3 on the **Billboard Top 100** in the US and #1 in the UK.

**Early Life:**

Styx was born Katherine-Ann Mendenhall Marshall at Emory Adventist Hospital in Smyrna, GA, to Robert Quinn Marshall, a minister, and Claire Mendenhall Marshall, a schoolteacher. Her upbringing was strictly conservative, and Styx first exhibited musical tendencies in middle school band.

After graduating from Lockwood Baptist Academy, she went to the University of Maryland to pursue music theory. At UMD she met **Kurt Bastian** and began playing in clubs in the Baltimore/DC area as Hurt and Hate. The duo played through college but broke up when Bastian received a fellowship at American University for his master's studies in sociology.

# CHAPTER FOUR

Two weeks later, and things were falling into a groove, at least. It wasn't normal. It wasn't comfortable, but it existed. Thankfully Kurt hadn't gone Jewish or Krishna on me or anything, so I was really valuing our morning coffee shop visits together.

Kurt was on his usual pop music rant. Funny thing about Kurt. He hates pop music with a passion (at least his definition of "pop" which is bubblegum, heavily-produced, and auto-tuned). It's his most frequent complaint among many. But the thing is, he's insanely well versed on the subject. He knows an uncomfortable amount of trivia when it comes to every pop princess and boy band. As much as he hates them, he fuels his hate with a very curious fascination that borders on fandom.

"... And it's not just that she can't sing," he was saying as he pushed around his *huevos rancheros*. "It's that the production level is pushed to the limits of digital intervention. I mean, at a point, why don't we just let robots do all the singing? It'd be a hell of a lot more entertaining. It's like Mr. Roboto taken to the next level. The musical singularity!"

"Not everyone has a Tom Chesley," I pointed out, which was my usual defense. Just saying Tom's name made me want to barf up breakfast. Every morning since his born again "event," I'd woken up, convinced he's up to some elaborate prank. No amount of drinking had been able to hide the cold, hard truth of his conversion.

Hi, denial phase. How's it going? It's me, Kate. Just wanted to let you know that you and I will be spending the next indeterminate amount of time together, hanging out, hashing out, you know, the usual.

The thing was though, even with his newfound faith, it was getting harder to hate the new Tom. He was on time to the studio, his voice was consistently amazing, and he was actually involving himself in the recording process. Our last two albums had been strong-armed into submission by James and me, piecing together Tom's takes with the magic of digital editing and a sincere hope the label wouldn't notice. Even sober, Tom was never the best in a recording environment. His voice was too big and wild. During his worst, drug-addled days, his live performances rarely missed. Once for "exhaustion" (read: near overdose) and twice for rehab-related issues. He was born to perform, but he rarely brought much energy to the studio.

Except now.

"And that's the problem, isn't it?" Kurt asked. "God. Remind me why I got into this mess?"

"Because Sara and James were going to kill each other, and I needed a bassist I could trust not to sleep around with the band." I smiled when I said it. It had been two years since Sara left. "Also, the paycheck. Even if you did come after the big bang, you're still doing better than you were in Atlanta."

"And to think I turned down Coldplay for this," Kurt sighed, one of our inside jokes. He hated Coldplay with the passion of a thousand suns.

"We can always ring up Chris Martin…" I played along.

Kurt laughed. "I. Would. Die."

"Well, we're all going to die if we don't figure out this Tom shit."

"As the band's official inside outsider, you know it's not just this."

"What do you mean?"

He sort of squinted at me, judging without words. "It's cracking, Kate. You can feel it; hell, I can feel it, and I distance myself from everyone at all costs. It's like an evolutionary imperative for my own self-preservation to keep away from your drama, but even I'm not immune."

"Yeah, you keep your distance until you're critiquing something. Then you're an extreme closeup. You're a musical jackass."

"It's because I'm almost always right." He gave me one of his brilliant smiles and hailed the waitress for more coffee.

I was glad James wasn't in earshot. None of them had particularly liked the idea of having Kurt along. And initially, our intention was just to keep him for a few live gigs, to make up for the space Sara left behind. But it wasn't going to happen because the label wanted another album and we were already strained enough as it was. Kurt was a solid bassist, in every sense. And we'd brought him on with the understanding that creatively he wasn't going to have much input. I mean, no one appreciates his eclectic musical sense more than me. We practically grew up together. But it isn't the right sound for October Revival.

Honestly, there were many days I just marveled that Kurt hadn't left yet. I'd thought the move to Nashville might be the end of it. He and James could hardly speak two words to each other without growling, and Kurt was entirely ambivalent to everyone else in the band but me. Which was unfair. I constantly felt like I had to tend to him and James—and always separately—to keep things together. Though James insisted it was my problem since, of course, Kurt was "mine" to begin with. I'd been his biggest champion. More than anything, it was because I didn't know what to do with Sara gone. I was furious with her, but I couldn't help but feel a void on stage every single night, not to mention in the studio.

Which reminded me. I was scheduled for vocals. Probably shouldn't have eaten all that cheese and sausage.

I was about to make a comment on the current country crap music seeping out of the house speakers, but the door on the diner rattled open for me just in time to make out a familiar face.

It was Tom. Again.

He was alone, which was surprising in and of itself considering his usual need to be flanked by at least six people. He had a backpack on and smiled very politely to Anne, our usual barista, who made him his favorite, though she was surprised to see him. Kurt and I were typically the only members of the band who actually hung out here—the rest had their drinks brought to them. No judgment, I just don't think they grew up in coffee shops like these as Kurt and I had. I did a lot of songwriting in those booths.

"He walks into a room, and I swear, you still turn into a little schoolgirl," Kurt said after seeing Tom too. He wiggled his fork at me again. "Tell me. Ms. 'I've been on a bender for a week because I'm running from Jesus'—what bothers you more, that he's found God or that he's hanging around so much?"

"I'm over things."

"The fuck you are."

"Okay, okay. It's both. It brings up all kinds of baggage, okay, Kurt? I'm fucking miserable. I want to run away."

"Well, running away into the bottle isn't the best long-term strategy."

"Fuck you, Kurt."

He averted his eyes and sighed. We'd had this conversation a few times over the last half year, him dropping all kinds of hints that I was an alcoholic, and it had only gotten worse after the breakup. I didn't think it was bad enough. I didn't feel like I needed an intervention. I was managing.

But it still pissed me off to no end that Kurt kept bringing it up.

Tom came by with his hot cocoa and sat down next to us. I barely greeted him with a grunt.

"What is it we're working on this morning?" he asked, all smiles and earnestness.

Kurt bit the bait. "Complaining about the general state of pop music. As we do."

I'm not sure how Kurt ever manages, but he speaks subtext into his own words with expert care. Somehow in those handful of words he was able to indicate to Tom that this was our special time, that he was not invited, and that he really should go somewhere else.

Tom, who's had his daft moments, understood.

"Ah, right," he said. "Well, I've got Bible study in a few, but I thought I'd stop by and say hello. Didn't mean to interrupt."

"We're just getting ready to go," I muttered, shuffling in my seat, then grabbing my bag.

He couldn't just let me go, of course. Tom took my arm gently. The physical contact certainly did enough to get my attention. "Listen, Kate. I'm sorry about the other day. About being so…overt. I'm just feeling very overwhelmed right now with everything, and I wanted you to share some of it with me. I thought you might understand."

"Just let's not bring it up again," I said. "Not until I do. Which is probably never."

"Kate…"

"Tom. I'm serious. Rule number one of being a shiny new Jesus freak: learn to back off when people say so. You'll never get your Salvation Points if people keep punching you in the face."

---

WHEN WE GOT OUTSIDE, I had tears in my eyes, and Kurt put his arm around me.

"I was so off," he said with a wistful sigh. His cowboy boots clicked, my Chuck Taylors shuffling despondently in concert.

"What do you mean?" I said, wiping my nose.

"It's not that you're mad about the Jesus thing. It's that you know it's like…it's the one thing that could really prevent you from ever getting back together with Tom. You just…you could never go there. End of story. Door closed. Except, he's even more visible than he was before. That's. Got. To. Suck."

I nodded miserably, and we headed to the studio as I gathered myself.

---

SINCE JAMES WAS at the board and Kurt could do his work later in the day, I ended up the only one in the studio for a while. I pulled out my notebook and went through the lyrics of what were supposed to be the other songs on the album.

But that was another problem. Since Tom had checked into the Jesus Train, I was finding it almost impossible to write anything useful. Three albums in five years is no easy feat, and before I'd always had a store to pull from. But the six songs we had at the moment were all I had in me. I didn't have any backup. There weren't any secret stores of songs left. James is less a lyricist and more a musical composer. We rarely sat down to write together. I'd bring him lyrics and sometimes some of the melodies, and we'd work on it from there.

At the moment all I had were blank pages. "Somebetween" was almost done, and it marked the last of my contributions. It didn't help that I was drinking away every last moment I wasn't in the studio, but that's beside the point.

James finally got some time away from the board and came to sit with me on the big leather couch while Jeff and Ian worked their magic in the editing room.

"Sara called last night," he said. "I hate that her calls still rile me so much. But there you go. I guess some breakups last a fucking lifetime."

"She's about to go on tour," I said, recalling her last, vague, self-obsessed email. We hardly talked since she left, but she liked letting me know the details of her musical success outside of our band. Rubbing my nose in it is more like it. "Did you tell her about Tom?"

"I couldn't get a word in edgewise," he said with a sigh. "You know how she is."

I nodded, trying to get the notebook out of sight.

He noticed.

"How's the writing going?" he asked.

I bit my lip and shook my head. I could let him know. For all his tantrums and perfectionism, he was remarkably kind to me and my struggle. I'd never let them down before, and I didn't plan on doing it again.

"Maybe you should go to a spa or something. Do one of those sea lettuce wraps. Detox. Hydrate. Relax and let all this stressful shit go away," he offered.

"I'm fine," I insisted, remembering Kurt's similar suggestion I purify myself earlier that morning. "I will get over it."

James squeezed my hand. "Let's go to dinner tonight, then. We can have a brainstorming session."

"Sounds like a plan," I said.

Except it never happened. James got predictably caught up at the studio, and I went out and drank, almost got myself arrested, and went home and blacked out.

# CHAPTER FIVE

Two days later, I was still miserable. To make matters worse, Tom was at the board while I was recording the background vocals for "Somebetween"—and he was actually trying to involve himself in the production process. It set my teeth on edge.

I had been on a genuine roll until he sat down next to James and Ian. I was feeling refreshed. I hadn't had a drink in two days. I was full of coffee and doing damned well. Then Tom appeared. I started fumbling over some of the lyrics in the second verse, the part about the sundering skies (one of James's lyrics I didn't quite dig in the first place), and it was made infinitely worse by Tom's input.

"You're flat, Kate," he said over the mic.

"I know I'm flat. I'm always flat," I muttered.

"Well, don't be. And when you come into the last line there, slide a little more into the oooh. Right now it's choppy."

"Aren't you the most observant lead singer in the history of lead singers," I said, feeling my cool evaporating. "What are you doing here, Tom?"

"Helping." He smiled brilliantly. "I'm enjoying this part."

"Well, I'm not. Listen, we were doing fine," I bit out. "Right, James? We're doing *fine*."

James said something to Tom behind the glass I couldn't hear, and I took some deep breaths to try and steel myself. I could hear Kurt's comment about everything cracking run over in my head. We had our process. I got to write whatever I wanted, and Tom sang it, and then he went away until we went on tour. There was none of this "you're flat" bullshit.

"He wants to help, Kate," James insisted, though he didn't look one hundred percent convinced either.

"It's annoying," I said, figuring today was the day to be open and honest. We'd all gone along so long pretending nothing mattered it felt weird just saying it out loud.

"You're taking it too personally," James said.

"I'm taking it personally? I already have to deal with you and Kurt holding me up to impossible standards, and now I've got a third expert with his own vision?"

"Kate, darling," Tom tried.

"Fuck you, Tom," I said clearly and perfectly into the mic in the tune of the vocals I was setting down. It wasn't even flat. Then I was just done. "I need to take a break. Turn off the fucking mic and give me some air."

Tom leaned on the heel of his hand, giving me his blue-eyed innocent look I found painfully charming. It made me even angrier.

I threw off the headphones and left the sound booth, making a good show of slamming the door shut in the process. Most of the time, I'm not the dramatic one. But that day I'd just had too much of everything, and what elation I'd had from not drinking quickly evaporated.

They all knew better than to bother me, so I spent about ten minutes banging out some melodies on the grand piano. It was surprisingly good, I had to admit it. It was something different, lower tempo with less meandering than most of the things I'd been writing lately. I knew they could hear me, and I made sure it was as impressive as possible. Sometimes a little showing off is good, especially when one is surrounded by so many boys. I didn't want them to forget that it was my songwriting that got the first album off the ground, that impressed the record execs, that made the band go from boring British import to something more. I just wasn't good at saying it aloud.

"It's good," James said. I'd heard him come in but had chosen to ignore him. "I like the minor resolve there at the end. It's got a sort of Beatles/Travis feel, doesn't it?"

"Or it's got a Kate Styx feel," I said, not looking up at him. "You don't always have to make me sound derivative."

"I'm sorry, Cakes. You're right."

"Of course I am," I said.

"Tom's left."

"Finally."

"I thought it would be constructive to have him in here. But it's a bit too much too soon."

I looked up at him over my glasses and stuck out my tongue. Yes, the picture of professional maturity, that's me.

"I can't deal with all of this at once," I said.

"You're not over him."

"Of course I'm not fucking over him."

"Or…not over fucking him?"

I slapped James hard on the arm, and he grinned stupidly at me. Sometimes I wondered why I didn't get on romantically with James. It seemed like a logical relationship. I guess he and Sara had always been so entrenched in each other, but at that point I was with Tom and… relationships gave me headaches. Yeah, I liked him better than anyone else in the band, for sure. Not just because we worked together so well, either. Kurt, he was critical and had constant strings of complaints; Tom was mercurial at best; Paul was distant. James was a pillar, someone I could always trust and lean on. Even if he was a moody bastard sometimes.

Even now. It was James who'd come to talk to me.

"Seriously. It's hard. It's one thing when he's not around. But this…"

"You know," James said casually, "you were never good together to begin with. You don't seem to remember that so well."

Trying to avoid his comment, I glanced to the control room. No one at the mixers.

"They're all on break," James said, sitting down next to me on the piano bench.

"My hero."

"Laying on the sarcasm really thick, aren't we? I know this is all shitty, but we've got to keep moving on."

"What if this is the last album?" I asked him. I kept playing the melody I'd been working on, more softly.

"Then it's the last album. And we move on to other stuff. We can't keep doing this forever. No one wants to be the Rolling Stones."

I figured out a change into the middle eight I really liked and fiddled a bit with it before asking, "Do you ever think about what's next?"

James started playing a plinky little accompaniment to the progression, and it sounded really cool. "I don't imagine it's much different than what I'm doing right now. Playing music."

"Where do I go?" I asked. "Paul and Kurt, they're like a Velcro rhythm section. You've already got side-projects. Tom will likely front some religious band if this whole thing sticks. But I feel like I've gone as far as I can go."

"Solo gigs aren't fun for me. I don't have the voice for it."

"Neither do I."

"So we should keep writing together," he said, stopping what he was doing at the keys.

I stopped playing, too, and let out a big sigh. "I'm tired of writing about Tom, but it's like…just when I think it's all out of my system, he goes and does something like this."

"It takes time. I bet fifty quid that you'll write a final song, y'know, something that sums it all up nicely, that you'll be able to walk away from. Put it all in the ground. But for now, let's put this track down," James said. He'd retrieved his acoustic guitar from the other side of the room.

"What track?"

"The one we just started writing."

---

I'VE BEEN TOLD I don't talk enough about Tom and myself. It's for good reason. I don't like talking to people I don't know about personal stuff. I never have. I write about it, and I always pass it off that way to journalists: if they want to know what I think about Tom, what our relationship was like, all they've got to do is listen to our music. The night I first saw Tom perform, I wrong a song about him called "Johnny Come Lately" which was, in every sense of the word, terrible. Since day one, that beautiful bastard's been my muse.

I think what scared me most about breaking up the band, which I saw as inevitable at the time, was Tom would be out of my life entirely, and I wouldn't be a good writer anymore. Which is painfully selfish of me, I realize. I'd written for Tom for so long I wasn't sure what to do with myself if he wasn't part of my day-to-day existence.

So, for the record. The rundown. I started officially dating Tom Chesley in late 2006 during the *Blindside* tour. We broke up for good around Christmas of 2007, which was after breaking up in October and briefly getting back together. So, we managed barely a year. I'd fallen in love with him in 2003, the night I'd seen him sing in Baltimore. The math is sad and simple: nearly two years of pining, one year in love and suffering intensely, and going on four years regretting every bit of it.

No, it wasn't the drugs that caused the breakup, though it was part of it. I'd be lying to say it didn't matter. Keep in mind, in case you haven't noticed, I'm an alcoholic, so I've got a different perspective on addiction. I don't talk about it much, mostly because I don't buy into the whole Serenity Prayer bullshit. And at that point in my life, I hadn't learned to face the world without reaching for bourbon every time I had a problem. And when I was with Tom, there was a lot of bourbon. Sure, he did harder stuff, as everyone knows. In the end, we both wanted to drown out parts of ourselves, and we were painfully codependent. Mine just happened to be perfectly legal. And I've always been really good, really consistent with my drinking. Tom was always up and down, on and off the wagon. I was more like a marathon addict.

Sometimes I think if we'd kept up our relationship, one of us would certainly have died before it was over.

To pull a Tom, I'll quote one of my own lyrics to boil the whole thing down. "I could never be the person you could see." Yup. No, Tom's drug addiction was not easy to live with. He was volatile and self-obsessed and a little mad. But the whole time we were together, I didn't let myself believe it. I kept seeing things that weren't there, certain he couldn't really love me—let alone be faithful to me— because, well, he could have any girl he wanted. Girls with bigger boobs and brighter smiles, girls with silky hair and no stretch marks who could rock lingerie rather than old worn out Radiohead t-shirts. It didn't matter how many times he told me he loved me; I just never could really let it through my skull.

So when he cheated and nearly died, when things got just unbearably bad, it was as if I was just watching a recording of something I'd imagined a thousand times before. I was a horrible girlfriend, and the songs I wrote while we were together were shit. It was the raw, broken-hearted aftermath that fueled the songs for *Blindside*. Which, of course, would go on to be even more successful than our first album in a wonderful ironic twist. None of us thought it was going to be as big as it got. Nothing feels so weird as your fans rejoicing in your suffering.

But I'm getting ahead of myself.

I'll always love Tom Chesley, and at this point, I'm finally okay with it. It's stupid to think you can move on in life and just leave people behind, people who come to define you. And it's worse for people like me and James, songwriters who fold our biggest hopes and fears right into the fabric of our vocation. It's like tattooing the heartbreak on our souls, then being forced to show each other the scars every night on stage. Sure, sometimes it gets monotonous. At a point, songs become songs, and after you've played the tune seventeen nights in a row, it gets a bit watered down. But there still some nights when we're playing "Lost and Loving" or "Midnight in London" when I look over at Tom, hearing him sing the words I wrote for him, and I get choked up.

I don't even remember the logistics of how it first happened, how it became clear we were a couple. There isn't a lot I keep around from that time in my life, but I still have a framed picture of the *Rolling Stone* cover I did with Tom in 2006, where we recreated the *Rumors* cover with Stevie Nicks and Mick Fleetwood. It was right in the middle of our time together, and I remember being shocked they wanted me on the cover, let alone that they wanted me to look like Stevie. She'd always been something of an idol of mine, right along there with Tori Amos and Marla North and Ann Wilson, and I remember the photo shoot, feeling both like a lousy imitation and absolutely giddy being dressed up like one of my idols.

Inside the issue are a bunch of other pictures of us in Fleetwood Mac gear. Me with a Gibson girl hairdo and draped in scarves, Tom in perfect suits and ties and big hats. I got rid of all those prints, especially the ones that didn't make the issues (too many genuine smiles for the magazine, but you could see the loving looks we gave each other; I used to treasure them—hell, I had delusions our children would look on them with awe and wonder). But I kept the cover because, try as I might, I'll never stop being proud of the moment we were together.

We got together just as Sara and James were starting to fall apart. You've got to understand, for years Sara and James were the bedrock of the band from a dynamic standpoint. But with our initial success, the stress cracks started. Sara wanted more creative control; she wanted to be as important to James as I was. But, when push came to shove, she just wasn't a very good songwriter. She has a beautiful voice and can hold her own as a bassist, and as far as stage presence goes, she's got it. The initial October Revival lineup was made iconic by her shock of hair, y'know? But she didn't write October Revival music. She wrote Sara Plummer music.

Now I think about it, it was Sara who pushed me toward Tom the most. She knew from the beginning. I mean, when we started, Sara and I sort of clung to each other for life. Those boys were intimidating, I'll tell you. Intense doesn't even begin to describe it. I was painfully shy when we first started working with October Revival, but her natural ebullience helped me break through. Before long, we were both part of the boys' club. Sort of. At least, as much as we'd ever be.

But Sara's motivations pushing me toward Tom were primarily to prove a point, I think. She was convinced James had a thing for me, despite both of our protests to the contrary. If I was with Tom, my golden paragon, rather than simply pining away after him, there was some safety for her there.

Good Kentucky bourbon got me into Tom's bed the first night, brought at Sara's insistence after an absolutely amazing show in LA. Tom was high, I was drunk, and it didn't take much goading.

Waking up in a bed at the Ritz-Carlton, I was so disoriented I fell out. Seriously, the ridiculousness of it is hilarious now. But at the time it was like being in some horrifying dream, tangled in sheets tinged with smoke and booze and God knows what else.

"Oh, damn, Katie!"

Tom's voice drifted down to me. I was face up, still struggling with the sheets (thinking the higher thread count made them significantly more perilous). When I got the sheets clear of my head, I saw him dangling over the edge, his curls falling down, almost brushing my face.

I blinked up at him, drowning in a sea of pure puke-stained Egyptian cotton.

"Hi, Tom," was my delightful reply.

"Did you hurt yourself?"

"Uh, no… I don't think so…" I felt around my hand, and something cold and wet was seeping into the sheets. Vomit has its own special feel when it's had the chance to soak in good.

He smiled. "Well, I suppose *that* happened."

"Yeah… um…"

"Can I help you up?"

I nodded and disentangled my arm enough to take his hand.

Conveniently the sheets fell off, and I made a half-hearted attempt to cover up and almost fell again.

Then I started to cry.

A fun note about me, really. I'm not an angry person. Sarcastic? Crabby? Moody? Sure. But real anger, it doesn't happen. I don't get angry, don't stomp around and yell. When I'm really mad, I just cry. Which is extremely confusing to most people, and absolutely infuriating to me. Not to mention exceptionally useless and ineffective. All my life it's been endlessly frustrating.

"Wait. You're crying. Katie, come on now. It wasn't so bad, I don't think," Tom said, trying to make a grab for me, but I darted away, as graceless as a three-legged baby elephant. "I don't know if I'm speaking for myself, but I'm glad we … I mean I'd been thinking quite a while…"

I shook my head. "I have to go. I have…to go." I needed my clothes. I found my t-shirt and slipped it on, found my skirt and panties, and started for the door.

Tom was there to meet me, though, staring at me as if I'd just done the strangest thing in the world. I suppose he wasn't used to girls flipping out and leaving him after a night of intimacy: that was his bag. We'd all had our turns sneaking him out of random hotels over the years, that's for sure. I just never thought I'd be on the same end.

He caught my eyes and put his hand gently on my shoulder, flipping my hair out of the way. "You don't have to go, Kate. I…don't really want you to go, honestly."

When I didn't respond, he wiped my tears with the back of his hand. He bent down and kissed me, soft and sweet, and the anger and fury (and let's face it, a bit of shame) I'd had moments before just evaporated away like the resolve of sustained chord to the major. I know we kissed the night before, though I had no recollection of it, so for me this kiss was the culmination of years of waiting and feeling sorry for myself and watching Tom from afar. His hair smelled like cigarettes, and he was so much taller than me he had to bend down; I practically had to get on tiptoe.

And cute and romantic as the scene was, it was probably the highlight of our relationship. Yes, we had a few good moments. But between my drinking and his addictions, mixed together with James's jealousy on both counts (his best friend and songwriting partner together) and the other band drama, it was a constant train wreck.

Which begs the question of why I can't seem to let it go, even now.

# CHAPTER SIX

THE SONG JAMES and I began ended up as "16th Street Lights," which didn't make it on the final album proper but was a hidden track after the last song. We'd done that since the beginning, taking the cue from Travis, one of our mutual favorite bands. We'd even gotten the chance to tour with them briefly after Keane did the same in 2004. I'm pretty sure I made myself a fool in front of Fran Healy, but he'd been extremely generous since then, even inviting us on some tour dates a few years later after my atrocious fangirl stupidity.

Anyway, this is a bit of a musical tangent. You'll have to forgive me. I'm not very good at this whole journaling thing, and, in fact, most days I think I suck royally at the whole musician thing. At least popular musician. I never had issue being an indie act. I mean, I could hide in plain sight there, if that makes sense. But now, even after everything, I feel like I walked through the whole October Revival adventure like some wayfaring stranger, like someone who acciden-tally walked on the set of a television show. That couldn't have possibly been me. I couldn't possibly have been there on stage; Tom Chesley could never have sung my songs, made love to me, promised to love me forever.

But he did. And I digress. I was talking about "16th Street Lights" and how the rest of the album came to be. It's probably helpful if I talk about what our process used to be like, so you can understand what was so off about the Nashville sessions (aside from reportedly sharing space with Taylor Swift and Tom finding Jesus).

In our New York days, recording was a hot mess. Our third album was cobbled together; Sara left in the middle of *Blindside*, and Kurt came in with his swagger and his zeal, pulling us through the *Blindside* tour, and since most of us were too tired of fighting, and recording, and touring to argue too much, it went in a bit of an unusual direction. Lots of synth. Lots of genre-hopping. We even had a rapper on one song, which was universally a laugh. The rapper guy was plenty nice, but ultimately, I think it was abundantly clear to everyone out there we were just trying hard not to fall apart. The tension glued the album together, and while I don't think it was a failure, it was odd, even for us. I don't remember much of it, honestly, but it's likely because I was after Tom. Also, I drank a hell of a lot. And liquor is very good at erasing memories. One of the reasons I love it so much.

But even before Sara left, at least after the first album, recording was helter-skelter. Tom was ushered in at the last moment, and most of the time was filled up with James and me getting the demos in working order and trying to get Tom to do the vocals over the finished tracks. If we could keep him conscious and consistent enough for long enough. Not easy.

It's one of the curious things about Tom and me. We have almost the same range since I'm sort of a middling alto and he's got this crazy nearly four-octave thing going on. Now, I don't have such a range, I'm fairly certain it's reserved for Freddie Mercury, Aretha, and a blessed few others, but both of our comfort zones are approximately the same. So, as a result, most of our demos feature me singing Tom's parts since James can't manage it (and Tom never got to the studio early enough in the cycle to be part of demo process). So, oddly enough, every one of our albums features almost finished versions with me singing almost everything. Once in a while one will surface, and the fans will get all giggly about it—or so I'm told. I stay away from the internet when October Revival is involved as much as possible. It makes me break out into hives.

Back to recording. The first two albums with the full set were very overproduced. James and I worked at the mercy of the label, and while our new producers were wildly popular, the studio work was also one of the worst experiences of my life. I'd never been under such scrutiny musically and personally. But I always sensed this constant undercurrent of dissatisfaction—with the direction of the albums, with the way we looked and acted, with the way we were singing—so I really didn't sleep much through those first two years. When I slept, it was because of weed or booze. In my defense, I wouldn't have been able to work if it hadn't been the case. I mean, seriously? What other options did I have? Meditation is bullshit. I'm far too uncoordinated to even attempt yoga. And the schedule they had us on was grueling.

Once we were given the reins to do what we wanted with *Lester Hotel*, I think we just didn't know what to do. Sara was gone. I was drinking my way through the album. Paul was getting married, and his fiancée was pregnant. Meanwhile, I was trying to argue for a different direction for the album, trying to distract myself from everything spinning out of control. I went experimental because Kurt was there and because I didn't know where else to go. Tom was at his worst then, and I spent a whole lot of time tracking him down all around the city, extricating him from dark alleyways or drug-fueled parties when I wasn't too drunk to function myself. I had all these half-finished overly emotional songs leftover from our breakup and *Blindside*, so James had to go in and severely reroute the hatred and anger and regret. But I still felt responsible for him.

So, going to Nashville was our attempt at saving ourselves. At saving the band. At saving the music. With Sara out of the picture (but not out of mind for neither James nor I) James and I had a lot more time to really figure out what kind of sound we wanted and what we wanted to say. Both of us were single, and neither of us was over the last heartbreak. So, *Something Else* was, no surprise, a total catharsis.

And really, when we stepped away from the whole thing, we realized it was far less of a band album and more of an album where our band happened to play the songs we wrote. Dusty and James insisted Kurt stay out of the process, aside from just playing what we told him, and Tom and Paul sort of danced around the periphery.

Oh yeah, there's another story there, too. Because halfway through *Something Else*, a few weeks after we were mixing down the first demo of "16th Street Lights," I started having delusions that I loved James. That I wanted to kiss him. That I wanted nothing more than for him to put his arms around me. That the love I felt for him just sort of skipped the elevator and slipped down the stairs another level.

We'd worked together so long, and he'd always been Sara's. And honestly, I thought they were going to get married (though God knows Sara's parents didn't take well with James to begin with; part of me would have loved seeing what they'd do with a half-Indian grand-child). I'd constructed an impressive wall around my perception of James, and it'd been up so long—and, I should mention, expertly forti-fied with liquor and delusions—and when it came down, I almost crumbled too.

"Kate? Did I say something wrong?" James asked after me.

The epiphany was enough I had to take off my headphones and get up from the leather chair to go stand on the other side of the room. It wasn't a big room, so it wasn't terribly effective. But I needed some distance to untangle what was going on in my head.

"I think I've got to call it a night," I said. I was literally shaking, having to ball my hands into fists. What the hell was I thinking? I couldn't have feelings for James. If I really had feelings, they'd have surfaced five years ago.

Right?

"Did I say something wrong?" James asked, getting up from the chair. He leveled me with his serious face, something he rarely had to use with me and mostly reserved for Tom when he wasn't behaving. "I was just going to say I think I actually like your vocals on this song, and in some way, it's a shame Tom's got to sing it."

"That's…not going to happen," I responded, fumbling for the door-knob and giving the signal to Jeff through the glass that we were wrapping up and he could go home.

James started to walk toward me, his hand reaching out. "Kate...?"

"G'night, James."

As I drove home, I went over it in my head. I couldn't figure out what the trigger had been. As far as I was concerned, we were just doing what we always did.

Except that's not true. No, it was a certain line in the song. Not one I wrote, one he wrote. *Something about the light in your hair, the light in your eyes.* The line was about Sara. Even though she was gone, we conjured her up like a ghost. All that damned beautiful red hair and those green, green eyes. It'd been over two years, and still we brought her back again and again. I never discouraged him, and it wasn't like I didn't write songs about Tom.

But the overwhelming tide ushering in the current of love? It could be only one thing: raging jealousy.

KURT WAS WATCHING reruns of *Matlock* when I got home, and he followed me into my room when I didn't say anything to him. I've got to say, he makes a far better roommate than Sara ever did, and he's always tuned into my emotions. Even when I try and run him off. He had a glass of wine in his hand when he showed up at the door to my bedroom.

"You look like you're pissed off."

"Is the wine for grabs?" I asked.

"Uh, yeah. Sure, sure," he said. "Be right back." He returned with two glasses and another bottle.

"Something stronger might be in order," I replied as he sat down on the bed and started pouring, nodding.

"We can start with this."

"Thanks."

I could hear the TV from the other room, caught the theme song and almost laughed. It was something my dad used to watch all the time and was one of a handful of cute memories I had of him that didn't make me want to throw up.

"So? The song sounded really good when I left. What happened?" Kurt asked. "It was solid." Though it didn't sound like it, it was pretty much the best praise Kurt could possibly give. He made no bones about not really liking the sound of October Revival, but when he did, it usually made my night.

Usually.

"I think I'm fucked up," I said. "Kurt, I'm exhausted."

"I know." He put his arm around me. "More Tom shit?"

"I wish…" I sighed. The wine was helping already, and I could feel myself unwind. "Just a difficult business arrangement sometimes."

"Was James being an asshole?" Kurt asked.

I knew I couldn't talk to Kurt about this. Tom was one thing. Kurt had his own crush on him, could appreciate his wildness and reckless-ness. But he hated, loathed, James, on principle. Maybe he worried, at a level, that eventually we'd end up together, that I'd screw up the best friendship—the longest enduring friendship—of my life, for James. He's prescient sometimes, Kurt. I bet he knew it was just a matter of time before we finally figured it out, then broke each other's hearts.

If that's not rock and roll, I don't know what is.

"James?" I asked as if he were the last person in the world I was thinking about. I knew it was a shitty job of pretending, but Kurt was too busy texting someone to notice. He was half present, which was to my benefit. "No, just stressed out. I'm being too…hard on myself with some of these songs."

"I can always help," Kurt offered, giving me an eyebrow wiggle. He knew well enough it wasn't going to happen.

"Dusty can hear your musical experiments three hundred miles away, so no. Though I guess when this album crashes and burns, we can always do a little side project together. I promise, plenty of synth," I said, crossing my heart.

He snorted through his nose. "Only if I get to play the Theremin."

"Anything for you, darling dear."

Half a bottle and a bourbon in, I started getting James's texts.

**James:** What's going on, you?
**Kate:** Just tired. We've been holed up for weeks.
**James:** You were practically flaky tonight. Not like you.
**Kate:** Maybe I need a break from the album.
**James:** I don't get it. Seems to be going so well. It's the best we've done yet, and we've still got more songs to write.
**Kate:** I dunno.
**James:** You're the worst on yourself sometimes. Was it what I said about the singing? I mean it. You should sing more.
**Kate:** Not going to happen. Listen, I have to go. TTYL.

KURT HAD SETTLED on the end of my bed and was flipping through the channels, smoking a cigarette. It's one of the things about him that gets under James's skin since he views smoking as one of the worst things to occur to humanity ever. It doesn't help, his father is dying from emphysema and all. Sometimes I think Kurt continues to smoke just to piss off James.

Anyway. I was tired of James's texts and feeling sick to my stomach. The wine was sort of roiling around rather than doing anything effective. Wine's never been my preferred vehicle of alcohol delivery. It's just too filling, like beer. You need a lot to get a real buzz off of it, which is why I've always been a straight bourbon kind of girl. On ice when it gets really hot, to be specific. You'd be amazed at how detailed my liquor fantasies are, even years out and dry. I know, the total rock-and-roll cliché, right? But once you're an addict, you're always an addict. One of those little gems I learned in rehab I don't consider total bullshit. I'll never go a day without thinking of good Kentucky bourbon, and I'll never go a day without thinking about Tom. I guess it says a lot about me.

Liquor aside, though. James, and everyone, in fact, knew exactly why I didn't sing. In the beginning, we'd had this idea I could sing some of the songs we wrote, a la Fleetwood Mac. But our first gig out with new material, just before we went into the studio, I apparently lost whatever abilities I'd had in the past. I'm not sure if it was because I had to follow the voice that was Tom Chesley or because I was becoming painfully aware everyone adored Sara, but I started forgetting lyrics. My own fucking lyrics. I only had two songs to sing in our initial set, and no matter what I did, I would screw them both up.

And I don't mean like a brief flub. I mean the kind of mistake that brings about a singular horrifying silence of "holy shit I can't remember a single damned word of this entire song."

After three gigs, the band just gave up. No. Scratch that. I gave up before they had to say anything to embarrass even more, but I could see what they felt written all over their faces. I'd lived out the greatest fear of a musician, to fall silent when music is supposed to be happening. We adjusted the key of the songs slightly, changed some "he" to "she" and *voilà*. Tom had two new songs, and essentially all the vocals. I'll admit giving up was freeing, but at the same time, I definitely lost track of a part of the music I really liked. Sometimes I'd drop subtle hints about trying something other than background vocals, but I just didn't have the courage. Years later, I was still mortified.

Sure, early on, Sara could have done it. But her voice didn't gel so well with the rest of the sound. She was great with the harmonies, especially when we all got in on it. Four-part, man. There's nothing like it. It's the sort of sound that gets right into your brain and makes the nerves vibrate. Chills. But even though Sara wanted, really wanted, to do more lead vocals, even James pushed back. Kurt had called her style of singing "precise yodeling" because it really did have a sort of Lilith Fair lilt. Yeah, she's had her own successful little solo career, but hearing her sing the sort of songs James and I wrote never felt right. Even when we were The Blue Trixies, I took the lead.

So James bringing it up was overwhelming. Not to mention the whole feelings thing. I'm not good at feelings. But it's probably obvious. To add to the fun mix, I'm even worse at relationships. I'm good at breaking things. It's like the world's most useless superpower. And having spent almost two years watching James tormented by Sara—both while they were together and afterward—I just felt depression rising up all around me. I couldn't tell him. I couldn't tell Kurt.

When Kurt realized I wasn't going to confide in him, he took his leave of me, knowing full well I was keeping something from him. But he could tell I wanted to be left alone. I was trying to avoid too much drinking, but I still polished off the rest of the wine.

Though it wasn't all that pathetic because I started writing "Some Summer Song," and it turned out really well. I still hear it playing now and again when I'm out shopping or whatever. And it always makes me smile. It's one moment where I didn't break anything, myself or otherwise. Pure musical catharsis. And people get it. People like me who've felt those same conflicting feelings. Sometimes it's important to sit back and pat yourself on the shoulder and say, "That thing I did there. It was just good."

# CHAPTER SEVEN

THE REASON it's so important to savor good moments, I've learned, is you never know when you'll get slapped in the face with something horrible. Looking back, I'd expected it to happen in the band. You know, another overdose on Tom's part after lapsing back to the real world (which never happened, to everyone's shock and surprise) or Paul quitting or Dusty wrecking her Porsche.

Maybe I'm a terrible pessimist, but it's sort of the way of the world, isn't it? I mean, I've always felt stupidly lucky. Most people in the world live lives with more pain and anguish than I can even imagine. I enjoy freedom of expression, the right to vote, and the right to rock. Not the same can be said for women around the world. So, knowing that, I always felt as if bad things were my due. I can't go on enjoying life, doing exactly what I wanted to do rather than suffering through some menial job, without expecting something to tip the scales in the other direction every now and again. Especially when it comes to my past.

I was on my way to the studio the night after the horrible epiphany I'd had regarding James and the feelings I promised to Never Ever Speak Of. The first time my phone rang, I didn't even bother taking it out of my purse, since I was running late and I was 99% sure it was

"

someone calling from the studio to make sure I wasn't hung-over and still sleeping (which, sadly, was still a rather common occurrence).

When it rang again, I stopped mid-stride and fished the phone out, startled to see a metro Atlanta number, 404. Granted, I'm related to half the folks down that way, but as a rule, they don't contact me. Between having a kid at thirteen and running away and becoming a godless singer/songwriter, you could say we don't have the closest relationship. And, well, the last time I'd seen my father, I'd asked him to do something very uncomfortable to Jesus. Family fun.

So, when Dad's voice came over the phone, I almost threw it across the street.

"Katherine?" he asked as if he had never heard me ask ten thousand times to just call me Kate.

"We're not talking." It was a stupid thing to say, but I was already too angry to say anything else. "Or did you forget?"

He paused. I could hear him clear his throat. "We need you to come to Smyrna. I need you to come home."

"Uh…" was my reply.

"Your mother…she's…"

* * *

THE NIGHT BEFORE, my mother had been out with her bridge club. Painfully cute, I know. Apparently the game went a little later than normal, and she'd had one too many with her friends and collided with a car filled with six teenagers. None of the kids were more than slightly injured, mostly because they were in a Hummer H3.

But Mom…

Listen, this sort of thing is really hard to write about. But I'm told it's the part that actually brings about healing. Or whatever. Not sure I buy into all of it, but the worst part about the whole car accident, almost, is that Mom was alive when Dad called, but by the time I got to Atlanta, she wasn't. All that great closure in movies and stuff? Yeah, I didn't get that. Even though it was just quick trip from Tennessee, and while I'd been prepared for seeing her in the worst state I could imagine, I hadn't readied myself for death.

Mom was broken. Smeared. Gone. No open casket. Barely identifiable.

Shocker, we've never had a good relationship.

Claire Marshall did everything she was supposed to do. She learned how to keep a house, how to cook for her husband. She entertained. She made chitchat with all the right church ladies. But she always had a dark side. She was depressed. She was distant. I sometimes wondered if she had a whole other life inside her head that we couldn't see. What started as casual drinking when I was younger became a problem by the time I hit my preteens.

Dad would get this look on his face when she started to pour herself a drink, and while he never said anything about it around me, soon she was self-pickling around the clock. So, when Dad wasn't home, I misbehaved. I wanted Mom to yell at me, but she always left the discipline to my dad. He was the head of the house; he was the one she submitted to. I remember talking about this to a therapist once, and she asked me if I thought my dad ever hurt my mom, like beat her. I don't think so. And yet, I think their emotional distance was a kind of abuse.

I knew my mom had a drinking problem. And I know why she chose to drink. It's what makes it so hard. I hated her for drinking when I was a kid, and then when I was thirteen and… Okay, clearly I have to back up even more because this is just getting nebulous.

A FEW TIMES, it's been noted I have a sister thirteen years younger than me. Except Rhee isn't my little sister, as any idiot could deduce. She's my *daughter*. When I was thirteen, I got pregnant by this eighteen-year-old named Jason Miller in high school, who I very stupidly and naively got myself involved with. Since it was so easy with Mom hammered most nights, I was running away almost every week, and even when my dad had my door nailed shut, I'd find ways to get out. And I did. I didn't know birth control existed. The only advice I had was not to have sex until I got married. And when Jason and I started fooling around, it felt good. Damned good. And I wanted to feel good instead of a constant failure.

Anyway, that horrible thing they promised would happen if I disobeyed the law of God happened. I got knocked up. Abortion wasn't an issue; by the time I figured out what was going on, I was halfway through the pregnancy—seriously, people go on and on about how it's a personal choice, but I didn't have one.

My parents' response wasn't support. It was utter shame. They pulled me out of school and moved under pretense Dad had been wooed by another church in the Atlanta suburbs (we lived in Athens at the time). I was adopted by a reluctant homeschooling group to finish out ninth grade and then enrolled as a sophomore after I had the baby as if nothing had ever happened. We were new enough no one really raised an eyebrow.

I never wanted to be Rhee's mother, and after going through pregnancy and childbirth, I decided I didn't ever want children, to even make the attempt at motherhood. But I never wanted my mother to be her mother, either. Years later, when I half-heartedly tried to fight it, Mom got legal custody out from underneath me, and Rhee never got wind as far as I knew. I was twenty at the time, just finishing college, and had the idea that I'd have a great job (or maybe be famous) and have the chance to give Rhee a good upbringing. Which was a joke in and of itself, but my mom was a drunk, and my dad is a terrible person.

So, Rhee was raised thinking I was her sister and as shitty as I am as a human being, I never tried to tell her otherwise. I was her quasi-famous but usually drunk and/or hungover "Sissy," and that was that. Cutting myself off from my parents meant I didn't speak much with Rhee as she grew up, only emails every now and again or a text message. Rhee's always been everything I'm not, which is a miracle considering the significant lack of diversity in her father's genes. She was valedictorian of her class—graduated a year early, even—and was studying pre-med at Emory; also, she drank the Kool-Aid really young and embraced Jesus like I never could.

That sounds old and bitter. Listen, I don't hate God. I don't hate Jesus. Sometimes I feel like I have to point that out. I hate my father, and it doesn't take a shrink to realize my vision of God was shaped by his dark, awful secrets. I can't deal with the gossip mill of churches and the fact most Evangelicals run from historical readings of the Bible like it's one of the plagues of Egypt. I find the Bible fascinating; I think Jesus was a really great guy. But when it comes down to it, I suppose I'm just a non-practicing Christian. In my mind, Jesus always looked a bit like John Lennon. Maybe I conflated the two after a while. I don't know.

What was so bad about my father? Well, the worst of his grievances were the affairs. It's the hypocrisy that gets me.

I was about nine when I found out. Mom was at a women's retreat. I remember it was late summer, sweltering, and disgustingly hot. I had been playing at our neighbor's house, and it got late and dark before I even knew. Dad hadn't called me home, but I was still worried he'd be mad if he saw me come in so late. Thankfully I was old hat at entering the house without him knowing. My current method of re-entry was going in through the basement, through a conveniently placed window (our old house actually had a dirt basement, uncommon in the South).

I had to skirt the driveway to get to the basement, though, and that's when the shit really went down. The house is set back quite a bit from the road, in good old Southern style, and the driveway snakes around the side of the house. Dad's Chevy was parked, as I expected. But it was moving. Shaking. The shocks squeaking in a comical rhythm.

Sounds emitted. Dad thought I was inside my room, so he knew he couldn't do the deed in the house. So he'd taken this hussy out to his car to fuck her like some lovelorn high school kid. Ironically, she was saying, "Oh God, oh God," over and over again.

Masochist as I am, I found Dad doing this same thing at least a half-dozen times, with three separate women, over the course of the next few months. All church ladies, one of whom was married. All in a fucking Chevy (yeah, it really was a fucking Chevy, as my mom's was the *driving* Chevy...) It's like my dad was some sort of pastorly Don Draper.

I never told Mom. But I think she always knew. Their relationship was all smiles in the pews but freezing cold to each other at home. Mom got everything she needed from Dad, which was a secure home (something she never had) and enough money to drink. Dad got a relatively attractive wife who stood by him and never caused a stir at church. And didn't seem to mind him boning on the side. Claire and Bill Marshall. What a pair.

So no, I wasn't ever a good kid. But at the point I learned of my dad's wayward ways, what resolve I had in being a Christian completely evaporated. This wasn't just my father; this was a man in charge of a whole congregation, responsible for the spiritual welfare of two hundred people who looked to him to be an example. It was fine that he failed me; honestly that didn't hurt so much as knowing he lied to all those other people—some of them were my friends. So maybe my pregnancy was a good excuse to move away from them, to detach my own umbilical cord. I don't remember Dad being particularly upset about it, not as sad as I thought he'd be, when I finally left home.

I know it's really hard to love an addict. I've been told as much. I don't know how much my father knew about Mom's drinking, but I suppose he had to have some idea. Maybe that's why he did what he did. I don't like to think about it. It's not the easiest thing to hide. And I don't know if she drank because she knew about the infidelity or if she thought no one would ever find out. But she was always out of control about it. She denied the problem to herself, and with Rhee out of the house, I imagine it got even worse.

I don't hate my mom. She was wonderful to me when I was pregnant, and she took care of Rhee which, admittedly, I couldn't have done. But she gave up on herself, on her own dreams, so long ago that talking to her was like talking to a recording. I wanted to have a relationship. And I think she did too. But whatever her demons were, they prevented forging that bond. And it never happened.

---

MY PARENTS HADN'T MOVED out of the house in Smyrna where I'd lost my childhood and finished high school. It isn't a pretty house but rather one of those late eighties contemporaries that, even at the time, seemed too modern to be practical. The slanted ceilings, the huge windows—not a house to be viewed on the outside, not like the big Georgian we'd had in Athens. Though despite the odd architecture, the house itself was pristine. The cedar siding had been recently stained (I could still smell it), and Dad's gardens wrapped around the house in a dappled embrace.

There was also a for sale sign by the mailbox.

I'd rented a car, nothing too flashy—really, my family was very weird with the whole quasi-fame thing—and walked up the flagstone pathway to the front door. There were three cars in the driveway, so I'd had to park in the street, but I had no idea who was inside, who would greet me. It had always been Mom. Or at least, four years ago when I'd last visited it had been her. She always acted as if I'd just been out across town, falling into the same scripted conversations. She asked me how I was feeling. If I was eating well. Suggested I read the *Wall Street Journal.* Then we'd sit in the living room and watch TV until Dad or Rhee came by, order Chinese takeout, and go our separate ways.

So, taking a deep breath and wishing I'd packed a flask (I figured it was a good time to make my best attempt to stay sober in a while) I knocked on the door. When no one answered, I rang the bell.

My cousin Rita answered the door, looking at me as if she had no idea who I was, until I took off my sunglasses, when her muddy brown eyes popped open. She'd expanded since I last saw her, edging comfortably into middle age. We'd last talked as teenagers. She looked just like her mom, my aunt Diane, had. Sort of like a hippy hobbit.

"Oh, Katie?" Rita asked, hand on her chest. "I didn't think...you..."

Before she could be more insulting, I saw Dad approaching from behind her. Dad was tall, handsome still, even though he was past sixty. His hair had gone completely white in the last few years, and he'd lost a good amount of weight from working out. He was wearing a plaid flannel shirt and dark jeans, a look that gave him the air of a man trying to appear younger.

Rita backed away, and my dad just grabbed me and hugged me, so no time for me to say anything stupid or angry or insensitive—which, I may add, I'm quite good at, and had entirely planned for—but I found myself holding back tears. You can hold years of anger—really I was working on decades here—but no matter what you do, family is family. I idolized my dad when I was a kid, and with the smell of his flannel and cologne, there I was again, seven years old with my knee skinned, blubbering in his arms.

I let go of the hug. Couldn't let it out. Couldn't let them see what a fucking mess I was. Without words, he kept the door open for me, calling for my cousin Jack (Rita's brother) to get me something to eat.

Walking into the house, it smelled exactly the same: fresh paint and, just under it, baked bread. Not that Mom ever baked. Just that somehow, the smell was in the bones of the house.

They had updated their furniture, replacing the brown couches with white streamlined ones and the thick curtains with tailored valences. But it was still the house I remembered, still full of the same knickknacks my mother collected (Precious Moments and Hummels, mostly) lining the cabinets and most surfaces, the same snapshots of me and Rhee growing up, Dad's favorite Last Supper reproduction above the couch.

I wiped my eyes with the back of my hand, and someone gave me some water. Rita's son, I think though I'd never met him, introduced himself as Kyle. He was in an Army uniform. I saw no sign of Rhee, but I could feel her hovering around the periphery.

"I'm so glad you could come," said my aunt Kathy, my namesake and my father's other sister. "Katie..." She had aged well, her hair as white as Dad's, but her face was almost unchanged. She still dressed to the nines, as if she'd raided a Coldwater Creek, and was covered in scarves and jewelry. I'd always liked her—she was an artist—but it was overwhelming enough to see her, and everyone else, I was a bit dumbstruck.

Staring down at the glass of water, I tried to collect my thoughts. Really, my thoughts didn't amount to a hill of beans. It was like static. My lips were still trembling from fighting the tears, and I couldn't look anyone in the face.

I just wanted a drink.

People were whispering all around me. I swallowed. I could just get up and leave. But it would be such a diva thing to do, and I was terrified of coming off that way to them for some reason. All the Zen feeling I'd had on the flight over had evaporated.

Then Rhee walked in from the hallway. God, she was so beautiful. Taller than me by at least three inches, she was dressed like you'd expect of a clever co-ed, her long dark hair (just like mine and Mom's) up in a messy bun on her head. She had glasses, too, big and hipstery. I almost laughed, but I did manage to smile at her.

She did not return the smile. She just stood there in the doorway to the living room, staring at me.

The Desperation Squad (that's the aunts and cousins and everyone who'd descended) all started talking among themselves. I mean, they knew about Rhee. You can't hide that sort of thing from your family. Mom had a hysterectomy after I was born, so medically it was completely impossible she could have had Rhee.

I stood up to start walking toward Rhee, and she bolted for her bedroom (my old room) and slammed the door shut.

My cheeks flushed red; I felt it creeping all the way up into my scalp.

"She knows, now," Aunt Kathy told me gently.

"How the hell did she find out?" I asked.

"You should talk to her," Dad said to me. "She's in your old room."

"How did she find out?" I repeated.

Dad frowned. "She found her birth certificate when we were going through your mother's desk looking for her Rolodex. The original copy. I didn't know your mother had saved it; perhaps she was waiting for a good time to tell her…"

IT DIDN'T TAKE much convincing for her to let me in the room. When I entered, Rhee was standing by the window, her hands crossed over her chest, staring across the street. She looked terrible and defiant. And scary. Seriously, what the hell am I supposed to do with a twenty-year-old? I was shaking.

I had expected a room stuffed with pink and ruffles, as her own room had still been when I left, but it's not what I found. The room was still painted the same color I'd left it, dark purple, and sported the same awful gray carpet. She was a tidy kid, but every square inch of her walls was covered with posters. Most of the bands I didn't recognize—they were Christian rock groups judging by their names and poses (after a while, you just get a sense about these things).

But by her bed were three posters, one ripped in half but still dangling. It was a poster of my band, the promo shot from *Round the Bend* with all of us silhouetted against purple and green lasers. The poster was conveniently torn down the middle of my body.

Next to it was a poster of Tom, staring and simpering at the camera in his younger days and scandalously without a shirt (making me feel eleven shades of awkward), and then another of our album covers.

I felt like such an asshole.

"You know what sucks the most?" she said as I approached her carefully. She turned her head to me, giving me a "congratulations you caught me" look.

"It's hard to pick. Lots sucks right now," I said. Yes. That's me. A paragon of motherliness.

Rhee made a teenaged noise, a sort of strangled groan of frustration I'd made a thousand times in my years. Clearly she hadn't grown up too much in college. "As fucked up as you are." She said the dreaded f-word as if it had been newly minted. "I still wish you'd have been my mom."

"But I—"

"I mean, really. Like, I wish you'd have been here. You knew about her drinking, didn't you?"

"Uh…"

"Now I have two moms. Except one is dead."

"Rhee, I tried…"

"Tried? You sent elaborate Christmas presents and birthday gifts every year. Now that I think about, it makes sense. The car, for instance. Too much. All those shows of affection were just guilt presents."

"It was just a little Honda," I said as if it made the difference. I had sent her a car when she passed her driver's test, mostly because she told me my folks weren't letting her drive Dad's car, since it was technically church property, and they couldn't afford anything else.

"The song, 'One More Try,' that song's about me, isn't it?" Rhee asked, accusing.

"You listen…to our music?" I asked.

"Are you kidding me? Dad and…" she stopped and corrected herself, letting her enthusiasm overtake her anger, "I mean. Yes. I listen to your music. Of course I do."

I nodded. Really, I've never been equipped for this kind of thing. She was right. I wrote lyrics years ago, but we hadn't recorded it until we hit the studio with the first album. Not exactly a #1 hit but a decent B side. It was about my parents snagging custody from me.

And it was painfully, painfully honest. Exhibit A: *Someday you'll see, I'll never be the one you remember; I tried, I tried, but it wasn't in me / Dream your dreams, and I'll dream mine.* Probably the most selfish song I ever wrote. And I was stupid enough to think she would never figure it out. That's the danger of cutting yourself off from family and coping with large and frequent amounts of alcohol; distance deludes you into thinking secrets stay in the dark while you're away, and the booze is a soothing lie. You think makes it all just go away.

"Why didn't you tell me? How am I supposed to process all of this, now?" she screeched.

"I suck at being a mom. And a person." I winced as I said the words. "I'm sorry, Rhee. I suck at being a sister too."

All these years, I'd honestly never thought of myself as a mother. More like a vehicle for a person being born. A meatbag, a vessel. I didn't mother Rhee; I didn't help her survive. I never soothed her or changed her diapers or picked out clothes. I didn't take her to school or help her with her homework or talk to her about boys. That was entirely my own mom's doing. I remember watching Mom with Rhee, when I was finishing out high school, absolutely shocked by her maternal instincts. She could get Rhee to smile at just a few weeks old, could soothe her with the wave of her hand. I didn't even bother getting close to Rhee.

"Rhiannon? My legal name is *Rhiannon?*" she asked me. She was crying, but there was still a curious glint in her eyes.

"Yeah."

"What kind of name is Rhiannon?"

"Don't tell me you've never heard of Fleetwood Mac."

"I've never heard of Fleetwood Mac," she replied drolly. "I know you didn't name me after the singer because she came along way after I was born."

"She's *Rihanna.* And this Rhian*non* is from a song. A song Stevie Nicks wrote. It was my favorite song around the time you were born," I said. "'Rhiannon rings like a bell through the night?'" Rhee looked confused, so I sang the first few lines.

"Oh, I think I've heard it before," Rhee said, but I could tell she had no idea. Just didn't want to lose face. I'd done the same trick a thousand times in front of musicians I wanted to impress. Especially as a chick musician. No matter how high October Revival went, some dude with an inflated sense of self who could play Dave Mathews covers wanted to make sure I really knew my shit. Whether it was gear or influences, chord progressions or music time served. I could write a whole other treatise on it.

"Listen. You're the only reason I came down here. Not for Dad. Not for the hens and biddies in there."

"And you were just going to keep on lying to me?" she asked.

Rhee had stopped making eye contact, so I put my sunglasses on to make it sting a little less. She was shutting me out. I'd let her down by being a grand disappointment. I hadn't taken her in my arms; I hadn't told her everything was going to be okay. Her mom, the real one, was still dead, and I was still a miserable excuse for a person.

My phone started chirping in my purse, and I pulled it out. James texting. I put it back, rather than responding. But I saw the dreaded name: Sara. I knew the conversation couldn't wait long.

"Yeah. I was going to keep lying," I said. "Rhee, I had you when I was thirteen. I was not, and never have been, equipped to be a mother. When you were little, I was…selfish and rebellious, and…"

"Listen you don't have to…just…this is all really hard."

"I've got to check in at the hotel. I'm at the Magnuson, so it's not far. You can give me a call there or on my phone."

"Thanks," Rhee said, turning away from me. I opened the door halfway before she said, "Hey, Kate."

I was already fishing in my purse for my keys and phone, ready to bolt as soon as humanly possible. So I was a little distracted when I responded, "Yeah, Rhee?"

"You could have done it. I just don't think you wanted to."

I walked out of the house and didn't bother to respond to my relatives. They wanted something I couldn't give them, so I did what comes most naturally to me: I ran away.

I was so mad I finally cried.

# CHAPTER EIGHT

"Wow. Just wow."

It was Kurt. I wanted to call Tom. He was the only one in the band who actually knew some of the story. It's hard to hide stretch marks from a very enthusiastic lover. It's just how it is. But with my muddled brain, I just couldn't reach out to him at that moment. It wouldn't have been fair. And I couldn't deal with more religious bullshit. I really would have lost it.

Plus, James had texted me about Sara being in town—in Nashville, recording some sessions with her solo act—and I couldn't cope with his still-pining heart. He wouldn't have understood, either. He'd find out eventually, sure, but I wasn't about to walk into another broken heart, feeling as I was for him.

So I dropped the whole thing on Kurt. At first he was offended I hadn't told him earlier, having met the family when we were in college. But then the drama of the whole situation became far too delicious for him to stay mad at me.

"I mean…I thought the girl was a miracle baby. You really had me duped," Kurt said. "And I can usually smell gossipy deliciousness miles away."

"Yeah. She's not taking it well. And I figure since she knows, everyone else should know."

"Everyone?" he asked, dubious.

I stuck my tongue out at the phone. "Okay. Not everyone. Tom knows, but no one else does. Not even my agent. Not even Dusty."

"So what are you going to do?"

"What do you mean, what am I going to do? What *can* I do? I can't adopt a twenty-year-old like she's some puppy left in a will."

"I don't think anyone's asking you to adopt her. I just think you need to be there for her. You both lost a mom. I mean, regardless of the technicality."

"Right."

"She likes the band?" he asked.

It had seemed that way. "I...think so."

"Maybe it's a place to start. Talk to her again. When's the funeral? Do you need me to come down?"

"Maybe. I don't know."

---

**James:** Just saw Sara downtown. Ugh. Felt like punching a wall until my hand fell off.

**Kate:** Sorry took so long to respond. Been dealing with stuff.

**James:** Shit. I know. I'm sorry. How's it going?

**Kate:** Funeral's on Monday.

**James:** You okay?

**Kate:** Yup. All's fine.

**James:** Any idea where Tom is? He's not answering his mobile.

**Kate:** No. No idea. Hopefully not dead in a gutter.

**James:** Christ, Cakes. That's morbid even for you.

**Kate:** Give me a fucking break, James. My mom is dead, and I'm trapped with my insane family I haven't seen since I was a teenager.

...

...

**James:** You're right. I'm such a sodding selfish prick when Sara's involved. Condolences and all that shit.
**Kate:** Thanks…

---

I SAT HOLED up in my hotel until late the next day, drinking overpriced shitty wine at my leisure, when the pressing guilt about Rhee started to really take its toll. I knew there were unresolved conversations between my dad and me, between Rhee and me, and lots of family members who were waiting in the wings to see what I'd do next. Waiting to see what gossip would keep them afloat for the next decade.

It became clear I was going to have to confront them one last time if I truly wanted to cut ties again. Which meant cutting ties with Rhee. I'd already proved a colossal failure and had no intentions on metamorphosing into a good mom. It just wasn't going to happen.

I purposely didn't pack any flashy clothes, not that I had much anyone would consider haute couture. But I had some nice stuff, good foundation pieces that were more expensive than I wanted to admit, even if, as my mom had once told me, they looked no better than Goodwill purchases on a good day. I was, and still am, embarrassed at my success around my family.

Still, even my basic stuff felt out of place, and my hands shook as I tried to gather myself. It wasn't working. Nothing worked as well as booze. I was rooting through my luggage when the room phone rang. I looked around as if expecting someone to materialize, then picked it up.

"Hi?" I asked.

"Cakes, how's tricks?"

"Tom?"

"Mind if I come up?"

"Mind…if you…what?"

"I'm in the lobby. With Kurt. Quaint place here. Even more charming than Nashville. Or not. Quite the sprawl, innit? It just goes on forever. House after house. It's like out of some American Christmas film."

I threw the receiver on the bed. It gave me a half minute to think before I said something, even though all I wanted to do was throw the entire hotel phone out of the window.

Nothing came to mind, so I picked it up again.

"Katie?"

"Yeah. Hi. Sure. Be down in a few minutes."

Part of the lack of mental acuity on my part had to do with the whole drinking three bottles of wine the night before. I mean, even for me that's excessive, especially alone. When I first got the news, I went into the usual spin in my head: I was going to finally kick the whole booze thing. I was going to start new. But it's not how addiction works. One minute I was contemplating one last drink, then next thing I knew I was waking up with a mouth of vomit breath. Cut scene like in a bad movie. Not even a decent cross dissolve.

Yes, the dream of rock and roll. Living it, folks.

Still, I should have remembered Rhee had called me that night. I should have written it down. I should have looked at the clock or put my glasses on and checked my cell phone.

But I didn't. I walked headfirst into a disaster. Which I'm really quite good at, inebriation required or otherwise.

---

THE ELEVATOR DOORS SLID OPEN, and I immediately felt something was off. Too much noise in the lobby—people talking, shoes squeaking—for anything good to come of it. Listen, it's not like any of us were ever crazy celebrities in the States. We'd never travel so light in the UK, but I honestly was deluded into thinking people would leave me alone, what with my mother dying.

But apparently that wasn't the case.

I turned the corner to see Tom Chesley standing next to Kurt Bastian, the latter with his arm protectively around Rhee, surrounded by cameras and microphones. She looked terrified, Kurt looked distant, and Tom was a little smug. They were surrounded by the local news. Seriously, the local fucking news.

So I did the only rational thing I could. I called the police.

Someone pointed to me, and I took a step back, then saw the look of fear on Rhee's face and steeled myself. There were about fifteen people from the news stations all told, both Fox and ABC local affiliates present, but they were very pushy. And they kept asking Rhee questions. And one person said, "So, you now know Kate Styx is your mother—how do you feel?"

Something snapped. Went red. It was like a crazy, dissonant chord just ripped through my body, and before I knew it, I was shoving people aside (which is difficult considering I'm not exactly a linebacker).

"When did you find out you were Kate Styx's daughter?"

"How long have you suspected?"

"Are you a fan of the band?"

"Did you ever suspect…?"

So here's what happened. Someone made the mistake of putting a microphone right in my face and asked me a very rude question about covering up my pregnancy and my rebellious years. I'd never felt anything remotely maternal when it came to Rhee, but in the moment, I did.

I punched the lady. It wasn't that hard (she later claimed I knocked her tooth loose, but listen, I've thrown about six punches in my life, the majority of which were directed at inanimate objects, and there's zero chance my punch resulted in that much damage). The police arrived just in time to restrain me from doing anything further. Not that I would have. My hand hurt too much, and the impact sort of woke me up to reality. Plus, broken fingers don't gel so well with keyboard players, no matter how drunk they are.

Posting bail wasn't an issue, but for safety reasons, we ended up at a hotel in downtown Atlanta. This meant significantly more driving on my part to see the family, but it was harder for us to be tracked. I should have known staying in Smyrna would land me in trouble, but I made the mistake of thinking people just didn't care about me and my life. I've never been good at perspective.

The bigger hotel also meant Tom and Kurt had their own space since the last thing I wanted to do was share rooms with them.

Rhee had found her way to the hotel though, and I had her sitting in the living area when Dusty called me. It was inevitable. Dusty had gone eight hours without reaching out, and I knew since my face was all over the local news (and that James had filled her in) it was just a matter of time.

"You okay, pumpkin?" Dusty asked. I could hear the whooshing wind on the other side, most likely from her being on a hands-free while driving her Porsche.

"I'm fine."

"I know it's tough with all the drama, but try and stay low as you can."

"I'll be as low as a snake. A snake at a funeral."

"Good. 'Cause you're the one I can usually depend on, Katie. I've already talked with Fred," the band's lawyer, "and she's willing to settle out of court. But it'll still make all the headlines. Probably more in the UK, of course, since they care more about you there."

Underhanded compliments are one of Dusty's specialties.

"Right."

"They've got pictures of Rhee, y'know. Not sure there's anything we can do, legally, to stop them. She's over eighteen. Have you prepared her?"

"I'm pretty sure she's still dealing with it herself. I'm not sure we're talking right now. I don't know. I inherited a teenager, and I'm not sure what to do." I didn't know why I was saying this to Dusty, but I had to say it to someone.

"Buy her a pony or something. Hell if I know. At least she's a lovely girl. That's helpful. They could have torn her to shreds."

"Could have? You sound like you've already seen it in print, Dusty."

I didn't like the way Dusty was talking but really had too much going on in my brain to start jumping to conclusions. It's not that I don't trust Dusty. It's just she's in a business I don't understand. Public relations, interaction with bigwigs and all that. I just really can't imagine what she's up to—or I can, and I wish I couldn't. I'm grateful we don't have to deal with it as a band, but those behind the curtain dealings just make me a little itchy.

And like I said, I was feeling really overprotective of Rhee in the first place. My hackles were up, and Dusty wasn't helping matters.

"Calm down," Dusty instructed. "Chances are a big scandal will eclipse you in a few days, anyway. It's just the way these things work. October Revival isn't exactly Coldplay."

Rhee was sitting on the leather couch when I returned, flipping through something on her iPhone with a determined expression on her face. She didn't notice me standing there for a good solid minute, but when she did, she stood up. She sat back down again as if she'd decided not to run away in that short second.

I didn't know what to say to her, so I offered her some coffee or room service or something. She declined with a mumble.

"I'm not planning on going anywhere," I said. "Except...the funeral. But if you want to stay here, you're more than—"

"Listen. I called the news," Rhee said.

"You what?"

She gave me an incredulous teenaged stare, making me feel like I was the stupidest, oldest, most out of touch human being in the entire world. It seriously aged me fifteen years in the span of six seconds.

I sighed. "Right. You called the news to get back at me."

She nodded and started to cry.

# CHAPTER NINE

My mother's funeral was thankfully uneventful after that rousing interlude. Tom had offered to sing something at the ceremony, but I declined. While it might have made Rhee's day, it was a little too excessive for me to be comfortable. Tom and Kurt, the world's most unlikely duo, stayed until the next day, and there was an array of famous friends who sent flowers (including an elaborate display from the band). Rhee collected all the cards, morbid and weird as it was, but she wanted to prove her provenance to her friends. My dad delivered the eulogy and said all the expected things. We ate crappy catering after, took condolences, and that was that. I didn't talk to many people beyond accepting their condolences and moving on.

I'm not sure how to feel about how we left things. I wish I could tell you I started calling Rhee every day, and we began this magical, wonderful relationship that's treasured and amazing. But it's not so easy. We buried her real mother that day, as flawed and broken as she was. Nothing can change that.

At the funeral home later that evening, after I'd had my weight in Jack Daniels, Dad wanted to talk.

"Katherine," he said. I had tried to make my way back out of the funeral home, but he found me anyway. Old habits die hard. "Can we speak for just a moment?"

Behind him, I could see vague shadows of people in the parlor, smell the onion sweet odor of hors d'oeuvres. I was predictably drunk, and my ride was waiting for me outside, Kurt and Tom ready to whisk me back to the airport and my real life.

"I don't really have anything to say to you," I said, waving my hand as if it might dispel him.

I was embarrassingly unsteady on my feet. And drunker than I had thought. Shit. Shit. Fuck.

"We should have told Rhee. But your mother was afraid of what might happen."

"Rhee could have handled this whole bullshit if you had eased her into it. You were sloppy."

I was getting sloppy, too. But I never would have admitted to it. I was at the point of drunkenness where I was aware it was happening but feeling rather proud and invincible and entitled.

Dad sighed. He looked so old. The lines under his eyes crinkled like wax paper. His eyes were starting to dull with age, especially around the edges of his irises. He had hair growing out of his ears.

"We made mistakes; we've all made mistakes."

"Were any of them here tonight?" I asked, craning my neck. "Do you have a new cadre of fuck buddies?"

"Lord, Katherine. Your mouth."

"You're fucking right, my mouth."

He gave me the look. But it didn't scare me any longer. "I probably deserve that." There were no tears in his eyes, no lines of grief on his face. I'd be willing to bet he was relieved now that the old lady was gone. He could mess around all he wanted. Nothing as appealing as a silver fox, after all.

"We should have done better with you." I didn't expect the level of bitterness that came from him, and even in my drunken state, I faltered a bit. The wit is never well lubricated when I'm on my way on the drunken train.

"You know what, Dad? I think I turned out pretty fucking great," I told him, leaning forward about three inches too far. Pesky equilibrium. "I graduated college. I make a living doing what I like, and you know what? People like it. They pay me to write songs and play music. To top that off, I even fucked the man of my dreams. I'm sorry if that's not your definition of success. But that's okay. I take responsibility for every action. So I'm a shitty person. That should come to no surprise to you. I take after you."

"Katherine..."

"What?"

"I'm glad you have your friends. And I'm sorry. I pray the Lord shows you the way."

I didn't hear anything more because I staggered out of the funeral parlor, and Kurt was there, and I was in his arms sobbing.

Then I threw up.

Because that's my jam.

———

Do I regret having zero relationship with my mother? Do I still blame her for lots of things? Sometimes. But, in general, I've let it go. I hadn't talked to my mom regarding anything of substance in almost ten years. Going to her funeral was a mark of respect, really. That's all it could be. Visiting Georgia reminded me that I had chosen not to be a family person, that they wouldn't control me. Even Rhee couldn't keep me there. And my dad certainly never would. I may have made a fool of myself in front of him, but at least I proved that I am my mother's daughter.

A day of a hangover, and we were back at it. I had an album to finish, after all. And in the grand story of Kate Styx, when given the choice between family and music, music always wins.

———

WALKING BACK into the studio never felt so needed. The smells, like cedar and dust and metal, almost brought tears to my eyes. It was the scent of music and creativity and something altogether my own. For the last week I'd had enough of childhood memories, bad mistakes, and that pervasive haunting I'd felt since I'd left.

I needed some personal time there, and I found it. Knowing that we had the place booked for the next month solid, and that James never came in much after eleven a.m. (and that Sara was in town, and he was likely doting on her as usual) I found my way into the piano room and did some work on a bit of a song that was flitting around in my head.

It's hard to explain my songwriting process. I don't have any hard and fast rules, and there's no real alchemy in it. It's just that I'm horrible at expressing myself to people in general, and the only way I was ever really able to do it and achieve catharsis was by way of music. Before I ever started writing songs, I wrote notebooks bursting with poetry. I studied the songs I liked and rewrote lyrics over their rhyme and meter. I fiddled with chords until I had a different piece of art, close but not the same. Eventually, I found my own comfort spots. It didn't take long for me to move from guitar to keyboard—the latter a gift from my parents because I could practice with headphones in.

Shortly after Rhee was born, I started to disappear at home. Part of it had to do with the fact there was a baby in the house, of course. My mother took every waking moment to focus on Rhee, because damn it, she had hoped her granddaughter wouldn't be the same royal fuckup as her mother was. It was basic mom thinking. I let her to it. I mean, what was I going to do? I didn't want anything to do with having a kid or being a mother. I wanted to finish high school and get the living hell out of Georgia.

Two things happened right around my fourteenth birthday, just as I was starting to figure out who I was after Rhee's birth. I got a guitar, and I discovered the Cure. I don't remember which order it happened in because I can't recall ever playing anything else on the guitar other than Cure songs early in my repertoire. Sure, there were lots of other bands out there I eventually clung to, but the Cure was my own, personal, deliciously dark obsession. My dad had no freaking clue I'd gotten one of their tapes (from the library of all places) and had been listening to grossly un-Christian music.

Of course, my infatuation was years too late, the band embroiled in lawsuits and disagreements. Robert Smith started packing on the pounds, performances got sloppy, the band became a punchline like so many underrated eighties acts. But it didn't matter to me. That they were falling apart had a weird sort of appeal. They were dark and sexy and British. At the time, listening to the Cure felt like the most subversive, devilish thing I could possibly do. You know, aside from the whole unprotected sex and having a baby thing.

(Which, let me point out, was entirely consensual. I was stupid and ignorant and really, really misinformed. But I wanted to have sex. I couldn't think of anything else. The dude I was with was attractive, and I felt sexy and amazing with him, even though I was thirteen and he was eighteen. I had lots of very sexy feelings, and I didn't know what to do with them, and my parents sure as hell weren't going to tell me. Wait, they said. Just wait because that's what Jesus wants. Well, I didn't want to wait, so when Rhee's dad pressured me, I let him because it felt good. It felt damned good. I never saw any sperm, and, thinking they floated through the air or something, didn't think pregnancy was going to be an issue. Sure, I endured bleeding and pain, and when it started happening, I wished I hadn't done it. But Rhee's dad knows who he is, knows where I am if he ever wants to be involved in her life. He's never shown up. Which is his choice. Not that I exactly had the choice to *not* have her. Listen, I'm not pro-life by any stretch. This just happened to work for me, though the cost was amazingly high. I didn't start having sex again until my mid-twenties, after years of taking birth control. I still harbored a lingering fear I'd get pregnant again.)

The Cure was my gateway drug into the music of the eighties and beyond. Before them, it had been the classics that, despite not being Christian (and Stevie Nicks being decidedly witchy), they approved of. It was the music of their twenties and thirties, and they let the CSNY slide along with the Beatles, the Stones, and Simon and Garfunkel.

So it was the Cure who made me love music, who gave me the inspiration to start learning to play (I found piano suited me better but picked up the accordion, the flute, the clarinet, and the bass along the way). My parents didn't know what to do with me, but music lessons seemed to make sense to them, even if I was taking what I learned and applying it to Brit pop.

Later, in 1997, when I was a junior in high school, I heard Marla North for the first time on a mix tape my friend Kelly put together and slipped me during social studies class; she wanted me to branch out, fearing I'd become a little too obsessed with the Cure to be healthy. She was right. And all of a sudden it started making sense. Marla's voice was low and sweet, her songwriting off the charts and utterly off the books. She swore on stage. She was famous for her lovers (lots of novelists and foreign sorts) and her addictions. Coming along on a sea of female artists on the Lilith Faire wagon, she set herself apart by refusing to be defined. Alt country? Alt pop? Alt rock? She was either loved or hated, and I worshiped her.

I cut my hair like hers (those bangs!) and started making my own clothes. I started mimicking her singing voice, though I never really got it right, which is probably a good thing. I didn't have the same range or that hair-raising wail going on. But I did have, I discovered, a knack for songwriting and, it turned out, for playing piano. After years of playing other people's music, I wrapped all those melodies and harmonies around me and started making new things. Once I was in college, I was a regular open-mic sort of gal; then I met Kurt. Then I met Sara, the first other woman I connected to so strongly with music (though she argued Tori Amos was, by far, superior to Marla North; I will never concede, as much as I like Tori).

By the time The Blue Trixies were playing and getting the ear of some minor indie labels, when James and Tom found us, I was a pretty decent songwriter. Adding James to the mix made us great. I'm not saying it because I am full of myself; I'm saying it because it's true. That's one of the things that's so amazing about being a writing team. Sometimes you can just step back and see it more objectively simply because it's not entirely yours. October Revival wouldn't exist without both of us. No, we're not Lennon/McCartney (and even their partner-ship lasted only a few years as a true co-writing duo), but I like to think that Styx/Vayne has some staying power.

Back at the studio in Nashville, thinking about all this stuff, I was fiddling with what I called the Infinity Progression. It was a bit in A that I'd been playing almost all my life but never put words to. It wasn't exactly a complicated piece, but the melody was interesting, and it got me in my comfort zone. It's cyclical. Keeps on going. I could play it for hours and never get sick of it. I remember learning A is the perfect wavelength, so maybe I just tapped into a great metaphysical wavelength. Who knows? I doubt I'll ever put words to it, or even share it with anyone else, but James knew what it was and damned if he didn't sneak into the studio when I was zoning out to it.

"Hello, Katie Cakes," he said over the intercom. "Would you mind the company of a sullen Englishman who's not had enough sleep?"

My heart did one of those really annoying flippy things, half because I'd been startled and half because it was James's voice. He hadn't come to Georgia though he sent some beautiful flowers and a very lovely note. Tom had come, I kept reminding myself. Not James. But I had still spent more time than I should have thinking about James, James and Sara.

I waved at him to come in if he wanted.

He looked tired, his skin a bit on the sallow side, but he gave me a bright smile anyway. "Morning."

"Hi," I said.

James sat down on the piano bench next to me. "You, ah, look different. I almost didn't recognize you if it wasn't for the Infinity Progression."

Ah, yes. *That.*

I ran my hands through my very short hair. Yeah, people do weird things when their parents die. And once I got to the hairdresser, I just told her to cut everything off except the gray. She did a light rinse to sort of bring it all together, but where I'd had cute bangs and hair down to my elbows, I now had a pixie cut.

"I look like a little boy," I said, self-consciously running my hands through my hair and glancing sideways at him. "Dusty's going to be furious. It doesn't fit with our aesthetic."

"Ah, fuck Dusty. It's fetching. Very Jane Wiedlin. Makes your eyes stand out."

I laughed. "I get a lot more ma'ams, I notice. I should just get a cane."

He shoved me playfully. "Oh, hush you. You can't take a compliment to save your life."

"Sorry. It's been a weird few weeks, and I'm already second-guessing my impulse haircut."

"Well, I wouldn't worry about it. It was just surprising to see, that's all. People do odd things when they're grieving; I'm no stranger to that. When my gran died, I got a tattoo of a pineapple, which was largely considered a bad move."

He did have a badly drawn pineapple tattoo on his bicep. I had never asked. "James Vayne, the pineapple king," I declared.

He smiled, eyes crinkling at the edges, genuine warmth in his gaze. "I'm glad to see you back at the keys. I'm sorry I couldn't make it over. Just too much to do in the studio, and honestly, it was good to have Tom and Kurt out for a bit so I could focus on mixing down some of the tracks."

"How'd stuff go while I was gone?"

"Well, Paul's back in town, and we worked on drums. I think he also appreciated the absence of Tweedle-Dee and Tweedle-Dum."

I smiled, almost laughing. "Total and complete control. Not something you typically have, is it? You must be drunk with power."

"A little. Not that I mind. Tom's newfound happiness means he's forcing himself into every fucking corner possible, when before we just had to prop him up enough for vocal takes and do the rest ourselves. D'you know that before he left, he was suggesting I change some of my fills? He was giving me guitar advice. He of the three chords and stuck out tongue." We'd made fun of Tom behind his back for years because of his ineptitude at playing guitar. After a decade of trying, the best he could manage was a handful of Beatles songs all in the key of D.

"Are we sure he hasn't been body snatched?" I asked. "I mean, I'm all for the collaboration and participation, when it comes early on in the cycle. But he does realize we're set to go on tour in sixteen weeks, and we need an album before that, right? We can't change our process now. His opinion isn't part of the deal. He's the pretty face. He sings. All else is forfeit."

James laughed. "The actual nuts and bolts of album production have never been his forte. But now he feels he's required to participate because, as he told me, he *loves* us."

"Ugh. 'I love you, man.'"

"What?"

"Just a line from *Wayne's World*. I think we watched it together once. Mike Meyers and Dana Carvey?" I stammered a little, almost blushing. Bad timing.

James squinted giving me that blank, polite British expression he always did when I made American references he somehow missed or, in this case, disapproved of.

I tried again. "Tia Carrere singing 'Ballroom Blitz'?"

"Oh! Yes, that shining paragon of American film. How could I forget?"

"Oh, come on. It's practically rock canon!"

He giggled in his way, sort of a restrained gurgle. "My dear, I think something was lost in translation. Though I admit the 'Bohemian Rhapsody' bit was clever."

We started at the keys, and then he went and got his guitar, and in an hour, without speaking, we had the backbone of a song. I even had some lyrics. It's not the way we usually write, together and so in the zone, but it worked that day. I was still dealing with Mom and all the difficulties related to grieving, and the song had absolutely nothing to do with any of it. I was so thankful.

I want to say writing pop music is profound, that it's this amazing, cathartic process, that it comes naturally and perfectly. But it's never been that way for me. You can't predict what exactly is going to be the thing that unwinds you and sets you free in the course of writing. It might be the melody. It might be the progression, or the way a chord resolves just right. It might be the whole damned thing, or nothing you can point to precisely. But it's the *music* that does it, even if it isn't particularly deep. I'm not a very spiritual person; you've probably figured that out by now. Still, when it comes down to it, I think music is as close to magic as we'll ever get here on Earth. Sure, the Beatles said "love is all you need" — but they sang it, didn't they?

And writing with James? That evening, as we fussed over basslines and transitions, I forgot what I'd thought of him earlier. Whatever glimpse of romance I'd read into the situation vanished as we ceased to be Kate and James and became something bigger, grander, perfect. I'll be honest, there's time when being a rock star is just plain work. Over the years, James and I had gone to the well and it'd been dry, dry, dry. In the early days, it was always easier, when we were reckless and didn't care about labels and all the baggage that comes with success.

But when we get in the groove, there's no stopping us. We ride the wave until the song's finished. It's more beautiful than sex. More enduring, anyway. I get glimpses of it when we play the songs live or the track turns out particularly well.

In this case, it was "Game of Love" which, really, is the quintessential moody rock love ballad on the album. Sure, there was a little pathetic turn of phrase every now and then hinting at the whole maybe I'm in love with James thing ("The weak and wasted / The fruit untasted" being rather obvious, right?). But all in all, it was a simple song, with a fun progression, and it came together easier than anything we'd worked on in years. For a few hours, we were kids again, just out of college, wide-eyed and entranced, bewitched by the music.

When we were done, and the demo was cut, rough and ragged (with me giggling through the middle eight) we sat down on the couch next to each other and smiled in the comfortable silence, basking in the amazing afterglow that comes with creating something you know is undeniably good.

"Tom's going to hate us."

He laughed at my words, but I could tell he was exhausted. Hell, it was almost two a.m. But we'd just had coffee a few hours ago, and we were both still a little hyper.

"Oh? What for this time?" he asked.

"'Wind-wracked heart?'—you know he's going to ask to change it. We might need to come up with some alternatives."

"Uh, I don't think so. It's such a good word."

"Broken? Battered?"

"Ugh. Lonely? No, no. Wind-wracked is perfect."

"It's from the book you tried to get me to read, isn't it?"

"*All the Windwracked Stars*, yes. Did you ever read it?"

"Can't say I did. Sorry, man. I always have a hard time with fiction."

My brain was still in hyper mode, but my body was tired. Maybe that's why I didn't notice he had taken my hand until he lifted it to his lips and kissed it.

"I love you, Cakes."

"I—"

Then, Sara burst in.

# CHAPTER TEN

I MET Sara Plummer my senior year of college. We both were taking this shit-for-brains pottery class that was mostly filled with stoners and continuing education students. I noticed she listened to music during our "free form" period almost every class, and I could tell by the way she tapped her foot that she was following the basslines. Not something you see every day. Then I noticed her backpack: Hartke and Warwick patches, sewn on with care, amidst a few bands I really loved, including a Tori patch.

At the time, Kurt and I were sort of on the outs. He had transferred to Georgia State and left me to fend for myself, and I was itching to play live with someone. The problem was I'd spent the majority of my first three years in college with Kurt and a variety of rotating boyfriends, so I really didn't have any friends to speak of. I mean, I had acquaintances, but since the second half of freshmen year, Kurt and I had lived and played together, and it hadn't left a lot of space for lasting friendships. Not to mention, I've never been popular girl material. At the time, I wore primarily black, had my hair dyed bluish purple, and wore way too much eyeliner. Not exactly approachable, if you get my drift.

Anyway, it turned out I didn't have to talk to Sara first. She found me, one afternoon, while I was in the CD section at the library.

"Hey. You're in my pottery class," she said.

I looked up at her and nodded. "Yup." Unlike me, Sara looked pretty much the same as she does now. Big, huge mop of red hair, willowy waist, aquiline features. Stunning green eyes. Freckles. She didn't need makeup, being model beautiful, and stood at least four inches taller than me. I know even in heels, I never could see her at eye level.

Despite rumors to the contrary, we never dated. I think she's beautiful. We might have kissed once when we were really drunk, but though she's openly bisexual (and major props to her because it's brave and awesome and wonderful), we were never *together*. Maybe that's part of what broke the two of them up, James and Sara. I don't know. James swears it wasn't an issue. I seem to recall him giving her leave to having lovers if she wanted. But he wanted marriage; he wanted to keep her. And Sara was never a person for keeping.

"Good taste." She gestured to the pile of CDs in my hand. I could have gotten everything from Napster, it's true. But I always felt like I had to do it legally, as a musician. It was a weird badge of honor, being so lawful good. Then she laughed. "That's a good one too."

"I've got a soft spot for The Smiths. Even if Morrissey and Robert Smith are mortal enemies."

"If you had to pick sides?"

"The Cure. Always."

"See, I'm a Smiths girl all the way. Morrissey's a fucking genius and smoking hot. Though I'm not sure if he's back into sex or not. That whole celibacy/vegetarian stuff sort of blows my mind. But maybe that's where he gets his *je ne sais quois*."

"I guess." I didn't know what the French bit meant, but she oozed confidence and poise and damn if I didn't want to be like her in every possible way.

"You play?" she asked. "Or just a musical connoisseur?"

"Ah, yeah, yeah. I play."

"What do you play?" she asked, batting her eyelashes. I was being slow-tongued and stupid, no surprise.

I flicked my fingers over an invisible keyboard. "Keys. And vocals."

"You got good gear?" she asked, turning back to the wall of CDs. "Or just like, for fun?"

"No, I'm...I mean, I used to—"

"Hurt and Hate, right?" Sara laughed, as if the entire band was her favorite inside joke. "I saw you. You're Kate Marshall, right?"

Hurt and Hate was not exactly the sort of act I was used to getting noticed from, so I nodded and gave her a half confused look.

"I play bass, coincidentally. And rumor is you're out a bassist," she said, still talking to the stacks of CDs rather than looking directly at me.

"Yeah, Kurt transferred to State. I tried some gigs alone, but...eh." I gave the universal shrug for mediocrity.

"We should jam some time."

"Sure...that would be cool." I probably looked like I was standing vigil at a wake, but inside I was bubbling over with joy.

I don't remember ever sitting down and saying, "Hey, let's start a group." It wasn't like that with Sara and me. The first night jamming was just our first rehearsal. We didn't need to make it official. It didn't take more than a few bars of "Brass in Pocket" to make it really clear we were complementary. And I'll tell you, she killed it. This sounds lame to say, but I'd never heard a girl play the bass like that before, to say nothing of her vocals.

When we were done, I said something along the lines of, "Well, we know who's going to sing lead."

She looked at me. "Not me."

"What do you mean?"

I thought she was joking, but she gave me a dead stare.

"I'm not interested."

"What...why not?"

"I don't want to sing. I mean, I want to play rock music. Not folk music. I have a folk music voice. You have much more depth to your voice."

"Thanks, but…"

She laughed through her nose. "Not that you'll blow people's minds, but you're passable. Besides, I can't sing the songs you write, but I'll be happy to do backup vocals."

The fact I was "not *that* good" was one of the things that put a wedge between Sara and me, especially later in our partnership. She is a better vocalist than me, and she's finally been able to branch out and embrace her folksy side. But at that point, I chalked it up to her charm.

We got high a lot. She liked hash, and she habitually smoked clove cigarettes for a while until they started wreaking havoc on her throat. She was too cool for school in my eyes, and I followed her around like a little puppy for most of senior year; after graduation we got an apartment together in New York.

Sara had a dream that we were watching The Pixies live, but they were painted like the Blue Man Group. The Blue Pixies sounded too cute, so we went with Trixies. Again, nothing profound, no man rising out of a flaming pie. Just two girls, stoned out of their minds, in love with music.

---

*SOMETHING ELSE* WAS the first album we did entirely without Sara. *Lester Hotel* still had some of her backing vocals (some of the songs were things we didn't use on *Blindside*) and she even had a song credit, as the whole song was built around one of her bass riffs, even if she didn't play it on the album.

But just because she wasn't recording with us didn't mean her presence wasn't painfully tangible anyway.

I'm not sure if I would have kissed James that night when she burst in, or maybe I could have said something more. I was already convincing myself that my deluded affections for him were panic or dependence or alcohol. But I know the minute Sara walked into the room, everything changed. James sat up straight, then stood up straight. I sank down further into the cushions, wondering vaguely if I could melt right into the creases. It'd been more than a year since I'd seen her. She hardly emailed anymore unless it was to rub in her success.

Really, she looked brilliant, wearing a calf-length faux-leather jacket (her Morrissey obsession extended to strict veganism in contrast to my personal devotion to the smoky gods of pork barbeque) trimmed with purple faux fur. Her hair was a perfect mess of curls, attended to by the best hairdressers in London, where she worked out of now. She was wearing a good deal of makeup, appearing like it was recently applied, like she was coming in from a photoshoot. Her shoes were gorgeous, her wrists bangled, a braid just-so in her hair. The image was cast; she was radiant.

At first, I took James's attention for excitement, but it wasn't. One look told me anger was the driving force behind his taut energy.

"Isn't it a little late?" he asked her, and the multiple meanings really hit me. It was late. And she was late. And their relationship was late. And I was late to whatever was going on. As usual.

Immediately, I was embarrassed to be there. Embarrassed of ever contemplating a relationship with James. I wanted to hide.

"I thought we left things badly," she said, sweeter this time, not making eye contact with me. I might as well have been furniture.

"I thought your flight was at seven," James replied, monotone. After years of enduring their arguments, it was astonishing to see them both fall into the same roles again. Sara always blazed, and James turned off. I don't think I'd ever heard him yell at her until that night. I could feel it building all around us.

"Delayed. Thought I'd swing by," she said. "I just didn't feel right—"

"Listen. Sara. You don't just get to walk in here. This isn't your studio."

"Oh, come on James." She laughed. "I'm practically family."

"No. I'm fucking serious. You need to go," James insisted, flapping his hand at the door as if hoping the gesture would bring it closer to us, and by extension, her.

"James. Seriously? We're not children."

"You probably should go," I said, my voice catching. I'm not confrontational by nature, and piping up at all was difficult.

Sara didn't turn her head, but her eyes fell on me. I could see her take in my hair cut, my ripped jeans, my crummy t-shirt, the day-old mascara. We couldn't have been more different in that moment, but I'm sure she could see it in my face, what I'd been hiding from James, from myself. We'd known each other a long time.

"Oh, okay. I get it. That's fine." She laughed. "I mean, it was bound to happen eventually."

"There's nothing to 'get.' Why can't you figure that out?" James said, practically shouting. He rubbed his hands down his stubbled cheeks, then let out a big sigh of frustration. "I feel like we've been having this same stupid argument for the last five years, and I'm sick to death of it. Your jealousy over Kate is just old, Sara. Old and bitter."

"Oh, James…" Sara turned to go, smirking over her shoulder. "It's okay. I've seen what I needed to see."

"There is nothing to see! This is me, where I'm happy. It's the one thing you haven't completely perverted with your fucking games. I. Don't. Want. You. I want this!" he said, apparently meaning October Revival. Or something greater, certainly, than the keyboardist chick sitting on the sofa trying to blend in with the leather grain.

"And here I thought it was all about love," she said, looking at me again. I gave her a sort of half-sneer, just in time to hear James shout: "It's not about fucking *love*. It's about *music*. That's all it's ever been about, but you've been so busy checking yourself in the mirror you never noticed."

He shoved past her, and she stood in the doorway a moment. We both heard the back entrance door slam.

"Bye, Kate," she said. She was about to dash down the hallway, when she added, "Sorry about your mom."

But her eyes, man. I can't even begin to describe her look, except I knew she'd gotten James to say exactly what she wanted him to say. It wasn't about love; it was about music. Her timing was impeccable.

What the fuck was she doing in Nashville? Why did she have to mess up my life, my moment?

I'll never know what the hell is wrong with people, I guess. I don't even really know what the hell's wrong with me. But that doesn't excuse what happened next.

———

THE NIGHT of Sara's little charade was the night I almost died. There's no way to split hairs about it. Kurt wasn't home; he was visiting one of his new boyfriends. Taking it as a sign, I drank too much. Way too much. On purpose. With gusto. I remember vaguely how methodical I was about it. Lining up bottles, checking the stores. I was on a mission to get completely and utterly pissed, as James and Tom would say.

Miserable and feeling far sorrier for myself than I had license to be about the James and Sara shit, I crawled up to my room and started pounding down bourbon. From what I can piece together after the fact, I wrote some song lyrics, ignored IMs from James, and called Tom six times (he was asleep, phone on vibrate, and didn't answer, but I left some very colorful messages that he was kind enough to share with me once I had my head in the right place). He's lucky that a) I didn't die and b) I have enough of a sense of self-loathing to have found them funny.

I'm told when they found me, Emmylou Harris was playing, and there was water all throughout the apartment because I'd started a bath and forgot. Thankfully I didn't go in the tub because I'm damned sure it would have been curtains for my drunk ass. That was their first thought when they found me, that I'd pulled a Whitney Houston.

This, oh readers, is that point in the book where you all shake your heads. This is rock bottom. Utterly the worst.

I am the worst.

It's cool, you can say it. Kate Styx, you are a hopeless fucking addict. You don't deserve to live while kids starve all over the world and countries rise and fall in chaos and better people than you die for no reason other than being born into poverty. You thoughtless coward. Go die in a fire.

See, I've rehearsed it for you. There's nothing you can think that I haven't already thought about myself.

How, you ask, did I fall into this well of absolute rock and roll cliché, like some Janis Joplin wannabe? Wasn't I just having the time of my life doing my favorite thing in the world? Why yes, yes, I was. But my mom was dead, and I had a whole fuckton of shit I hadn't dealt with. And then Sara breezed in, James basically admitted to the universe he only loved me for my music, Tom was lost to me forever, and I had officially completely fucked up every good relationship in my life. Including with my own daughter.

This is the problem with alcoholics with depressive tendencies. We're fragile and stupid, which is one bad combination. I like to think, in general, I'm a pretty stable person. I mean, compared to the rest of the band who like either get off on confrontation (Kurt) or are too sensitive (James) or are prone to making sweeping, life-changing decisions (Tom) or invisible (Paul), I think I'm balanced.

But booze *changes* me. I think that's why I've always gravitated toward it. That and a clear genetic disposition, of course. When I drink, I'm under the impression I'm cooler and more in control than I feel on a day-to-day basis. My whole life, and especially with the popularity of the band, I've just felt a bit of a poser, an impostor. I mean, who the hell am I to be so successful? To sell records? To get awards? Shit, there are musicians three thousand times more talented than I am, right now, barely getting by, who will literally never see the inside of a stadium or hear their own music on a movie soundtrack. Hell, they won't even get a record made.

Maybe drinking is something that makes me forget. Makes me feel worthy, or special, or relaxed about it. Clearly, I've got some anxiety issues. I mean, the whole not remembering lyrics thing? That whole never being able to say what I feel thing? That whole Ms. Non-confrontational thing? I'm never anxious when there's liquor in my veins. I'm funny and conversational and just happy to be hanging around. Music comes naturally. Well, I feel like it's coming naturally.

Judging by some of our live recordings, the beer goggles don't extend to reality.

I just don't know when to stop. Every time, without fail, I'm certain that after three drinks, I'll be done. But I never am. My fingers do the work; my throat ushers it in.

## CHAPTER ELEVEN

WAKING up was one of the most surreal experiences in my life to date. I remembered nothing from the night before, but I had this vague sense that I'd seen Sara. I wasn't sure if it was a dream or reality, and it was the middle of the night at the hospital (two days later) so all I could tell I was in an episode of *The Twilight Zone*.

But no. The feeling of the IV in my arm was very real; the empty, hollowed out sensation coursing through me wasn't the cool embrace of death or delusion. I felt like shit. So much shit. For a thousand reasons. And that was probably for the best.

I breathed in and out for a while, listening to the beeps and whooshes and sneaker squeaks of the hospital floor. It smelled like rubbing alcohol (not my preferred poison) and the sweet stench of sick people that permeates every hospital I've ever been in. The harbinger of death smell.

I must have fallen asleep again because I heard someone calling me Katherine and felt the pressure of hands on my shoulders.

"Kate," I corrected, shielding my eyes from the light now flooding the room. I blinked in the harsh fluorescent glow, but a quick glance to the window revealed a long, twinkling skyline. My voice rasped like the Crypt Keeper.

"I'm Doctor Grant. Tell us how you feel," said a young, high-pitched voice. She sounded like a cheerleader, not a doctor. I made out her form, the pieces of her slowly coming together through a filmy haze. Effing Regina George was looking at me with disdain from under her shellacked hair. I got a mean girl for an attending physician. Fantastic.

"I feel like shit. Shit scraped on the bottom of a shoe." I actually felt worse. I had a crawling feeling all over my body and a sense that I shouldn't be alive.

"You nearly died, you know," said another voice, to my right. I made out a male nurse looking down at me with disapproval. He had a heavy, seventies mustache I hoped was ironic.

He picked up my file, frowned, and peered at me again.

Ding, ding, ding.

"Wow, you really are Kate Styx," he said.

I sneered since it was essentially all I was capable of. The doctor, however, was unfazed and went to fiddle with some papers on the other side of the room.

"One of the other nurses said it was you, and I called their bluff. Apparently not," the nurse continued.

"Apparently not," I echoed back. My head was swimming.

"Jim. Do your job, please," the doctor said. She smelled like perfume, which was utterly weird. She must have been called in or something because I'm sure doctors aren't supposed to smell like the inside of *Vogue* magazine.

I winced as she checked my vitals, muttering some dosages and things to the nurse, who was still having a perpetually delayed reaction. I was just about to offer him an autograph if he'd leave me alone when the doctor pulled up a chair and sat down.

Dr. Regina George, aka Dr. Grant, probably weighed ninety pounds soaking wet. I mean, I think her hair made up for at least a third of her bodyweight. Classic Southern blonde. A runner by her looks. Maybe my age, maybe in her late twenties. My guess was that she was a Baptist. I saw the Pandora charm bracelet, recognized the Dior perfume, noticed her ginormous wedding ring. Even in the dim light, I could tell she'd recently applied makeup. A real beaut, contoured like a Kardashian.

"Hi," I said, when she said nothing. People who stare generally creep me out.

"Well. Jim is right. You almost died. You're playing a dangerous game, Katherine," she said, all sweetness and rainbows. Like talking to a fucking kindergartner.

"Wicked Game" started playing in my head, and I conjured up an image of Chris Isaak. But apparently, I was supposed to speak in response.

"I…drank too much," I offered.

"Too much? Well, let's see. When you got here, your BAC was hovering just under .4%. Really, it's a miracle that you survived at all. I've pronounced people dead with lower rates than that. It's tough for a woman of your stature to show such a high level, but it was more likely… oh…" She flicked her well-manicured hands in the air. "Ten. Eleven drinks. In the span of about two hours. Maybe one and a half."

"I wasn't counting."

"Clearly." She snapped the file shut. "You have a problem, Ms. Marshall. You need help. Your liver is in sad shape. We can patch you up and send you out, but I'm not sure if you can withstand this happening again. If you don't get help, you will die."

I nodded. Despite how much I loathed her on principle, I knew she was right on some level. Not with the whole tough love shit. I wasn't going to go sober because of her, or what she said. I was going to go sober because I didn't want to die. Not yet, anyway.

So I didn't respond. I just nodded.

I was scared. It had never been this bad. I mean, of course it had been this bad. I'd been wasted before. I'd blacked out, God knows, a hundred times in our early days and never more so than when I was with Tom. But then, it was always drinking for fun. To party. To celebrate. This was drinking to forget. Drinking because I was depressed and alone and grieving. And I'd been doing that a lot lately.

Doctor Grant softened. I had tears in my eyes; she probably noticed. She put her hand on mine, and her fingers were frigid.

"Listen. Whatever you're going through, you need to get yourself together. People look up to you. Girls. My niece, she wants to be you when she grows up. Jim tells me you've had some personal turmoil as of late. But from what I hear, you have an album to finish, don't you?"

I squinted at her. "Jesus. Is that all in my file?"

"We're a Nashville hospital. We make it our business. Musicians are sort of our thing."

"Right…"

"To be frank, if you don't get help, you may not finish the album at all. Or any album. Ever."

I sighed.

"Listen, rest up. We'll send you home as soon as we can. We just need to check a few more things, get you hydrated, and observe for a while. Perhaps the day after tomorrow—"

I started to say something, but she held up her hand.

"On the promise, you seek help."

I glanced over at Jim the nurse, and he was staring at me with pathetic, pleading eyes.

"Yeah," I said. "Sure."

---

I HAD no connection to the outside world that night. No phone, no computer. I didn't turn on the television. I just went back to sleep. When I woke up, I cried about everything, my lungs burning from sobs, until I fell asleep again. This happened a few times. I got checked by Jim, then the other nurse, Carol, who didn't seem to care who I was. Which was pretty much perfect.

A lot of questions went through my mind. First and foremost: who the hell had found me? I was betting on Kurt. Though if he was getting laid that night, I doubt he would have come home. Which left James or Tom. Neither prospect was ideal.

It was around eleven o'clock the next morning when the new nurse on rotation asked if I wanted visitors. I said no, at first, but changed my mind just as she went to shut the door. She looked annoyed.

"Who is it?" I asked.

"A gentleman. English, I think."

"Yeah…yeah, I guess so."

Tom? James?

"Wait—"

The nurse turned around, blank expression.

"I mean. No. No guests. Just…I think I need to be alone for a little longer."

She nodded and left. I fell asleep in the dark, listening to the strange mechanical music building all around me. No metronome, and no escape. Just the unpredictable mechanical chaos of beeps, squeaks, voices, and alarms.

---

I WAS DISCHARGED LATE the second day, but I didn't leave until it was well past dark. And, lucky me, I even got a special back exit. I was given reams of paperwork and more reams of advice and had the same lecture handed to me at least three times: *Get help. Get therapy. You're going to die.* The message was consistent, but I was in denial.

Oh, I wasn't in denial that I was an alcoholic. I was in denial I'd let it get that bad. In the back of my mind, I just kept thinking this was a slip-up. It was a mistake. I'm not *that* much of drinker. I function! I write music. People even buy it. A full-blown alcoholic could never be that successful, right?

That's the thing with addictions like mine. I kept imagining another hurdle in the distance, worse than where I was standing. Except this time the next hurdle was death.

When I got back to my apartment, I found it covered in flowers. Every inch of my living room was alive with flora: roses, lilies, daisies, zinnias, and a pineapple. A pineapple. Sitting in the middle of my kitchen table, on its side, as if it had given up all hope.

It smelled like my mother's funeral.

My phone was missing, so I went to the computer to check in on the world. Big mistake.

I opened my browser to about a thousand emails. Apparently some shitty entertainment website out of the UK had actually reported my death. They'd run an obituary, and I'd even trended on Twitter: #katestyxisdead. My Facebook account had a whole bunch of remembrances.

I read my own fucking obituary.

The short of it is I realized they had *expected* me to die. Someone had the whole thing written out. That's how it works. I read my own obituary, and I realized how fucking boring my existence had been. Girl born in Georgia. Goes to college. Is in a successful band. Estranged family. Awards. Dead.

I mean, what the hell is that? What did I do? No family mentioned. No great acts of kindness. Just some of our stupid awards and a mention of my "tumultuous relationship" with Tom Chesley was the "stuff rock-and-roll dreams are made of."

And that's when I sort of lost it.

---

Katherine Ann Mendenhall Marshall, known as Kate Styx, was born in Smyrna, Georgia, just outside of Atlanta, Georgia, to Robert Quinn Marshall, a Baptist pastor, and Claire Mendenhall Marshall. After what she cited as a "super religious" upbringing, she met Sara Plummer in college and formed a band called The Blue Trixies. That band went on to combine with October Revival, an English rock group traveling the US. Styx co-wrote many of the group's most well-known songs, many of which were about her bandmate, lead singer Tom Chesley, with whom she'd briefly had a relationship. She died in her apartment in Nashville, TN, while October Revival was finishing up their fourth studio-length album from apparent alcohol toxicity, TMZ reports. She leaves behind her father and sister.

---

**October Revival**
@OctoberRevivalOfficial

Our amazing keyboardist and co-songwriter Kate is in hospital recuperating. She is not dead. Good vibes appreciated!

2:48 PM - 6 May 2015

GOING off the deep end is such an overused phrase. I never in my life considered myself an unstable woman. That was always Sara's job. Her emotions were fuel for my drinking fire, sure, but I always felt like I was the stable chick in this rock-and-roll show. You could depend on me. I might get drunk after the fact, but it didn't tend to interfere with work. I was a stalwart, stand-up kind of drunk!

Or at least, while Tom was being Tom and drinking and using, I guess I sort of paled in comparison. Since he'd gone sober and Christian, I clearly was the one taking up the role of resident boozer. No contest, I guess, considering the rest of the remaining Revivals. I'd seen James drunk once, and it was after Sara left, and he really, really deserved it for what he'd gone through with her. Kurt smoked pot and drank the occasional beer, and Paul, in his early days, was a certified stoner but had since mostly quit. Families do that to you, I guess.

But coming home to an empty apartment filled with flowers probably pushed me over the Cliff of No Return. Lilies. It was all the damned lilies. Likely well-meant, considering that a fan favorite was always "Blue Lilly," one of our early tunes written while we were in London. But it still smelled just like the funeral parlor that I'd left a few weeks before. Cloying perfume, filling my nostrils until it burned.

I still hadn't found my phone. The battery was dead, but as I bawled my eyes out, I focused madly on the effort to find it. I tore apart my bedroom thinking it was the most obvious place I'd have been found. Because that's where rock and roll icons go to die, their beds, right? Laid out like some marvelous dark angel.

Nope, hold up, friends. No pretty pictures for me. I'd actually been in the bathroom, half in and half out of the hallway, with my fucking pants down. There is glorious, glorious humiliation in that. Apparently, I was trying to pee when I finally blacked out and stopped breathing. I fell on the bottle of Jack that I was holding, which didn't shatter but gave me one hell of a bruise on my chest. I wasn't even drinking decent liquor when I went.

I couldn't breathe. So, I started to scream. I was mourning my mother, I was mourning my life, I was mourning losing Tom. I was mourning losing Sara, who clearly still wanted to see me suffer even though she was out of the picture. I was mourning the loss of the daughter I never had and mourning the shit choices I'd made and what felt like, at the time, a complete loss of hope and passion for something that I had pursued with absolute tenacity my whole adult life. Something I felt I was losing.

Someone came in the door. I tried to run away, to make it to my room and slam the door, but I couldn't. They were on the floor, next to me, holding me. I tried to fight, but he was too strong, and eventually, I just stopped resisting and kept sobbing, my ears still ringing from my own shrieking.

"Come on, sugar, let it out."

Kurt.

---

AN HOUR LATER, we were drinking coffee at my kitchen table. You've got to understand drinking coffee for Kurt and me is a ritual that goes back to the late nineties when we used to sit in coffee shops and gripe about the music on the radio and make grand plans for taking over the musical world. It didn't happen like we imagined, of course, and I ended up "stringing" Kurt along, as he was fond of explaining to me. But still. Coffee is serious business with the two of us.

He didn't just make me a cup of coffee, knowing I'm a certifiable snob, he made me some single-origin Fair Trade, shade-grown Guatemala roast—these little tiny beans that smell like heaven smothered in happiness and procured from a very snazzy little shop downtown—in my Aero Press.

"I'm glad to see you," he said, a half a cup in. There were tears in his eyes. I couldn't remember the last time, if ever, I'd seen him cry.

I felt like the biggest asshole in the world. Guilty. Terrible.

"Did…did you find me?" I managed.

He shook his head, wiping tears angrily. "No."

I gave him my look that implied he needed to keep talking.

"It was Tom."

I winced. "Christ."

"Listen. I don't want to…to be the one to talk about it. It's not my place. He wanted to come up here, but I told him it was probably best if I did, first. We both went by the hospital, but they said you weren't taking visitors."

"Right."

"Katie…"

"I don't need another lecture. I already had ten at the hospital, and I still have the worst hangover in the history of hangovers."

He flicked my fingers. "Dude. I was not going to lecture you. I was going to tell you, whatever it is you need to deal with, you can deal with it with me. Okay? We've been friends for too long. I came to your mom's fucking funeral, and you just stood there like some statue. I knew this was going to happen eventually…"

"It's not just about my mom. I mean, fuck, Kurt. She was just as bad as me. And I'm glad you came, but I spent most of the trip sort of…I don't know. Coping with family shit I hadn't dealt with in long enough."

"We all have fucked up families, Katie. If it isn't about your mom…?"

He was walking around the room by then, pacing because he was frustrated with me. I know how he works. I mean, Kurt and I have been friends so long that at times we act like an old married couple. I can tell when he's about to get mad. I know exactly what will make him laugh. I know where he's most ticklish. Early on in our friendship, I can't tell you how many times I'd wished he wasn't gay.

"I know it's not Tom. I mean, I'm sure it's part of it. But if I'd have my guess, I know you left the studio, and James mentioned something about Sara."

I buried my head in my hands. I could feel him making the connection, the wheels of his brain turning and falling into place.

"Oh no. Kate. No. Tell me—Jesus, tell me you didn't…"

"Didn't what?" I asked through muffled lips.

"You haven't decided you're in love with James now, have you? Because…oh, shit, man. Are you trying to single-handedly destroy the whole fucking band!?"

I peered at him through my fingers with one eye. "I don't know."

"When…when did this start happening?" He was aghast but not entirely surprised.

"It was a few weeks ago. Before the stuff with Mom. I just couldn't help but think…but feel…I don't know."

"You're lonely. You're grasping at straws."

"We do great things together!" I protested. "I know it's silly, but you can't tell me that it wouldn't make sense for us to be close."

"Professionally! But you'd be a disaster together intimately. Kate. He's never going to be over Sara. Never. Not even if he marries a fucking supermodel with tits the size of grapefruits and a voice like frigging Adele. And you're never really going to be over Tom. And if the two of you shack up, it just can't last. Not without all the baggage."

I sighed. He was speaking sense. It still didn't make it easier to hear.

He sat down next to me again, taking my head in his hands. "Kate."

"Yes."

He wiped my tears with his thumb. "Promise me you'll let this go. Promise…just until after the tour. Let's get through it. Let's get you some fresh air, some good music, and some tail. Then, if everything feels the same, then…"

I nodded.

"And I'm not letting you out of my sight. I've already pulled a list of rehab clinics, and I am totally going with you."

"I can—"

"Hush!"

# CHAPTER TWELVE

It didn't get worse. At least there's that. But it doesn't mean it wasn't hard, harder than it had been before. We had two more songs to write, and to give me time to recover (and, I'm sure, the hopes I'd work some magic at home) the band went into the studio to finalize the tracks.

I went to rehab. Yes, yes, yes.

I'd never actually been before, though I'd encouraged Tom on his repeat visits. I decided it was best to take two days off at home, and then immediately checked myself in. I mean, there really wasn't a lot of beating around the bush here. I'd almost died. I needed some time, even if it was at some foofy New Age spa dedicated to detoxing the mind and soul. I was permitted a guitar, and I took it. I was told there was a piano in the music room.

I want to tell you that rehab was a transforming experience and I never looked back after absorbing all the good vibes and cleansing my soul. I want to tell you that the letter Rhee sent me was the thing that did it, the single moment that made me realize my responsibility to the world, to my fans, to my family. But it wasn't. Sure, it was a piece of the puzzle. But just like Mom's death, it wasn't the whole picture.

Eventually I just got too tired of the place and sort of accidentally fell in line. I got tired *thinking* about drinking. I got tired talking about my feelings and my baggage. I got tired of talking to people about it and figured, in my weirdly stubborn way, the best way to move forward was just to be done with it. To let it go. To find something else, whatever it was, to spend my time. And most of it was making music.

I made some friends. I even knew one of the patients, a music journalist named Jesse McLaren. You'd never have pegged him for an alcoholic; he was like a Polo poster boy. But his drinking had cost him his marriage. It was good to have someone to talk music with.

"Are you sure you're not a mole?" I asked him one night as we sat on the porch sipping tea together. I played music and we talked about music and we just got on so comfortably. "I mean, it's whacked that I'm here and a music journalist just happens to be along for the ride."

He was very cute. In the dark, his blond hair looked almost gray, his dark puppy eyes glittering in the lights from within the facility. He smelled like patchouli, but he was possibly the least Bohemian person I'd ever met. He was one breeze away from a popped collar.

"I promise this is all off the record," he joked.

I fiddled a few chords on the guitar, looked up at him through my hair. It was getting long again, getting into my eyes.

"It just seems weird."

"*You're* weird. But I'm not complaining. I was sure I was going to be stuck listening to Cat Stephens and Peter, Paul, and Mary the whole time I was here."

"No knocking on PPM!"

"No offense meant. You know what I mean."

"They do play Kenny G and Yanni in the spa," I pointed out.

"Yeah, I'm happy to endure torture if I get to listen to you play every night."

He sounded so sincere, so, dare I say it, smitten. So I did what you'd expect. I changed the subject.

"I can't wait to get out of here."

"I can," he said, turning away from me. Shit, I'd hurt his feelings. I played a little louder.

"You want to stay here at the Kumbaya Club? You seem to have it all figured out." He was quite the model patient. I'm sorry, I mean "wayfarer."

He almost smiled. "I'm afraid of what happens when I get back. Dealing with all the stuff I've been able to put aside while I'm here. The kids. The house. The mess I left behind."

"This, my friend, is a good reason to remain single and unattached. I take all my baggage with me. I'm like a hobo with her life on her back."

Which, of course, wasn't true, but lying to myself felt good.

I wrote fifteen songs in the month that I was absent from the studio, two of which made the final cut for the album. Jesse's encouragement and my boredom were good catalysts.

James had little to do with those tracks, but he loved them. He was beyond happy when I played them after discharge.

No, he didn't talk to me about "it" right away. He didn't mention the Sara incident. When I got back to the studio, he gave me a smile, squeezed my shoulder, and told me he was glad I was feeling better. It was good to see my face again.

Regardless of my true lack of epiphany, I did feel different. I felt thinner, frailer. I felt like my existence, for the first time, was just a complete and utter fluke of the universe. Who was I? Just some cosmic speck, really. A cosmic speck who had somehow landed this dream job while people suffered—really suffered—all around the world. I'd never been impervious to the plight of the poor or people in the third world. I mean, hell, I gave to charity plenty. I still do. I just felt sad for them and found myself feeling detached from everything around me. I felt like an actor in a play, like someone else was playing my part.

Sure, I was creative during that time. But I never felt truly connected to the music. Even though the songs came easily, they didn't resonate as much as they had once. Or maybe that feeling I was missing was booze. I don't know.

Which isn't to say it didn't all mean something eventually. In a way, it was nice to be distant, to care less. I'm sure the anti-depressants had a lot to do with it, but I'm not really complaining. The weightless sense of being almost nothing in the whole universe, in the long run, was comforting. I guess it's expected that musicians are always searching for the mystical, the unknown, the mysterious. We have the Beatles to thank, I guess. But even the majority of them walked away empty-handed. Lennon was still a heroin addict. McCartney was still a selfish bastard. Ringo was a drunk. Maybe George got something more out of it, but in the end, he just saw the hypocrisy and sought elsewhere.

Music doesn't make sense amidst the cosmic nothingness. It is something utterly unnecessary, this confluence of vibrations and wavelengths and volume and tempo.

At the end of the tunnel, it's the one thing I realized still gave me joy. Gave me hope. Made me want to get out of bed. It had saved me once, and it saved me again, more than Jesus or Buddha or Cthulhu ever could. When everything was scoured away, when my mind was raw with emptiness, music still mattered.

---

IN TIME, once I got back to the studio, everyone talked to me about "it." Even Sara. With Sara, it was an email, written in her usual, near incoherent rambling.

Kate

I know this is tough and I'm sorry for all. Not sure what I said and if I did not sure I meant it. James gets me... you know more than anyone since we've been through so much together... at this point. Every time I think we're finally done and through... he's always hanging around, we always find... each other.
Anyway... I'm not sure what I can do... and I'm not sure where we stand or if it ever will be the same. We had a good thing before and I don't think... going back is an option... you know. We're different

now, but I still remember… you as the little girl with the heavy accent and the eyeliner… in the library…

Xoxo Sara

I HAD to read it over a few times to understand the whole gist, grammatical errors aside, but it was there. The closest to an apology from Sara I was ever going to get. I'm not going to say we were ever that close; I think some people seem to be under the impression that because we were together in music so long we were BFFs. The truth is we always had a tenuous relationship, and we really didn't have much in common other than the music. Which was the biggest slice of the pie. It was the music that kept us together because we knew, at the time we started, we were the best thing going for each other. And we were right.

If James hadn't been in love with Sara, I'm not sure she'd have been asked to be part of the band. I know, it sounds mean and callous. She's a good bassist. She's solid. But she was never comfortable with the band dynamic. And when she was with James, which she was for about four years straight, their constant fighting was an impossible discordant melody throughout all our work. She's a tempest in a teapot, and that's what makes her beautiful and scary and powerful.

But she's also competitive. I mean, like, insanely so. I wouldn't say I'm entirely bereft of the competitive gene, but it's definitely dormant when it comes to music (Monopoly is another story; I swear to God I have cheated my way out of that game more times than I can count). Sara is a powerhouse of a woman. She's confident in ways I'll never be. She's statuesque, a presence. When she walks into a room, it's like the air changes. People stare at her even when she's in jeans and a t-shirt. She's cool beyond measure, and she knows it.

I was never cool enough for Sara. I'm just not a very cool person. If you strip away what our agent and manager make me do, I'm really just not that awesome. I couldn't care less about trends and hashtags and shit. I don't rub elbows. I always let Tom and James do it, or Sara in the day. The business is the vehicle for my one enduring obsession, songwriting, and it's paid off my student loans and put Rhee though college and basically allows me not to think much about money is just, really, almost stupid. People work a lot harder to just get by, and I've sort of stumbled into it.

Hashtag blessed.

Which isn't to say I don't enjoy playing live. I think, if we're being competitive, I'll say that I always enjoy touring and the associated trappings more than I admit. Certainly more than Sara ever has. She was never a fun touring partner. And not just because she and James were in perpetual dysfunction, but because it also cramped her style. It was a lack of convenience. It was outlets that didn't work and bad nights and creepy fans and Tom missing and James shouting and chaos.

I've always found an obscene amount of amusement in chaos. It helps me think.

Anyway. Reading her attempt to apologize was something. I'm not sure what exactly, but something. Normally my general alcoholic antics didn't bother her a bit, so clearly I meant more to her than I thought.

---

WITH THE REST of the band, talking about my overdose (okay, I wrote it, there you go) took the form of a faux dinner party at James's place. He claimed it was solely for the purpose of getting everyone together under one roof, even Paul, but I could detect an ulterior motive. James is not good at lying, and so long in cramped quarters with him has given me a very keen eye toward this sort of thing. I figured the "party" was an intervention, a time-out. But I didn't expect it to be so emotional.

I got there late because I'm incapable of making it anywhere in Nashville without getting lost. I live downtown and hardly ever drive (because I'm a damned cautious alcoholic, remember) but decided to that night. I never bother with GPS and always think I can remember my way around Edgefield, but I don't.

Anyway, James's place is nothing short of amazing and totally him. For British Indian, he really skews English, and the house was this brick Victorian monstrosity he'd lovingly decorated over the last year. From the hardwoods to the crown molding, the place was like a cross between Southern charm and a perfect English pub. It wasn't opulent, especially not by Nashville standards—some of those country singers, man, they give swank a new address. But it was stately. As a kid who grew up in Hounslow, James sometimes still got a kick out of houses with yards in historic neighborhoods with lawns.

I pulled up in my car, and Paul was standing outside the house on his cell. I hadn't seen him in months, between funerals and hospitalizations and whatnot, but I offered him a smile anyway as I passed him on the walkway. He gave me a concerned-but-happy-to-see-me look and almost started to end the conversation when I waved him off. We'd talk later.

James greeted me at the front door; I'd managed to avoid him entirely since I got back, sneaking late into the studio and corresponding mostly by text, and sparingly. He smelled like cardamom and was wearing a way too warm wool sweater that scratched my face when I hugged him. He hugged me for a long time, long enough for me to take in the smells of curry and roasting meat and hear the sound of the rest of the guests in the back of the house. It sounded like more people than just Kurt and Tom.

"Please don't hate me for this," James said, pulling me away and holding me out by the shoulders. "I tried to keep it intimate. But Tom's got some ideas, and he really wanted everyone here."

"Everyone? Please tell me this isn't some fucked up musical version of 'This is Your Life'…"

"No, hah. Nothing like that. Just everyone that's, you know, part of us. This. The band."

"Fun."

"And it's a dry party—so everyone will be sober."

I blinked at him.

"Please don't leave," he begged.

I didn't leave. I followed him like a dog shamed after pissing on the carpet and saw, indeed, "everyone" was there. Kurt and Tom, of course. And Dusty. And Jeff and Ian and Clarke, our engineers in Nashville; also, Peter and Clive, our producers in the UK, Kyle our agent, Ralph our lead roadie, and our own personal label executive, a chick by the name of Kelly, who, in an attempt to appear casual, had donned a lovely J. Crew ensemble to set off her positively middle-American girl next door looks. For some reason she made me think of Jesse, and his polished Polo looks, but I banished the thought. We'd barely spoken since we'd graduated. I didn't have time to think about him.

There were hugs and well-wishes, and some tears, but really, I could see through easily. Likely Dusty got wind and wanted to use this as some kind of proof to the label folks and everyone else that we're marketable without the album and I wasn't dying, or dead, or incapable of working.

The food was really good. James had my favorite Indian restaurant cater, and so we all ate way too much. There was zero alcohol to be found anywhere, which, I knew, was an attempt to keep me from feeling weird but, honestly, it just made things feel stranger.

James got the fireplace going, and after Kelly, Dusty, and Ralph left, it was just the core of the band, really. The people who had made October Revival happen for the last five years or so.

We were all sitting around in the living room drinking our not-alcohol when Tom stood up. He cleared his throat and glanced around for the remote to the speakers, which were playing a combination of jazz and early blues, and when it stopped, I realized how much I'd been tuned in to it. I really wasn't participating much in the conversations around me, sitting next to Kurt (who was texting someone every five minutes) and Paul who looked continually more uncomfortable as the evening progressed.

"So, well." Tom clapped his hands together. He was going into "talk to the audience" mode, which was rather adorable, I had to admit. He liked to address the crowd when we were on tour, and he always took this same stance. "Glad you've all made it. Hi, Kate. We love you."

I gave him a wince and a wave.

"Well. Yes. It's been lovely, but we wanted to talk about something —well, I did. I had this idea a few month ago, in fact, and while at first I think everyone thought me daft—which, let's face it, has been rather a common theme as of late—I think we've all come to agree my idea might be a good one."

Nervous laughter.

Tom put his hand to his heart, looking quite Emo but sincere. He's a stand-up guy, even if he's hopped up on Jesus. "Listen, Kate. No one here knows what you've been going through more than I do. Like you, I've got something…something inside of me nudging me onward toward absolutely stupid decisions after I've let crap into my body. It's maddening, isn't it?"

I gave him a little nod, feeling embarrassed. At least he was owning it with me.

"Anyway. The album's half done, but there's been such a shadow cast on everything with all the drama that I was thinking it was time we had a change of scenery. Y'know? Take a moment and step back and get to writing music like we should be."

"I can't really argue with that," I said. Everyone was smiling. Except Paul. I got the distinct feeling no one had consulted him. Again.

"So. I've been working on it for a few months, and it wasn't going to be ready until next month—but I pulled some strings. We've got a studio in Lamberhurst."

"Lamberwhats?" asked Paul.

"It's a town. Where I bought an old farmhouse and converted it into a studio," Tom said. "Enough room for us all to live and work and play—and a train's ride from London to do mixing."

"London?" Paul and I said at the same time.

"Yes. England! Sweet Britannia."

# CHAPTER THIRTEEN

AND THAT, of course, was the end of Paul being in the band. I'm still not sure why Tom ever thought he'd be okay with packing up and going overseas, but then again, I'm not sure Tom ever thinks things through when he's in that sort of mood. It was going to be one thing or another when it came to Paul, and it was actually impressive that he'd stood so long through all our drama.

We knew his heart wasn't in it. His heart was with his kids. His wife. Dina met him when the band was still starting up, and she was fangirling all over him. But I can't blame her for wanting a semblance of normalcy in her life. I won't say Dina's the kindest, loveliest person I've ever met. She's not really the sort of chick I'd normally hang out with, and in recent years she went all mommy-chic (short hair, Coach purses, strollers, SUVs). But she was looking out for her family, and that's why she insisted Paul leave.

Also, we were all getting older, and our line of business ever favors the young.

It wasn't much of a fight once things got going. Paul just stood up and made his point. He's always been a small, rather quiet guy. Killer chops on the skins but not exactly an explosive personality.

His throat caught the first time he tried to speak.

"I've...got to quit," he said, finally. He looked toward the door as if assuring himself there was a way out to safety. "I'm sorry, guys."

James looked shocked, for some reason. As if he hadn't picked up on the thousand signals Paul was drifting away already.

"Come on, Paul," he said, standing too. He didn't realize how threatening he looked, but he's always had something of a scowl when he's afraid. It's not like Paul was irreplaceable, but the band had had so much instability in the last few months, I could see James starting to panic.

"You'll find someone in the UK. For sure. There's dozens of drummers tripping over themselves to join you on tour. I just can't... I can't do the album out there and then go on tour, not with the kids in school," Paul explained. He was getting choked up. "I promised Dina."

"Is there anything we can say?" I asked. "I'm sorry, Paul."

"No, I'm sorry. It's not about me. It's never been about me. The heart of the band is the three of you—sorry, Kurt, but it's true—and as long as it's intact, you'll do fine. You're all rock stars. I'm just a session musician who lucked out."

He walked away. Shut the door. That was that.

There wasn't much to say. Kurt had a few potential drummers he knew of in London, and Tom had a few friends. But it felt like a blow we weren't prepared for. I liked Tom's idea. An English country villa, sunshine and fresh air, time for James and me to figure out the rest of the album and get things done without the stress and hustle of our normal routine. Nashville was nice, but maybe we all needed a change of scenery after two years. We'd come for Tom, and now...this felt like it was for me.

<hr>

I WAS the last one to leave. I didn't remember ever being sober at James's house; it was sort of our go-to party place. I noticed for the first time how much of a home he'd made himself, how comfortable and grownup the place was. My apartment had expensive gadgets and some pieces of art, but no one would ever call it well-appointed. It was just sort of *there*. Walls to keep away the rain, stock carpeting and flooring. Most of it was prefabricated. Walking away from it wouldn't be hard for me; Nashville never felt like home.

"Just a train ride from London," I said, helping James put the last of the dishes in the sink. "You think Tom will be up for it?"

"Lamberhurst's his home. It's going full-circle, you know? He'll have his friends. His Jesus friends, I'm sure. I don't know. He seems... it seems to be working for him."

"You're not angry anymore."

James laughed. "Not at his religion. Not at him, not really. It's been rather rough as of late, and with you nearly shuffling off this mortal coil, I figured I ought to take stock of my friends a little better."

I felt my face flush. "James, I—"

"No, listen, Cakes," he said. He took a deep breath. "I know you didn't do it on purpose. And I'm so proud you got help. I'm just sorry I wasn't...*there* enough. I was caught up in Sara shit, again... D'you know what she told me before she finally left town?"

I didn't really want to know, and didn't see how it was relevant, but I said, "No," anyway.

"She's getting *married*. To some lawyer bloke in California. She came to just make sure I was okay with it. Married! The woman who vowed she'd conflagrate herself before taking marriage vows."

"And?" I asked, feeling a weird hollow sensation in my chest again, the sense I was about to fall down a set of stairs.

"Are you serious? She's mental."

"She loves you."

"That doesn't stop her from being mental. In fact, it fuels the fire. She's always been so sodding jealous of you, of your talent, and for once she actually thought that *I'd* be the jealous one. But I couldn't care less about her personal life right now."

"I'm glad." I was feeling tired and really didn't want to talk about Sara.

"But—Kate, hold up a sec."

I'd gotten my purse and jacket from the pegs by the door. He knew my tricks. My avoidance tendencies.

"What?" I asked.

"You know I didn't mean that it was just about the music with you and me. It's not…it's more complicated than that."

I nodded, throat dry. Here it comes.

"What we have, in this moment, together, is the very heart of this band. When we make music, we're greater than the sum of our parts. We've got the fucking awards to prove it. But I don't want you to think that I never thought of you…as just a songwriter. I see you as a woman as well."

He'd put his hands on my shoulder. I shivered. "Thanks," I said. "I think?"

"You need to start seeing that too. Seeing yourself full of talent and promise and adventure again…you can't…God, Kate, you scared me so much."

James broke down on my shoulder, sobbing. I held him and said, "It's okay," like he was the one who'd lost his mother and almost died of an overdose. I didn't know what else to do. I couldn't change the fact I'd nearly died and taken the whole band along with me. I admit it, my drinking had reached some huge selfish proportions. I wasn't thinking straight. But they depended on me and loved me, even if it wasn't the way I wanted.

It's weird. I remember this happening at my mom's funeral too. People crying on my shoulder while I sat, dry-eyed. Comforting them, telling them it's going to be okay when, you'd think, it should be the other way around. Grief and fear make people act strangely some-times. James had held it together for so long, had thrown this party and contrived along with Tom to rescue me. But I still almost destroyed just about everything he'd ever worked for, and he could only keep up the act for so long.

Tom had nearly died twice, two major overdoses in two years. But I'd never seen James this broken up about it. I guess, with Tom, he was so used to the threat of death that when it happened, or almost happened, he had a sort of numb resolve. Like, well, we always knew we'd be here. But for whatever reason, I had surprised James. Maybe it's because I didn't live with him like Kurt, who did try to curb my drinking by plying me with coffee and food, but he saw the best in me. Even when I was at my worst.

And I knew Kurt was right. Whatever crazy thoughts I'd had about hooking up with him, they were just desperate. I was reaching out for someone. But being together meant we'd break up inevitably. I'm not the marrying kind. I've never had dreams of a picket fence and stability and kids and SUVs. It's just not in me. Just looking around James's house, I could see how easily a family would fit in. No, it wouldn't be cliché, but he'd be happy. He'd be a great dad, someday. He just had to get over Sara, and I would never allow myself to be his rebound girl.

***

**Kate:** Hey, man. How's life

**Jesse:** Long time no hear, Georgia girl.

**Kate:** You avoided my question.

**Jesse:** I was thinking about the funny way you say words yesterday.

**Kate:** I don't have an accent.

**Jesse:** LOL – not a big one, but it's subtle. Like, a pen, a pin, and a pan, are all pretty much pronounced the same way in Kate speak.

**Kate:** Kate speak? Wait, it's my own dialect now?

**Jesse:** And pink. You say it "penk." It's adorable.

**Kate:** Adorable is not a word people use when talking about me. Where are you?

**Jesse:** Zurich. Chasing a Very Well-Known Musician who won't show up for his damned scheduled interviews.

**Kate:** Musicians are the worst.

**Jesse:** There are a few exceptions.

***

I FLEW out to the UK with Kurt. Surprisingly, the label was quite copacetic to us leaving Nashville. I'd called Rhee briefly to let her know where I'd be and if she wanted, I'd pay for her to visit. She said she had a lot of work to do with school and couldn't make the time. I understood what she was saying between the lines; really, she didn't want to be around me. Her mother had been killed and me, her technical mother, had almost died. College years are hard, and, unlike me, she didn't have something yet to throw herself into, to wrap herself up in. If it hadn't been for music during that time, I don't know what I'd done with myself. Dad had sent a cloyingly religious card after my incident, and she'd co-signed her name. That's all I'd heard from her.

We flew first class, and Kurt was kind enough to abstain from the complimentary champagne. It wouldn't last forever, I knew. Eventually, they'd realize I had to be a big girl and let them to their lives while I worked on my own, booze or no. At the time, I was sure it wasn't going to happen again. I had a sort of queasiness when I thought of alcohol, but it was most likely just in my head. If someone had put a bottle of bourbon in front of me, I'm sure at that point I'd have taken it.

"Any luck on the drummer front?" asked Kurt.

I'd taken it as my personal crusade to line up as many drummer auditions as I could the first two weeks we were in London before we formally absconded to Kent. I'd never spent as much time in London as I wanted to, and hotel rooms were just as good a place as any to write songs. I had a lot to go through from the rehab stint.

It wasn't worried about songwriting, but I was worried about finding a good drummer to fit in. If you haven't noticed by now, October Revival is a group of some impressive personalities. None of us does anything without voicing an opinion, and we only get worse when music's involved.

"Hmm," I said opening up my notes on my phone. "There's a handful. An Irishman named Aidan who's played sessions with just about everyone we know seems like a contender. Two Americans who've both come from defunct bands and are looking for something stable. A Scotsman with known temper issues, and some chick Sara and I used to know. She's more of a percussionist, but it'll work I think, if we want something a little different."

Kurt made a sour face. "Paul was good."

"Paul was a git." I was quoting Tom. It was one of the kinder words he'd adopted since going all Jesus on us.

"I know," he said, rolling his shoulders. "But even if he was a git, we worked. I liked playing out with him, even if he was sort of a lump otherwise. We'd get in this pocket, the two of us, when we were playing. It was really impressive how intuitive he was. You need to find that."

"He's not dead, y'know. He's just moved on. I can't say I blame him. We're a tough group to warm to, and he's been absentee for long enough."

"I guess you're right. But I want this new person to be good."

The flight attendant brought by some warm towels in preparation for the upcoming meal which, horrifyingly, smelled like seafood of some sort.

"And you think we can do this?" I asked him. "I mean...we're all kind of a mess."

"Speak for yourself."

"Okay. Excepting you."

He gave me a surprisingly warm smile. "Yeah. I think Tom's idea was a good one. He needs to be home right now—it'll encourage him to stay on the straight and narrow, y'know? He told me he hasn't seen his own father in six years. I hate my old man, and I saw him two weeks ago. Granted, I live in the same country but still. Just seems weird."

"He had a close family. His dad's a good guy, but his stepdad beat the shit out of him," I said, knowing more about Tom than was probably healthy after my long infatuation with him. "I think he was always embarrassed about his lifestyle, his addictions. But now that he's found something else, I think he can face them a little better."

"I hope so. I mean, I think so. My money's on you, not him."

"Oh?"

"Yeah. I mean, religion is fine. But it's scary. It's fragile. Especially when it's so rigid. He's got to have something more than just Jesus to keep him from falling apart."

I nodded. I knew what he meant. "Well, you won't have to worry about me doing anything stupid with James. I've…gotten over it."

"Really? Just like that?" Kurt, as usual, sounded entirely unconvinced.

"Well. I just…you're right. It would kill the band. If not now, eventually. What we've got going, the two of us, is special. I almost destroyed it by dying. I don't…we're not done yet, y'know?"

He grinned, accepting a mound of flabby looking filet of sole. Then he scowled once the smell hit him. "Why do I always order the fish?" he asked. "I should know better by now."

---

THE TWO WEEKS we spent in London were awesome. We didn't do as much clubbing as we might have done in the past, but we saw quite a few great shows and auditioned some kickass drummers, and Kurt indulged me in some museum hopping. We went shopping. We had an extensive list of what the new house needed, and we'd all promised to chip in to get it furnished. It wasn't out of necessity, but James thought it would make it feel a little more like we owned it too. I got some great lounge chairs for the studio along with a leather couch (which is just, let's face it, one of those ubiquitous necessities) and a half-dozen Oriental rugs. Kurt was in charge of the living area, and he outdid himself at some Mid-century modern place. He was in his "Mad Men" phase, so it was pretty good timing.

London in June was beautiful and blooming. We ate our weight in curries and rode the Tube everywhere. It was one of the best vacations I'd ever had, and Kurt seemed to be having the time of his life right along with me. We hardly talked about the band, but we talked plenty about music, just like we always have. Sometimes I think James and Kurt are like dueling angels on my shoulders—I won't go so far as to call one an angel and the other the devil because that would be supremely uncool of me (you can hedge your bets as to which is which). But Kurt's been my best friend for so long we've established the ability to tolerate each other for extended periods of time and, more important, accept silence. We don't have to talk. The pauses are good enough, comfortable enough, to be meaningful in and of themselves.

I started getting texts from James about three days in, mostly bits of lyrics and ideas he had for various songs. He promised Dusty he wasn't going to get all experimental, but he's always on the lookout for old school ways to improve the sound and leveraging new technologies too. It's admirable. He's always pushing me to fuzz out the keys more and to do things I never would consider—I'm just not much of a revolutionary in that way. And I think that's why James is so integral. I've talked about it before, but he's really part John Lennon, part George Martin. If anyone's responsible for our "sound," it's totally him. He's the baking soda to my flour.

We took the train out to Tunbridge, reading the tabloids and giggling to one another. There was even a picture of the two of us, holding hands, with all sorts of hilarious speculation. Kurt claimed he wanted to get it framed, stating that his mother would weep to see it since it would give her a glimmer of hope for grandchildren, sired naturally. Apparently, she's always thought I'd make the perfect match for him. I'm convinced if we had children, they'd break a hole in the space-time continuum.

And I guess that's sort of when it hit me. We were only a few stops from Tunbridge Wells, and we were laughing—one of those bright, happy, friend moments—and I saw something in Kurt's face. That expression he gets when he's trying to find the moment to say something, and can't.

We were stopped, and the hostess came by with the cart. We both fell silent.

"Kate..." he sighed. There were tears in his eyes.

I knew it would happen eventually. I knew Kurt wasn't satisfied, creatively, as part of October Revival. I knew he was staying there for me and, in all likelihood, my recent drama had made it nearly impossible for him to leave.

"You came all the way to England to tell me you're leaving the band?" I asked him, taking his hands. As always, Kurt was clammy. It was his nature, I guess. Just like James always ran warm.

He laughed bitterly. "I thought… Fuck, I don't know what I thought. I wanted to leave on a high note. I guess. I promised to deliver you to the studio, and then…"

"The album—"

"It's not about me. None of the albums are ever about me. You know that. I go in, I play the notes I'm told. This isn't my kind of music, and everything that's gone on lately… I just need time to… I dunno. Express myself in a more authentic way? That makes me sound like such a fucking douchebag when I say it."

"Who wants you?" I asked, trying to smile, even though I felt as if my stomach was swimming in sorrow. It took a ton of concentration to keep from bursting into sobs. I wasn't so good keeping my emotions in check since the overdose, but I was building the skills back up.

The train jerked forward, and he looked away, pushing his sunglasses back down as light streamed in. I could tell he was embarrassed; later he told me he'd been putting it off for days and he honestly didn't think he was ever going to manage it. He was worried about me, about my drinking, about letting me go. About blaming himself if something happened to me again.

Except I understood more than he knew. I was the albatross around his neck. I'd treated the whole thing like I was some angel, plucking him from obscurity and bringing him aboard. Giving him this lavish lifestyle, the touring schedule, the experience of being a rock star. But he didn't want it. In that way, I think, he's more of a genuine musician than the rest of us. He was ready to give it up, and none of us were. Not yet, anyway.

At that moment, though, I remembered what he'd told me before, about the cracks in the band. It wasn't just about Tom and Jesus or James and Sara or me and Jack Daniels. It was deeper, a sort of exponential weakness brought about by all of us.

"Live Monkey Trip," Kurt said. They were one of his absolute favorite bands, a sort of synth-pop electronica thing with a bluegrass vibe. The kind of music only Kurt could love. He'd become friends with Mark and Trina, the lead singer and drummer, a few months back while I was going through my pre-midlife crisis.

"Aren't they going on tour next month?" I asked. He'd been excited about it, and it made sense why.

He nodded, averting his eyes even more from me. Damn, but it was harder on him than it was on me.

"I feel like an asshole, not telling you and telling everyone else. It was before this shit with Paul, even; I didn't know he was going to quit. I mean, I knew it was going to happen eventually…but I just can't be this person anymore, Katie. You need someone whose heart is in it, and mine's not. I'm just worried about you."

"I'm a big girl," I said, kissing his fingers. "I can take care of myself. I mean, I know I don't have the best track record, but I think I'm getting myself into shape."

"I was never the heart of this, you know that. It's always been about you three. I was just the anti-Sara."

"You are. And we needed you. It still won't be the same."

"No, but it'll be better. You'll see. For all of us."

We pulled into the idyllic train station, like something out of the Narnia books, and even though Kurt wanted to take me to the studio himself, I told him I would do it alone. He was afraid for me, I could tell. He was practically shaking when we hugged goodbye. But I knew what he was feeling too, a sense of freedom after being absolved from something. It's the same feeling I'd had when I'd left home. And let me tell you, the last fucking thing I wanted was to be Kurt's obligation. He'd been my friend too long. He would never stop being my friend; he just wasn't going to be my bandmate anymore.

No matter how much I wished I could keep him around, I knew it was the best thing for him to get the hell out of Dodge. He needed a chance to do his own thing, to trip out with the kids in New York, play clubs, and be a rock star in his own right.

# CHAPTER FOURTEEN

THE DRIVER KNEW EXACTLY what I was talking about when I described Tom's dad's property, but he clearly had no idea who I was until I mentioned I was with the band. He did fill me in on all the details though, how the house had been renovated over the last half year and everyone in town had wondered what was going on. He was from Lamberhurst himself, the driver, and he said some of the folks were worried what a pop group might be doing, but then, it was remote enough that it shouldn't really matter.

We drove along the windy, hedge-high roads and through Lamberhurst itself—charming brick houses stacked along the side of the road with their squat little chimneys—before taking a sharp turn down a dirt road. It was horrifically bumpy, and just the thing for my motion sickness to start kicking in. We drove about half a mile before I noticed the house in the distance. It was about as typical as you could imagine, whitewashed and sprinkled with ivy and chimneys and roses. Except there were three conical parts to it I couldn't quite make sense of, painted white and black at the top. Not quite a castle, not quite a farm. Something else?

There was a Bentley in the driveway, which had to be James's, and some kids playing games with sticks in the adjacent field. I noticed some outbuildings around with other, smaller, practical British cars, and wondered if he had actual staff. Not that the house looked big enough to accommodate it, but I sort of figured it might be the way Tom had structured things.

And someone did meet me at the car. He was in his seventies or so, with a cap and t-shirt and dirty jeans, sprigs of curly white hair over his sizable ears.

"And you're Kate," he said, laughing. He peered around me and into the car. "And here I was expecting someone else along with you. The other lad."

"Kurt," I said, for some reason looking into the car after him, as if somehow Kurt would still be there. I cleared my throat, trying to stifle the emotions rising up. The house, the air, the birdsongs, it was all a little much. In the distance, the sun was starting its descent, and the tall grasses behind the house were dancing in the breeze. Seriously, you can't make this shit up.

I realized I hadn't answered the man's question. "I mean, Kurt went back to London. He's…got another gig."

The man nodded. "Oh! And my manners. I'm Mr. Chesley. Tom's dad, as it were."

Of course it was Tom's dad. I felt stupid for not noticing. I'm just glad I hadn't given him my luggage and a tip.

"Glad to finally meet you," I said, being as polite as possible. Tom really hadn't spoken to me much about his parents in the years we'd known each other—other than the terrors of his step-father—but I certainly had never expected this veritable hobbit of a man. It was then I noticed Mr. Chesley's old t-shirt was, in fact, a Revival's tour shirt from 2005. Our first tour together. It was so faded it was almost impossible to tell, but you could still see the second half of our name and the triangle logo.

"Well, let me show you 'round. The boys are locked up good and well, and I'm sure you'll be wanting to join them soon enough."

I followed him into the house, which had to be hundreds of years old by the look of it, and it smelled like cider and sawdust. The renovations were extensive; I mean you could just tell by a glance things were new, but they kept with the old style, too. I wasn't sure how much of a hand Tom had in it, since this was a place in his family and all, but the outcome was quite spectacular. White walls, dark wood, a smattering of antiques, posters, statues. It wasn't the cluttered coziness of James's house, that's for sure. Almost like a museum or a house out of some architectural digest (which, I think was actually in an issue a few months later).

"We're proud of my boy here," Mr. Chesley was saying. "D'you know Margaret Thatcher herself came from here as well?"

"I didn't, no…"

"Couldn't be more different than my Tom, but…"

"What kind of house is this?" I asked Mr. Chesley as he took me down a narrow hallway.

He glanced over his shoulder and said something that sounded like "oats" and, not wanting to appear stupid, I just nodded and laughed as if I knew exactly what he was talking about.

"This is yours," he said, opening a heavy latched door and gesturing inside.

Apparently, my room was in one of the cones. So, basically, the ceiling went up like forty or fifty feet. The walls were white painted brick and crisscrossed with thick wooden beams. In the middle of the room was a bed with blue linens, simple and elegant. There was an upright piano, a guitar, and a bookcase fit to bursting with books. Plus, a writing desk and some chests of drawers. The floor was sealed concrete, a sort of brownish gray, and carpeted toward the middle of the room with a rustic yellow knotted rug. I've never been a decorator or cared much one way or another how a room looks, but it was impressive, nonetheless.

I went over to the bed and smoothed my hands across the bedspread. I found a note, scrawled in Tom's childish script: "Make sweet music, Cakes!"

"Been in the family for a long time, but none of us has ever had the time or the money to do much about it. When Tom told me he was thinking of turning it into a live-in studio, and he'd be coming back home for a bit, well…" He trailed off, clearing his throat.

"It's amazing," I said.

"Well! I'll leave you to set up. There's a bathroom down the hall that's pretty much yours, if you're needing to freshen up any. When you're ready, the boys are in the studio—it's out behind the house, the one with the blue metal roof."

I made the mistake of lying down on the bed and fell into a blissful, if unexpected, hour-long nap. I guess I needed it. One of the tips from rehab: *Listen to your body.* Most of the time my body was just a grouchy old woman who needed a nap, so I knew that old song and dance pretty well. I still felt a bit out of sorts with Kurt gone—I was still getting used to the fact he wasn't going to be part of the band anymore. By the time I woke up though, it was almost dark outside, and the room was weird and shadowy.

I bathed, put on fresh clothes, and found some cucumber sandwiches in the refrigerator on my way out back. There was a beautiful lighted patio and a pathway leading to the very obvious studio. The lights were on, and the glass panes gave a clear view into the mixing room where, predictably, James was standing. I could see Tom as I got closer, a makeshift vocal booth through the interior glass, singing with his headphones on. He'd cut his hair—like, really really cut it—so at first, I had no idea who he was. I had never seen him without his mane of curls, and it definitely took me aback.

Walking into the room quietly as I could, I sat on the black leather couch I had sent ahead of me and got a good look around. It still smelled like Home Depot, with a little underlying scent of sweat and incense.

James didn't see me or hear me, as he was listening intently, leaning on the soundboard and straining to hear Tom's notes. I couldn't hear much but could gather he was working on "Sunday Strives," which was one of the last instrumental tracks we laid before the hiatus.

"Oh, shit," said Tom, laughing as he missed the lyric again. My fault, as usual, for throwing too many consonants at him. He's always had this slight lisp, barely detectable, but I tend to give him lyrics that trigger it. "And there she is!" he said, spotting me and shaking his fists. "I can blame her to her face this time!"

James looked over his shoulder and smiled, taking off the headphones. "Cakes, you sneak. I didn't even hear you."

"Quiet as a mouse," I said.

Tom came out of the booth and gave me a big hug, and James followed suit. Tom plopped down on the sofa next to me, stretching out his legs so I had his feet in my lap.

"It's been a good day so far," James said, folding his arms and leaning back in the big roller chair. "What do you think of this lovely speck of Kent?" James, who'd grown up outside London, claimed he had a difficult time out here in the sticks, but you could tell he was in his element regardless.

"The room's beautiful. I'm a little overwhelmed," I admitted. "I'm not sure what I expected, but it's really amazing."

"My dad's the one with the vision," Tom explained, running his hands over his hair. He wasn't used to it yet, either. Maybe even a little self-conscious. "I just tell him what colors I like, and he's off. Loads of the furniture was from my mother's family, and it's just rather come together, I think. You like the oast room?"

"What the fuck's an oast?" I asked. "Is that like English toast or something?"

James and Tom laughed in their "Americans are so cute" way and explained the house used to be an oast house, where hops were dried before brewing. The humor of that wasn't lost on me, considering I couldn't have a drink, but I did think it was a cool idea to renovate it the way he had. We started calling the house "The Oast" in spite of the fact it had some foofy English name.

They filled me in on where we were in the progress, and James had some basic sound sketches for a few songs he was dying to share. They were both energized and excited, and I wondered if that's how they were when they first started playing together, like little kids discovering something new.

When they finished talking about the progress they'd made that day, as well as some of Tom's more in-depth descriptions of what had gone into the studio, I told them about Kurt leaving and me giving him the blessing to do so. They both watched me intently as I told them about our conversation on the train.

"I don't want to hold anyone back," I said. "Least of all Kurt. I'm just sorry it took so long to get to this point."

"We should have told you," James said.

"Probably. But I get it. Kurt just wanted to say goodbye the best way he knows how, which is to have a good time. And we did. We had a great time."

"You're okay?" Tom asked. He'd pulled his legs up under his chin, wrapping his long arms around his calves. "I mean…"

"He wasn't happy, and I think we all knew it," I said. "Sure, I wish he'd be here. And I know if I'd asked him, he'd probably have stayed. But it's not fair of me, is it?"

James was still chewing on his lip, looking worriedly at me.

"You're all going to have to stop hovering over me at some point," I said. "I might fuck up. I might fall off the wagon. But I'm okay. Right now, I just want to hang out, have fun, and make music. That's the whole point of this, right?"

"Of course." James shook his head like a horse getting rid of pesky flies. "We just worried. You and Kurt are close. You live together… It's just…"

"Transition," I said, standing up and going to the soundboard. "Now let's get to the album making, then we can talk about finding ourselves a rhythm section."

# CHAPTER FIFTEEN

FINDING an entire rhythm section is no easy task, not even for a seasoned band. Especially one with a track record for burning through them faster than coke at a Fleetwood Mac show in '78. It isn't fair, really, that bassists and drummers are so often relegated to the sidelines. After the failed attempt in London to score a drummer, the idea of bringing in new blood had me uncomfortable enough I suggested getting session musicians to finish out the album, but James was adamant we had to find the right people.

We were not far from London, which meant we had plenty of talent to choose from. All of a sudden, I found myself the lone American, the lone woman, in a sea of British men. As much as I'd have loved to find a couple of chicks for the group, the truth of the matter is they're so few and far between—and the ones who are super talented are taken. I rang up a few ladies I knew, and, although they were nice about it, none of them were particularly enthused or available. It's sort of hard to claim to want to hire a new, fresh face when you've just lost half your band and your primary songwriter nearly died of alcohol poisoning. Not to mention totally awkward.

The tabloids were not nice. Not that I expected it. But we've—or, I should say, James and Tom—have always been higher profile in the

UK, and with Kurt leaving (he set Twitter afire with his announcement that he was joining Live Monkey Trip), I was pretty sure no one was going to touch us with a ten-foot pole. Why would they want to? Sara had badmouthed me to half the record industry, and the other half was probably sure I was about to turn up dead any minute (I recall Kurt telling me there were websites devoted to such things, but I never bothered looking it up—I've never had a good relationship with the internet).

"What about Clive whatsits from Posh Maul? Didn't he leave to do some solo stuff?" Tom asked over breakfast one morning. It'd been two weeks at the Oast, and the three of us had settled into a neat little routine, which, even I had to admit, was fun. Musically, we were spot on. But as the final album lineup was becoming more and more apparent, so was the huge gaping hole in our own band.

"I'm think he's on tour with Casper Trash," I said, remembering reading that somewhere. "Besides, he was a tool." I didn't want to say it so inelegantly, but it was true.

"Jesus, woman," James said, "you turn everyone down."

"I'm just dreading it. And Dusty's threatening auditions if we don't come up with someone soon. It's…just so high school. I don't want the tour to be all hermetic and uncomfortable with someone we don't know, y'know? I need a good bassist."

"Fuck, Kate, we all need a good bassist," James countered, rolling his eyes and elbowing me.

Tom pushed around his oatmeal. "I've been praying about it," he said, staring into the bowl. "And I just have this sense we need to go back to our roots."

James and I exchanged looks while Tom stuck his fork in the marmalade.

"Our roots?" James asked. "Like, trolling clubs in New York? I hate to break it to you, Tom, but we're on the wrong fucking side of the lake."

"Yeah, yeah, precisely right," Tom said. "I mean, not New York, obviously. But here. If it's one thing I agree with Kurt, it's that we need someone fresh, new. Someone with passion."

I laughed. "No way. We're too old for that. The last thing we need in our lineup is some hipster kid with an Imagine Dragons obsession."

"Not everyone out there is like that," Tom pointed out, wagging an accusatory spoon at me. "I'm just saying we can't expect the label to find us suitable people, not if we want them to be more than studio musicians."

He had a point, even if he claimed it was heaven sent.

"I don't know shit about the music scene here, but my guess is you two would be fairly conspicuous if we were just to head out and start sitting in on local gigs in London, right?" I asked.

Which was a problem. I didn't know how I felt about being let loose on my own. There were plenty of ways for me to get the music to them, hell—my phone could practically edit half the music on its own. But I had a lot of work to do on the album, and I didn't fancy the idea of trolling around the big city on my own. It was a depressing thought and made me miss Kurt all the more. It's just the sort of thing he'd have loved to do, even if he'd be a snarky bitch through most of the critiques.

"Not if we skip London altogether." James drummed his fingers on the table. "There's other places we could go. Bristol. Brighton. Birmingham…"

"Bath and Bexhill? Are we just naming cities with Bs?" I asked.

"I just mean, slightly off the beaten path. I'm as out of touch as anyone, but I think it might be fun."

"You have an odd definition of fun. Sitting through painful sets waiting to hear a diamond in the rough isn't my cup of tea," I said, feeling every bit of a music snob. But it was true. One of the nice things about being a professional was not having to deal with shitty music. We'd all been through our share.

"What about YouTube?" James asked.

I threw a bagel at him. "Are you fucking serious? We're not Journey, dude."

ULTIMATELY, that's how I ended up on a showboat called the Thekla listening to a never-ending rotation of mediocre bands, wearing a shoulder-length black wig and red lipstick. I'm pretty much the only one able to manage visiting a club without being recognized. I took Mark, one of our London engineers, along with me, while Tom and James took a mini spa retreat in nearby Bath. I was under explicit instructions to report anything exciting to the boys, but that was unlikely.

The Thekla is its own special thing. Seriously. You play in the hull of the boat, this German ship parked in the Bristol Harbor. We'd played there a handful of times when we were starting out, and it always struck me as warped and wonderful. They had a constant string of up-and-comers, but I had no idea what James and Tom were expecting out of it. Was I going to steal someone's bassist? I guess it made sense, tangentially, that I was the one acquiring the rhythm section, but it was still worth a shot.

I barely made it through the first two bands. They were post-pop awful. In the first band's case, instrumentally they were impressive. The lead singer was of a mind he was the lovechild of Axl Rose and God Himself, gyrating like a drunken Mick Jagger in heels. Nothing to write home about. Except maybe for a laugh later.

The second group was a girl band, and they were doing an impression of the Bangles meets Alanis Morissette. It wasn't very bad, but it wasn't very good, and most of the members just looked angry and unhappy about being shoved into the hull to begin with. I could concur; I'd been there. It was hot and cramped, but it was definitely an experience not to be missed.

And that's when this tall guy with red hair and a black t-shirt comes out on stage to tune up the instruments for the headliners. He plays a few chords on the guitar, and it sounds vaguely familiar, but I figure—well, I just can't accept some random dude is playing a song I wrote on the guitar. My ego's not that big.

But then he picked up the bass and started playing, no joke, "Round About the Wrong Way" and I just about spit out my ginger ale.

Yeah, sure. People play my songs. But they don't play *that* song. It's not on regular rotation, never has been.

Mark was looking at me, wide-eyed, and I was caught between excitement and resentment. I didn't want Tom to be right. Well, I didn't want some miracle. I just wanted a damned bass player.

I kept listening. He played through a few more bars, and stopped, but it was amazing. It was a little meandering, but I didn't need to be convinced of the guy's skills. I had full-body goosebumps, all the way up into the roots of my hair. Serious musical dopamine.

I was fully prepared to see him come on stage when the next band was announced, but he didn't show. Apparently he was just some wildly talented techie who happened to have a thing for our music.

So I sent Mark to find out who he was. I waited, gritting my teeth and wanting to order half the bar to settle my stomach. I was having flashbacks of hearing Tom sing for the first time and wondering if James had felt the same way when he'd heard my lyrics.

"He's not interested," Mark said, sitting down next to me, looking a little bemused.

"Did you tell him I was asking about him? Or at least, that we're a big deal, relatively speaking?"

"He laughed at me, and sort of threatened me." Mark shrugged. "I think he didn't take me very seriously."

That made sense. Mark's a good guy, but he does come off as disingenuous sometimes. He's just got a perpetually snarky streak, kind of like Kurt but a bit more difficult to decipher.

"Where was he?" I asked.

Mark said he'd last seen him heading for the dock, and I figured now was a good a time as any to leave. The main act was painfully disappointing, so much so I was pining after Kurt. We'd have had a ball of it, tearing them apart. And feeling depressed was making me seriously consider alcohol, which was not even a remotely good idea.

---

HE WAS HARD TO MISS, smoking a cigarette out on the concrete walkway, under a street lamp. His hair looked like it was on fire, it was so bright. The music reverberated around the air, muffled by the boat and yet oddly amplified over the water.

"Hi," I said, coming up to him.

I got a grunt in response.

"Listen, about your playing…"

"I told that wanker to leave me the fuck alone," he growled, flicking his cigarette angrily into the water and taking a step toward me.

I took off my wig. I've never been one for theatrics. Sure, when we're in the middle of a live set and the music's flowing, I'm happy to toss my head back and sway with the music and hop around. There's sort of an expected keyboardist stance, y'know? But generally speaking, I don't do stuff like flaunt my fame or do big, impressive reveals.

But in this case, it worked, and it was fucking amazing. He totally recognized me.

"Oh… God. Shit. I…"

"I'm Kate," I said. Mark was some distance away, and I caught him laughing into his sleeve. "I heard you on the bass, but I've been told you're not interested in entertaining any professional gigs."

"Um…yeah, that's…that's what I said. I'm mortified at the moment, honestly."

"I'm sorry—I should have talked to you first. It was kind of a diva thing to do."

"No, no, it's… I'm sorry, but you're really Kate Styx?"

"It's not on my driver's license, but we can jam and I can prove it to you," I said. I was nervous. Like I was asking my crush on a date. I shoved my hands in my pockets to keep them from shaking.

He took out another cigarette and held it between his fingers. He had a nice voice, probably a solid baritone. If he had half the ear he did on bass, he could sing backup now and again, which would be an improvement over Kurt who struggled, at best, on vocals.

"Listen," I said when he didn't reply. "We're looking for a bassist. You seem like you know your shit. If you're around, and available, you should come drop by the studio sometime."

I gave him my number and said goodnight and went back to the hotel with Mark. I texted James and told him I'd found someone. He was a little grumpy I hadn't heard him play more than a few bars, but I promised him that my Spidey senses were right. He said he'd caught up with Ron Clairemont, formerly of Spicemilk, and he was totally game to test the waters with the new October Revival lineup. Ron was one of the best in the business and a known quantity—he didn't get into trouble, he was creative and friendly, and he wasn't married or religious or a drug addict. At least we had a drummer.

# CHAPTER SIXTEEN



"We have a problem."

Back at the Oast, James announced this at breakfast, at approximately ten in the morning, after going to the front window. He was still lounging in the closest he ever got to actual nightclothes, which was comprised of natty green fleece pants and a patchy old sweater over a t-shirt. I had come to think of this as his morning uniform.

Tom was half asleep at the table, curled around his coffee and humming to himself, but the tone of James's voice was still apparently enough to rouse him. Since my visit to Bristol, we still hadn't found a rhythm section. The "Mystery Ginger," as the bassist was now referred to, had not returned my calls. And Ron Clairemont had failed to return James's calls and emails after being initially quite enthusiastic.

"Is it the cow again?" Tom mumbled. "Stupid creature."

We did have an errant cow. Before the renovations, the house had been in relative disuse, and some of the town cows frequented the fallow fields. Mr. Chesley never minded much since he didn't think anything was going to be done with the house to begin with. But now that the construction crews were gone, there was one particular cow who felt as if her space had been infringed upon. Tom wanted her voice on the album.

James put down his toast and started fumbling around for his phone while I poured more coffee. For my part, I was with Tom.

"Who're you going to call?" I asked. "I don't think animal control really cares one way or another…"

"There's a girl standing outside." James pointed at the door with his half-eaten toast. He looked horrified. Granted, he and Tom—and even I—had suffered from zany fans now and again, but typically it wasn't a lone girl that would freak him out.

Tom got up and went to the window, perpetual curiosity one of his most charming and occasionally irritating features.

He came back to report. "She looks like she's fifteen. And she's talking to someone on her mobile."

"Shouldn't we talk to her?" I asked, feeling as if everyone else had collectively lost their minds. "Maybe she's just lost."

Tom and James clearly weren't going to be gentlemen about it, so I pulled my robe around and slipped my shoes back on, then grabbed my sunglasses for good measure. I've always made the mistake of wearing sunglasses just about everywhere, going so far as incorporating them into almost every hairstyle. It's convenient but terribly lazy.

I opened the door to see, indeed, what appeared to be a young girl of indeterminate race standing in the morning drizzle, shaking her phone in hopes it might start working. A second glance gave me pause because she wasn't as young as I'd thought, just sort of impish. She was shorter than me, and her thick, curly hair was dyed dark purple and shaved on one side. She wore very dark lipstick and her nails were painted hot pink, to say nothing of her outfit, which was an amalgamation of preppy wear—a white sweater vest and plaid tights—with jeans, chains, and bangles. Couldn't miss her for the world and, in James's defense, she did have a little of a creepy doll child vibe going on.

"Can I help you?" I asked.

She didn't notice I'd opened the door.

"Oh, shit. Uh, hi," she said with an attempted grin. "Is this where October Revival lives?"

I nodded. "At the moment, yes. We haven't trumpeted it to the skies though, so we weren't just expecting fans to drop by."

I knew she wasn't a fan. Our fans generally don't look like the lovechild of Prince and Joan Jett. But I couldn't ascribe any other motive to her at the moment.

"Huh?" she asked me, tilting her head as if she was just seeing me for the first time. "I'm not—well, it's not that I'm not a fan, exactly. Just not that kind of fan. Not the sort you're thinking of, I don't think."

Despite her rather harried appearance, she had a soft, Suffolk sweetness to her voice. Her voice itself had a good, strong sound. Probably a mezzo soprano, if she worked at it. With good singers, you can tell they're quality just by hearing them speak. Which is what sort of cued me on to the next insight.

"You're a musician." I said it, didn't ask it, because for much of my own existence, people have always sent the statement courtesy of a question mark. Nothing makes a chick feel less professional than people starting off with their general disbelief.

"Yeah. How'd you guess?" she asked.

"Intuition," I replied. "I guess I'm at the point where I can spot another one a mile away. But, uh, that's sort of beside the point. You are hanging on our stoop."

She cleared her throat and pulled at one of the braids off the side of her head with actual hair. "Right. My dad told me you'd be here."

"Your dad?"

"Yeah. Ron Clairemont."

"Shit. You just made me feel really, really old. You're telling me that Ron sent his kid instead of coming on his own?"

Tom and James were intrigued by now, and they were both standing behind me. At the moment, all I could imagine was us looking like a rag-tag mid-thirties washed up version of the Three Stooges, peering out the door at this little teacup person smiling expectantly up at us.

"Hi," James said.

"Hiya," Tom added.

"Yeah, hi," she said. "I'm Dee."

"Like the letter?" asked Tom.

"Right. Short for my first name," Dee clarified.

"Which is?" James asked.

"Which is rude to ask." I shoved them both back with my arm. "Here, Dee. Why don't you come inside, and we can talk about what it is exactly that your, uh, dad was thinking."

---

Turns out that Dee is the nickname of the most unfortunate Dorcas Mathilda Clairemont, whose mother was from Fiji and is one of Ron's tangential children. He's been married for something like twenty years to a woman too good for him, and even though he's about fifteen years older than us, talking to his kid was quite an experience.

It wasn't that she was that young because, really, she was only eight years younger than Tom. But she still felt like another generation altogether. Not to mention her whole look.

"Pardon me if I'm rude," said James, which was always an indication of impending rudeness, "but you don't really give me the vibe of an October Revival... uh..."

"Appreciator," I added.

"I get it. I have a look. But whatever. It's not about that. I mean, it's no secret I don't give a shit what people think of the way I dress." She wiggled her silver Chucks like an antsy kindergartner. "It's completely irrelevant when it comes to who I really am."

"Yeah?" James asked.

"Yeah. Because the only thing you should care about is how I sound. On the drums."

A chick drummer. It could work, I figured. But she had to be really good. As good as her old man. And able to withstand the rest of us. Which, so far, virtually no one had managed to do for any duration more than a few years.

"Let's hear it." Tom was already smitten with her. Not sure if it was genuine love and adoration, but I think he admired her pluck. Dee had an attitude, it's true, but it was part and parcel with her general confidence, which was extremely comforting. God knows I have none.

I won't say she was the tightest drummer in the world, and she'd obviously listened to a lot of Paul's stuff because on most of the tracks she was just sort of mimicking him a bit. But I could see part of the problem: the kit we had at the studio was too big for her. I immediately thought she'd do better with something custom, and perhaps some more percussion. Her instincts were straight on.

James was on the same wavelength as me. After she'd played through three of our tunes with me on the keys and James filling in on bass, he walked around the kit and studied it appraisingly.

"Your set's different, yeah?" he asked her.

Dee nodded, wiping sweat from her brow with the back of her forearm. "You'd never guess from looking at me, but it's sort of this hybrid jazz/rock kit. Dad helped me put it together."

"Makes sense," James said. "But now that you've played Paul's drumming back for us, let's do 'Rolling Around in My Heart'—but do it the way you'd do it, 'kay?"

And that, well, yeah. That sealed the deal.

None of us wanted another Paul. Listen, Paul's a good, solid drummer. He does what we ask of him, he never tries to be invasive. But sometimes with the expected, there's also a lack of passion. Dee's rhythm was amazing. Her timing, impeccable. Her ability to take a beat and spin it just right... James and I were practically slavering at the lips by the time we were done, ready to show her off to Dusty and get the paperwork, so to speak.

We kept her the rest of the day, showed her some of the new material. Turns out she was a big Smiths fan too, but she thought Morrissey was a twat, so she got my vote. Her influences were newer, weirder, less standard than ours, but it was a welcome new heartbeat to the center of the group. Young and vital and alive.

"So what's the rub?" Tom asked, as we all sat on the back porch, smoking a joint. It's the one thing Tom and I allow ourselves, and it's only now and again. For two addicts like us living under one roof, especially considering our general state of codependence, I'll take it without comment. Tom has told himself it's natural and God-given. Whatever.

Dee was fiddling with her phone, so it took her a second to realize Tom was talking to her. "Oh, what?"

"Tell me what's flawed. What's wrong with you. Why you aren't signed, etc." Tom waved his hand in little circles like some king holding court with the fireflies.

Dee laughed. "I'm young. I'm small. I'm a girl. It's not that I haven't played—I have, tons. Sessions, mostly. I could name six records off the top of my head, but it's been nothing more. When Dad told me... I thought, I mean, there aren't many groups out there who would take a chance with someone like me, and I figured if we had a chance, it was here."

"Drugs?"

"Not really. Not more than this," she said, gesturing to the weed with a silly smirk. "I was sick as a kid. Shit kidneys. So anything else is sort of asking for it, y'know?"

"Your dad's protective?" I asked.

"Sometimes."

"So he sent you?" I asked. "Or you asked?"

"Does it matter?" Dee replied.

"Not really, I guess," I said. "But it does..."

I was going to say something witty and clever when my phone vibrated and I reluctantly pulled it out. There weren't many people who would be texting me, at least not other than the ones sitting next to me. Kurt was just about to head out on tour, and I'd stopped hoping for his continual connection. He didn't have to say it, I knew. He needed space from me. For a while.

I didn't recognize the number. Then again, most UK numbers looked like crazy garbage to me, so I held up the phone to Tom.

"That's Bristol," he said, and his eyes widened. "The magic ginger!"

"It was 'mysterious' I distinctly remember," James pointed out.

"Mysterious ginger. I think he's maybe a sparkling vampire. Or, oh! An MI:5 agent."

Dee laughed because we were weird.

The text was short. "Want to come try out. Not sure if 2 late. Let me know—fellow from the Thekla."

# CHAPTER SEVENTEEN

I WAS NERVOUS. Really, really nervous. More nervous than I had any right to be. Instead of the trial by fire Dee had, I thought maybe it was best if the Mysterious Ginger and I had some time to talk before things got weird. He didn't strike me as resilient as our young new drummer, and I didn't want to scare him off. Besides, Tom and James were sometimes oddly territorial when it came to me and the band, and I didn't want machismo being an issue.

There were a couple of places to meet in the center of Lamberhurst, but I chose the Chequers Inn because it was infectiously darling. They had good beer on tap—not that I was drinking, but still—really good food, and a comfortable environment. I wasn't sure if this guy was a lifer from Bristol. We'd only exchanged a handful of words, so I had no idea what his accent was, really, other than general English.

They knew me at the Chequers because I was slightly obsessed with their chicken liver pâté and ordered it on a fairly regular basis. But whether they knew me by reputation or just generally as an American girl with a thing for liver, I don't know. Certainly they knew who Tom was—town boys rarely go without notice. But if people whispered about me behind my back, I never noticed. And the rare day a photographer found their way into town, they never seemed to find us exactly. A bit of a slice of heaven, really.

He was almost an hour late, and I'd have left altogether if not for the polite text message informing me the train had some maintenance issues. So I ordered another ginger ale and fired up some of my favorite playlists and fiddled with some lyrics for one of the last two songs that would be on the *Something Else*. That title was a bit of a joke. For months we'd been calling it *Something Else* to one another because we knew the name was going to change. Except it never did. It just stuck.

When the guy finally arrived, it was no secret. He was taller than I remembered, and his hair was even redder in the daylight. Like, seriously the color of fresh blood. You don't see redheads without the tinge of orange. And he was a lot more handsome than I remembered too. A rare dark-eyed redhead. He took off his sunglasses and scanned the room twice before seeing me.

My hair had grown out a bit and had since reverted to its default unruly waves, and I briefly worried he might not recognize me without the wig. So I waved my hand sheepishly, and he made his way across the pub.

"Well, hi," I said.

"Hi," he replied, holding his cap in his hand. He was wearing the same sort of outfit he'd worn the night I'd seen him, browns and blues and black slacks. No intention of dressing up, apparently.

"Sit?"

"Sure," he said. The waitress came, and he ordered sparkling water and the Ploughman's as if he'd been there a thousand times.

"I'm Kate." I held out my hand. "Professionally Kate Styx, but legally Katherine-Ann Marshall Mendenhall. That's a mouthful, so in a drunken bout when I briefly had a thing for Tommy Shaw, I decided Styx was the perfect stage name."

"Yeah, I know who you are. And I still feel like an arse for shouting at you."

"Well, you have...um...passion. So it's a good thing." He looked at me blankly and then glanced away. Shy. Guarded. Embarrassed? I wasn't sure. I cleared my throat. "And I suppose you have a name?"

"Jon. Jon Blake."

"Always good to put a name to a face. Right. And so, Jon Blake, how long have you been playing bass, and why aren't you doing it professionally?"

"Because most of us don't make it big," he said, already with a bit of attitude. "You ask me that like it's the easiest thing in the world."

"Okay. Good point. I'm a little out of touch." Part of me bristled, but part of me liked the fact he wasn't star struck.

Jon Blake might have been a little bit of an asshole, but he was a handsome one. I realize how messed up that looks now I've written it down, but there you go.

"Well, how long have you been playing?" I asked, starting with the basics since, apparently, pleasant chit chat was beyond my capabilities. I missed the mental don't-give-a-shitness that liquor brings. Being sober sucks sometimes. Which is a gross understatement. Life is generally a lot easier to cope with when you can drink it away; however, given the choice, it's not as bad as being dead. Sobriety does have that going for it.

I could smell the beer across the table and had to force myself to stop looking longingly at it.

"Music in general, or bass?" he asked.

"Both?" I was sort of losing steam, starting to second guess myself. Thinking about drinking and shaking my foot to distract my addict brain. Before I said something else stupid, I went for another mouthful of pâté.

"I was raised with the classics, and my dad, he's been playing guitar since before it was cool. So it was sort of everywhere, y'know?" Jon said, talking down to his hands. "He's passed on now, and I used to work with him—shipping—but that went to shit, and I've been working at the Thelka since. Part bartender, part techie. Hasn't left much time for music, I guess."

I didn't know the whole story, but I could sense there was a deeper, darker, far sadder story than he was letting on. So I tried to change the mood.

"Well, what I heard was amazing..."

"It's not my favorite song," he said.

"It's what?" He was losing me, and I was distracted.

He wiggled his fingers like he was playing an invisible bass. The waitress brought over his food, and he pushed it aside. "The song I played that night. I mean, all the Sara stuff...her basslines were so meandering. Not bad, just not my style. The last album—especially Kurt Bastian's tracks—they just sing. I should have played 'Yesterday's Girl.'"

God. In between every snide remark was a silky compliment to my soul. I wanted to slip away in a puddle of warmth. No one ever liked "Yesterday's Girl"—it's too much synth and all weird, sort of like "Within You, Without You" by the Beatles, but newer sounding.

"Either way, you impressed me. And I think you'd impress Tom and James." I almost said "and Dee," but it didn't feel natural yet.

He licked his lips and frowned. "I'm just not sure I can."

"What do you mean?" I laughed. "Of course you can."

"There's...I mean, Kate. Can I call you Kate?"

I nodded.

He cleared his throat. "I live in Bristol. My family's there. It's always been a perfect arrangement with the club, 'cause I don't have to leave. It's home, and it's play. I make enough to get by, but I've responsibilities."

"I know people don't approve much of—"

"Listen. I'll audition. But I can't promise."

"Fair enough," I said, not wanting to argue the point. "If it's about money—"

"If it was about money, don't you think I'd have said yes that first night?"

<hr>

"I told you. Divine providence."

"It's not divine providence. It's a coincidence. And it isn't like it's all rainbows and unicorns, Tom. He is very reluctant."

Tom and I were whispering back and forth in the control room while James, Dee, and Jon jammed. It wasn't perfect, but hell it was beautiful. It was *fun*. James couldn't stop smiling, and Dee was really hitting a groove. You could hear the new sound happening, building and swelling and changing the way we played our old songs and how we'd arrange the new ones. I kept catching James's eye, and he had this grateful, amazed look.

I'd realized, up until that moment, we'd all been running scared. None of us were sure after everything we'd been through we could sustain another album and another tour. None of us were thirty-five yet but, I swear, we were feeling old. Music was losing its excitement, its power over us, as the dramas of real life and relationships and addictions wore away at our hearts and minds.

But even if Jon said no, I think the three originals among us realized we could still go on. That we'd weathered the storm. Tom might be clinging to Jesus, but overall, he'd acclimated well. He was involved again. He was sitting next to me, his hand on my shoulder, leaning in and experiencing the music. James was in his element. We had more than enough songs to fill up an album. And we were happy with what we had.

"But what could possibly be keeping him? I mean, listen!" Tom flailed his hands in the general direction of the group. He was so excited he could hardly control himself. Sitting, standing, hugging himself, poking me.

"I don't know. He said family. He said it wasn't about the money. He didn't give me much in the way of details," I said.

"Maybe he's a little, you know, touched," Tom joked, and I rolled my eyes at him.

"This isn't exactly 2008. We're not on the top of our game. Maybe he's…I don't know. He could figure this won't last long. That it's a sinking ship. Although, I did find him in an actual sinking ship, so maybe it was just a bad portend."

I said the words casually and, to me, they felt natural because I'd thought it so many times. But I could see in Tom's face he hadn't. He sat down next to me again, putting his hands on his knees and leaning forward.

"Really, Kate?" he asked. "You think…you think that?"

"Tom…you can't tell me it never crossed your mind."

He chewed on his bottom lip, blinking slowly as if the strain of the emotion was making it hard for him to speak. "I spent a lot of time getting better. I mean, spiritually. Physically. I know I've been a horrid person to be around but—this—all this, the house and the break and the new start—you don't feel like we're doing something great? Something big? That this is just the start of it? That we're better, stronger? You don't have to worry about me like before. I thought it would help."

"I got through almost dying a few months back. Remember? I swear to you, Tom, this has been the only thing keeping me from the total deep end."

"Kate… If you just pray about it, take some time—"

The anger flared so fast I had to bite my cheek from growling. "No, listen. You have God, now, Tom. That's your thing. I am not going to talk smack about God, or whatever, but don't you start with me. Just. Don't."

"Kate, I just think if you—" He tried again, but I could see the fear in his eyes. He knew I was on the brink.

"God didn't work out for me, Tom. In case you missed the memo. Instead, I found music. And it'll be with me wherever I go, as long as I can flick my fingers and raise my voice and listen. But there's a point —there's always a point—when the song changes. When people have to move on. This won't last forever. Nothing does."

He didn't reply, but he stood up and went to the window to watch the jam session. We didn't talk about it again for weeks. I'd hurt his feelings, but damned if I was going to let him tell me to pray about my attitude toward the band. Eff that noise.

156

Shocked as we all were, Jon didn't stay beyond the jam session. He clearly enjoyed himself, and the excitement in the room was palpable. But he insisted he didn't have the sort of life where he could just stand up and leave at a moment's notice. Kent was, he reminded me, a long way from Bristol in English miles (which, he contested, were far longer than American miles). I wanted him on the album, but it didn't seem likely. Regretfully, we all had to contact Dusty and the label and tell them to arrange for a session bassist to finish off what Kurt hadn't recorded.

At that point, as the summer started coming to the close, we had everything but "Dalliance" and "Marvel" finished, and to all of our surprise, the label was really happy with what they were hearing. Due to the drama—not just on my part but on Tom's, too—they'd given us the hands-off treatment, and they were really pleased we'd risen to the task. Tom had revived his Twitter account and was actually posting, with a bit of handholding when necessary, and from what he could tell, the fanbase was getting really excited.

We started putting tour dates together, getting artwork for the *Something Else*. We announced Dee Clairemont as our drummer, and the industry welcomed her with open arms. There were naysayers, sure. But we knew once they heard her tracks and got to see her live, it would put their fears to rest. It felt good to have another girl in the band, especially one that was the precise opposite of Sara. Instead of begging for her to get out of the bathroom and get ready, we had to encourage her to get in there in the first place.

The album was slotted for a holiday release, which the label was thrilled about, with the tour kicking off in February, with a handful of more intimate performances beforehand, as well as the usual circuit of television and radio appearances.

We were winding down at the Oast when we got word they were sending someone over from *Rolling Stone* to do a cover on us. Dee ran around the house six times before we could calm her down enough and brief her—we knew there'd be lots of questions surrounding her. Her excitement was catchy though. Apparently, they were originally going to put us in the women's issue, but because the buzz was so good about *Something Else*, they wanted to switch gears a bit and do a lengthier feature. It'd been a long time since we were considered so worthy.

James was holed up in the studio most of the time, and even when I tried to spend a good number of hours there, I almost always felt extraneous. I trusted James, almost implicitly, at this point in the recording cycle. It's not that I'm not interested in the mastering and producing side of it, it's just he's just so fucking amazing at it I have always felt better letting him have the wheel, so to speak. As usual, he hardly slept, and when he talked to me, it was about nothing other than music, music, music. But I expected it and, on a level, adored it.

The morning the reporter arrived, I was pretty much holding down the house alone. We wanted them to see Tom in action—happy, healthy, talented—and so he was with James on some of the last tracks, doing some of the vocals he'd already done in Nashville, but with slight changes. I actually took the time to do myself up a bit, put on makeup and something that resembled a fashionable ensemble.

Studying the image in the mirror, I was surprised to see I looked better than I remembered. For the last twelve weeks, I really hadn't bothered to take stock of my own appearance. I mean, other than my hair (which was now practically regulated by Dusty's mandate) I appeared healthier than I had in a long time. I was still getting wrinkles, especially around my eyes, but they bothered me less than I thought they might.

When the doorbell rang, Mr. Chesley answered—he was excited and wanted to help keep everything in line, he claimed. I didn't want it looking like a butler, so I made sure he introduced himself right away. I heard laughter and discussion, the hall closet opening to accommodate a jacket. It was a cold morning, and I'd put on a scarf/shawl hybrid thing to keep warm at the last minute.

I tried to look natural but felt fabulously unnatural.

The guy who walked through the threshold was not an unfamiliar face. It was Jesse from rehab. We'd been writing back and forth since we graduated the program, but, since I got to England, he hadn't been replying as much. Travel was a bitch.

He was a good guy though. American. Handsome in a traditional, Midwestern way: wheat brown hair, clear blue eyes. He never pretended to be a rock star, and I think that's what I liked about him. He just liked music. Really, really liked music. We never talked much about anything else—not drinking or drugs or fast living or personal shit—we just made each other playlists, and sometimes I sent him demos, and he'd often send me flirtatious or funny texts and .gifs. Nothing serious.

"Jesse!" I slid off the stool and gave him a hug. "They didn't say they were sending you."

He hugged me back and told me I looked great. "They were going to send someone local, but I managed to weasel my way in."

"Smart," I said. My nerves vanished, and I felt immediately at ease. I could do this. I was confident.

"Coffee?" I asked gesturing to the countertop.

"Can't live without it," Jesse said, sounding extremely grateful. "I'm jetlagged as hell. I was in LA, following Rock Special on the last leg of their tour and, Christ, those guys can party. I got tired just watching them."

"Just watching?" I joked.

He cleared his throat. "Yeah. It wasn't easy, but…I left unscathed."

"Good for you." I fiddled with the coffee press. Tom usually made the coffee since Kurt's exit, and I had very little idea of how to do it properly. It was a good distraction from the weird feeling of two alcoholics standing side by side in a room. "Good…good for you."

"I hear you're doing better."

"Much. Yeah. Life's boring. I miss drinking every day. But getting older sucks. Reality sucks. I write more music now and wake up in far fewer puddles of puke. It helps with my life perspective." I set the kettle to going and sat down on the opposite side of the bar from him.

"Yeah, I know that feeling."

"How's the wife? The kids?" I ask. The last I remembered he'd had a daughter or two.

Jesse gave me a sad sigh. "Well, the divorce was finalized two weeks ago…which is why I've been sort of not replying to emails. That and the tour…"

"Oh, shit. Jesse. I'm sorry. I didn't know. I just live in this stupid fucking bubble sometimes."

"It's okay, Kate. I don't expect you to keep tabs on every journalist that comes your way. It's just nice you remembered me—and that I had kids—at all. Divorce is a pain, but I think all of us are happier now."

"Isn't that what you're supposed to say?" I asked.

He laughed.

# CHAPTER EIGHTEEN

Jesse stayed for two days, and everyone was on very good behavior. Dusty made a brief appearance since she was working with another of her bands, Holy Rolling Pope, out of London, and she wanted to make sure Jesse and the magazine weren't imposing. She complimented my hair but declared it was time for a cut, especially considering photos would be taken.

I knew Lamberhurst probably wasn't going to be the slickest place to get my hair done, so I decided to take a drive up to Tonbridge using James's Bentley. The car itself was at least twenty years old, so I wasn't too worried about attracting attention. Not that I've ever had the face for getting attention. I think ninety percent of the time I've been recognized in public, it's because of context, my bandmates. Not me personally. Dusty informs me I have a forgetful face.

Just as I was about to get in the car, Jesse came around the side of the Oast and waved me down.

"Where're you off to?" he asked.

"Getting my hair in an acceptable state. The manager has decreed," I said.

"Oh, come on. You're a rock star. You don't need to do your hair. I mean, hell, look at Dee. She's like some weird post-apocalyptic punk."

"Dusty says she has character. I, on the other hand, do not." It was always challenging keeping my mouth shut around Jesse; he was so easy to talk to. Even in my darker days, I liked shooting the shit with him. For a non-musician, he really understood music, really felt it on a sort of philosophical level.

He rolled his eyes. "I'd tell her to fuck off."

"It's not like I have anything else to do. James is going to be locked away in his cone of silence until he's dragged out for pictures, and Tom and Dee are finishing up some of their last tracks. I'm slated for some background vocal stuff later—" I stopped because Jesse was smiling stupidly at me. "What? Do I have something on my face?"

"No, no. You're just…I just thought, since it's such a nice day and not drizzling for once, you might want to take me on a local excursion, maybe see the sights instead of stay here and whine about Tom and James."

It was hilarious, the idea I'd want to do such a thing, but I indulged him anyway. "Excursion? Like, hiking and walking and stuff?"

"It's not far. You can make the trip in a little more than an hour."

"The trip where?"

"The castle! You're shitting me. You've been here for like, three months and you still haven't seen the castle."

"I've heard about it. I just…"

"Just?"

"I'm not a super motivated person, in case you haven't noticed."

"Well, let's change that. I'm from old Midwestern stock. We have wandering feet, my granny always used to say."

"I have tired feet. And they want slippers."

"Come on, Kate."

He looked at me with those stupid puppy eyes, and I consented, though not without a little more grumbling.

---

I'M NOT a walker or a hiker or an exerciser in general. I know it's shit for your health, but I hate sweating and I hate sore feet. Most of my life, I've spent what physical energy I have on stage, and I've always been fine with that. So the trek to the castle wasn't exactly fun for me. I wheezed while Jesse glowed and chatted about new bands he'd heard and horrible flights he'd endured.

He didn't ask questions about the band. He just wanted to talk about music and life, which was refreshing. Because I have to admit, I was quite sure he had an ulterior motive dragging my ass all the way up fields and hills and valleys to the castle.

And by castle, it wasn't so much a castle as a moat and some squat towers. In my head, I'd envisioned some towering marvel of the Middle Ages, but this was just barely more than a fort. Don't get me wrong, it was cool, and old, and we walked around the main house on the premises. I had a good time. But gardens and ruins aren't my thing. Clearly Jesse found them fascinating because he kept mentioning over and over how awesome it all was.

"There is nothing like this in Kansas," he said, staring up at the faux ruins on the estate that had been set up in the nineteenth century. "I mean, this place is so old they have fake ruins as decoration next to real, honest-to-god medieval masterworks."

"Imagine that," I said. Admittedly, his enthusiasm was kind of infectious. I wasn't about to go on an all-England ruins tour, mind you, but I could see his point. "And it's Kansas, is it? I had you pegged as Iowa."

He chuckled as we made our way back toward the genuine ruins. We found an easy outcropping over the moat where we could sit comfortably, and we did. It wasn't until that moment I realized how much of a date this all felt like. And I hadn't been on a date in a very, very long time. Being a touring musician isn't about dating; it's about hooking up. Aside from Tom, I'd had nothing remotely long term since I was in college. And even those were never with a thought for longevity.

"You're going to tell me you're the seventh son of a seventh son and your family has an idyllic farm grown with corn, and your mother makes you quilts and sends you baskets of cookies in the mail, right?" I said.

"Oh, that's far more interesting than reality. My dad was a car salesman. No longer living. My mom gets by on his pension, some social security. I have a brother who lives in the same town we grew up in, just outside of Kansas City, and a sister who lives in Toronto with her wife. She's a graphic designer. No one's owned a farm in my family in over a hundred years. At least."

"You guys close?"

"Not like, typical Midwestern close. Holidays and funerals close. You?"

"Oh, this is about me, now."

Jesse shrugged, pulling his scarf tighter around his neck. He was prepared for the weather, I wasn't. What body parts of mine weren't under my red leather jacket were quickly approaching numbness. "Not in an on-the-record sense."

"You probably read most of it," I said, slowly. "If you pay attention to that shit. We're just funerals close in my family. They're large, painfully Baptist, and entirely overwhelming. They always have been. Not just since…my wayward days."

"So, Rhee really is yours?"

I nodded. I hadn't spoken to anyone about it since her news stunt. I hadn't even really taken the time to talk to James and Tom about it because I didn't know what to say, honestly. What was I supposed to say? It was hard enough to deal with the whole overdose and rehab thing, let alone my nearly adult daughter who was raised by my alcoholic mother.

"I'm a terrible person," I said, trying to laugh it off, but it didn't feel any less genuine to say. "My family reiterates the fact of it every time I see them. It's cool, I don't take it personally anymore. They like a certain picture of reality. I challenge that. It's better if I'm as far removed from them as humanly possible. I'm only too happy to oblige."

"So you go by Kate Styx."

"I didn't want to drag the family name into it, no. I figured people might not make the connection because they sure as hell weren't going to go screaming to the rafters that their fallen relative was making headlines with a known drug addict in a secular rock band."

"You made some really bad decisions when you were a kid. We all do that. But you turned out fine. They don't know what they're missing. They could use a little culture in their lives."

I leveled him with a look and shivered. "My cultural currency is shit in their books. I've done everything wrong. All of the deadly sins, blasphemy on a daily, sometimes hourly, basis. Not to mention flaunting extramarital affairs and using my talent for the fallen majority."

"I can't imagine you pulling an Amy Grant," Jesse laughed.

"Whew. Yeah. Not exactly my style."

Jesse was quiet a minute, looking intently at me. I made a face at him.

"So, those awards and accolades don't mean anything?" he asked. "The Ivor Novello, the hits. At the end of the day…what?"

"At the end of the day, I'm sort of a loser, man." I stood up. "I'm a decent keyboardist, and I'm a fantastic drunk. But past those parameters, there isn't much there."

I was ready for him to throw up his hands, but he didn't. He slowly stood up and took off his scarf, winding it around my neck even when I protested. I don't take well to romantic comedy movie moves, but I was fucking freezing, so I didn't argue.

"You think you hide behind Tom," Jesse said with kind smile. "But there are those of us who listen. Who hear you, behind that majestic voice of his. We hear the stories and the heartbreak. You're a lot less guarded than you think you are. People understand you more than you'd believe."

"Oh, you get me, do you?"

"I don't know. I get bits and pieces. You might have done some stupid things, but there's no way you're indifferent about it. All the pain and regret, it somehow manifests in these amazing song lyrics and melodies and…shit, Kate. That's a gift. You're this lone rider in an industry built around men and machismo, and you put up with those crazy boys, day in and day out."

"They help, they—"

"No. They sing what you tell them to. They collaborate with you. But everything that's so fucking amazing about this band starts right here." He poked my shoulder.

"Looks who's president of the Kate Styx fan club…"

"Fine. Fine." He frowned, and I could tell I'd gone too far. "Whatever. I'm just telling you what you need to hear. I've got to go back to the States, and it's probably going to be another few months until we cross paths again. I just hope, when it happens, you've gotten some of this through your thick head. I had to tell you because last time…I wanted to tell you, and I didn't."

"Thanks…I mean…I'm sorry I'm not more grateful. I'm just tired. I'm just…still figuring it out."

"Do you honestly think you're ever going to totally figure it out, Kate? I hope you don't. Because it's the questions that make it worthwhile. Once you have the answers, you're no better than your smug family. People that have answers are a fucking bore."

---

WHEN WE GOT BACK, the house was full of photographers for tomorrow's shoot, and Dusty had ordered enough fish and chips to feed an entire army. It was so stereotypically British I almost wanted to leave, feeling embarrassed for Tom and James. She also ordered a crapton of beer, in keg form, and thoughtfully a bit of soda for me.

She didn't comment on my hair, which was weird, but most everyone had eyes on the two of us when we came in. I mean, I did still have Jesse's scarf on.

I noticed some of Tom's old friends from his entourage had showed up too. Dougie and Maeve in particular. He'd mentioned as much, that he was feeling the need to be around other believers, and we'd all given the go-ahead because, well, Tom had been doing so well we really didn't want to jinx it. We hadn't expected non-Christian friends though.

But, looking over at Tom talking to his old friends, I had one of those moments where I felt like the reality bubble of my life just went and burst. Tom wasn't going to need us like he did before. The album was so close to being finished I could practically feel it. James was watching me from across the room with a really strange look on his face, and I couldn't tell if he was irritated or angry or jealous or what. Whatever happened around us, we were doing it. We'd made it through the fire. I was moving on from Tom. I was getting better. Jesse, even more of a musical snob than me, liked me as a *person*. Like, seriously. What the fuck was my life?

Dusty, as usual, was the ethereal center of attention. Fifteen minutes later and everyone was situated, and she led us all in a toast for the future of *Something Else* and "Runways and Airplanes" the first single, which she was certain would be huge for us. She praised our hard work, our overcoming challenges, and made a really good show for the *Rolling Stone* folks. She did exactly as she was supposed to.

———

IT MADE A GOOD ARTICLE, in the end. I mean, Jesse kept it professional. Most of his quotes from me were things he'd gotten out of our more formal discussions, and nothing to do with our walk through the Scotney Castle grounds. I appreciated it. But the article was definitely slanted toward me as the central talent of the group and was comprised of lots of praise from my fellow bandmates.

The magazine was so happy with the result, my first post-rehab interview, they wanted us to do a special cover shoot for the issue, so two weeks later, we had to say goodbye to the Oast house and Lamberhurst, and even the cow. For me it was both exciting and scary. I never in a thousand years would have thought a place like Lamberhurst would feel like home, but it was. Sure, I had to do without lots of the conveniences I'd come to expect, but it was a place of beautiful music. A place of relaxation, centering, soul-seeking. Mr. Chesley made us all promise we'd record the next album there, and Tom had plans to turn it into a recording studio when we weren't visiting there. Made sense. James, even though he was the most adamant countryside hater of all of us, even said he wouldn't mind working on some projects himself.

---

… Kate Styx has a lot to be grateful for these days, but while her brush with death may have riled her and sent her toward the journey to sobriety, it's still the music that keeps her going. As we sit outside the small, bucolic recording studio Chesley put together, she's both contemplative and surprisingly talkative.

"I guess it took me a while to grow up," she says. "I had a delayed maturity in a lot of ways, for a variety of reasons. But everything kicked in when I found music. When I found rock music. The electricity of a four-piece band, y'know? The emotion. The power. Writing songs was totally the key to getting myself out of the darkness of my childhood."

Her influences run the whole gamut, but her own style has matured in the years since October Revival founds its audience. As is most common, their songs revolve around keyboard hooks, with Vayne's guitar echoing in a kind of call and response, whether up-tempo or not. The pulse of their music is, at the core, their signature sound. A kind of tension in the background of every lyric, straining against Chesley's astronomical vocals.

As to her personal life and struggles, when asked how it has influenced the new album, she's a little reluctant to admit it's had much of an impact, but then elaborates after thinking about it a while.

"I'm seeing things differently," she says. "Tom is, too. For different reasons. There are fewer layers between me and the music. Sometimes that's good, but it's also a struggle, too. Not having a crutch means that I see the fissures, the weaknesses in songs and in takes I might have not seen before. I rely on James to be our ears in that respect. He really does his magic in the studio. And out here there are very few distractions."

On the subject of material, Styx is clear that the track list is the same as it was before her incident. "Unless something changes drastically, I don't think we're ready for anything on the level of what's been going on in my head lately. I've got notebooks full of stuff, but it doesn't feel like it's right for October Revival. I don't know. That sounds worse than I mean it. My descent was very personal, and I think my climb back will be the same way."

   - Jesse McLaren for *Rolling Stone,* from "Kate Styx Strikes Back"

---

Tom went to London with his friends, and James and I drove up in his Bentley. Unlike most English people, James took any opportunity to drive when he was at home, and I preferred it to trains, anyway. We were going to be staying in Shoreditch, but we had a few errands before we got too settled. The tour was looming, but we had a big gala concert at the end of November and we needed a new bus. The last bus had died a most terrible death, having been pretty much reduced to cinders by the end of the tour (mostly due to Tom and my collaborative efforts—and Kurt was no help). I guess these things are expected, but when the smoke cleared, we were bummed. That had been our first bus, and we'd seen it across Europe. We had another in the States, but it was due for an upgrade too.

It's not a terribly long drive to London, but it felt long. James was not in a talking mood. For all the excitement going around, you'd have thought someone told him he was terminal or something. He informed me before we even got going that all he wanted to do was listen to music. So I let him.

What he meant by music was lots of Beethoven, which was a little curious to me. I'd never known him to rock out to the classics, but from what I could tell, it was his flavor of the week.

I knew, mostly because I'd spent so much time with him, that sooner or later he was going to crack about whatever it was getting under his skin. In days past, I'd have just turned to something to drink in order to get me through it because explosions with James were never nice. That's the beauty of hip flasks. Being drunk through his tantrums was always a preferred way of coping, rather than dealing with him head-on.

We were at the hotel, and I was about to get out of the car, when he started. My fingers barely touched the metal handle.

"So, that's it?" he asked me, as if the words were written in the sky.

"Hmm?"

"You've nothing to say for yourself?"

"I…what?" On most occasions, James is pretty clear once the eruption begins, but I had zero idea what he was talking about. I was briefly worried I'd blacked out at some point or was sleepwalking myself into trouble.

"Come on, Kate! This whole ride, this whole *time*, you don't… I mean, do you think I'm daft? That I'm…stupid?"

I tried to calm myself down, but he was already so wound up I was feeling quite combative. "Please use more descriptive phrases, James. I'm really confused."

"The article. The bloody stupid fucking article that twat wrote."

"Jesse's article?"

"Jesse's article?" he mocked at me, hitting the steering wheel. "Yes, Jesse's article. Did you fucking read it?"

"Of course…"

"Well, then I guess you got what you wanted."

I started to put two and two together, sliding back in time and remembering how things had gone down. Yes, I had spent a lot of time alone with Jesse that weekend, but it had been entirely innocent. Well, mostly, if you don't count the thoughts in my head. I never acted on anything. I liked Jesse, a whole lot, but it'd been off the record. He was a friend and totally not my type. Though he was fun to flirt with.

Trying to take James's hand, but failing, I turned to face him in the car seat, the leather squeaking around me. "Listen. No one's cutting you down, James. You're amazing. We're amazing together. Jesse just felt like…I don't know. Maybe it was important to bring my contribution to the light. Enhance it."

"Enhance it. Really."

"Yes, really."

"It was like the Kate show! He might as well have proposed to you."

"It wasn't that bad."

"You know, we've been bending over backwards for you, making sure you're always okay. Tom, this house, the retreat. We always have to be so careful because we're all afraid you're going to up and keel over on us, and the minute I look away, you go and do this."

"Jesus! I didn't do anything! We just got on really well, and you were holed up in the studio, and I guess he had more time with me."

"That explains it, then. I suppose you just fucked him for it. Makes sense, now."

All the words I had caught in my throat. James and I had weathered a whole lot together. I'd defended him time and again against both Sara and Kurt. We'd practically brought Tom back from the dead a half-dozen times. But I could not, and would not, be made to feel like shit. No way in hell. Not from someone who should have known better. I'd been a lot of things—a drunk, a slut, a bore—but I'd never been self-seeking. It's not in my nature.

My ears ringing with rage, I got out of the car, pulling my sunglasses on to hide the tears in my eyes. Tears? What the hell? No, I swallowed them back. And even though I heard him calling after me, I walked down the street to another hotel and checked myself in. James gave up after three blocks, kicking at a trashcan in resignation.

When I got into my room, I cried. For real. Not because I was angry or insulted, but I had a broken heart. That shit was low, especially from James. I never thought he'd be jealous of me, especially after everything I'd been through. But maybe it had been lying in wait this whole time, and I was just too absorbed in my own problems to notice.

# CHAPTER NINETEEN

THE NEXT MORNING, which I had achieved without drinking despite every bone in my body crying out for it, I read the article again. James had texted me about sixty times, but I deleted every single one of them. He was still way out of line, but reading the words again, I could see how he'd been marginalized. Jesse had painted me as some fragile and mysterious artist, brooding and thoughtful and sincere, while James was driven and focused and distant. Tom was portrayed as childlike and bright and full of hope, which was more or less right.

I didn't know what else to do, so I called Jesse up. It went straight to his voicemail, and I realized he was back in the States, and I was ringing him up at two in the morning, so I kept it short. I'm not sure I was terribly coherent, and I sounded like I had a horrible cold, but I didn't know what else to do.

I went about making myself some coffee when my phone went off, and Jesse's name showed up. I'd labeled him "Preppy."

"Oh, hi," I said.

"I can't change it, you know." He sounded full of regret. "I mean, it's the angle the editors wanted, and we're not in the business of stroking people's egos, y'know?"

"You mean, other than what's considered the right editorial direction?"

He laughed, and for some reason, I laughed back, and I felt all wiggly inside. I started pacing.

"Listen. I know it's not the sort of thing James wants to hear, but it's something the fans need to hear. There's a thousand articles on Tom and James and even more on Sara and her direction and influence, but sitting down with you is practically a scoop. Especially considering."

My bad mood intensified, and my squirming stomach turned to lead. I didn't know how to reply to that. "Right. A scoop. I'm a scoop."

"Hey, Kate, I didn't mean it like that."

"No, it's cool. I get it. Thanks, Jesse."

"Just found out I'll be covering your show in London—if you want, we can talk more—"

"No. I'm good. Bye."

---

**Preppy:** Kate, I feel shitty for what I said. Can you forgive me.
**Kate:** Drowning my sorrows in treacle tart. Can't talk now.
**Preppy:** Please don't be mad. Let me make it up to you.
**Kate:** Jesse, you don't owe me anything. You were doing your job.

...

...

**Preppy:** Sometimes I let that get in the way of my better judgment. We've got a good chemistry. I feel like...
**Kate:** Gotta go, buddy. Talk soon. [Poop emoji]
**Preppy:** Is that...why did you send me a poop emoji?

---

JAMES WAS SO angry he didn't show up to the photo shoot at the studio. The *Rolling Stone* folks were nice enough about it, but it only compounded the issue. Tom was prompt and surprisingly understanding when they offered to do some solo pictures of him for the interior—Mr. Photogenic is really impressive on the other side of the lens—but they decided to go with just Dee and me for the cover.

What followed was uncomfortable. Primping. Measuring. Pinching. Wardrobe. Makeup. Jesus Christ, by the time they were done with us, we were carrying fifty pounds of makeup and a few ounces of clothing between us. Even though Dusty wasn't there, I could feel her presence all over the shoot. It's just part of what this business is about. Sex sells. Two girls on the front of a rock magazine have to look a certain way.

I will say they did a relatively good job of getting me, regardless of the whole off-the-shoulder black lace thing. I was hiding mostly behind the prop keyboard they had and staring off the page. Dee's face is tilted up in the picture, laughing, with her sticks held high and her hair up. It's a good picture. I guess it does a good job of capturing us: me thoughtful, Dee exuberant. But it's not the whole band. And I knew when James saw it, it would only make matters worse.

Which, yes, was totally his fault for being such an ass about the whole thing. Even so, Jesse was right on that count. James had had more than enough moments in the sun, especially in the UK, while I languished in the background, the perpetual wallflower. But I think the difference is it was always about image before—now it was about talent, and that hit harder.

Tom came by later. I was up in my room doing some work on a piece I'd been dreaming about (seriously, all "Scrambled Egg" of me) when my phone informed me Tom was calling. He was in the lobby, looking for me. So I had him come up.

Thankfully he was sans the entourage. He looked so painfully handsome, so healthy. It's beyond fucked up, but I think I was attracted to his brokenness before, partially because it's something I related to. Seeing him so together was somehow less appealing, and for once, I wasn't feeling like the lovesick loser I was around him. I'm not sure why it took me so long, or what changed between our time at the Oast and then, but it was seriously disturbing. Even for me.

Certainly songworthy. Even if it made me hate myself even more. Which I didn't think was possible at that point.

He sat down on the generic sofa and put down what he'd brought in with him—a guitar. Which is surprising on a number of levels considering he'd never really branched out beyond the occasional tambourine or egg shaker, if you know what I mean. Musical accompaniment was never really part of his approach; it didn't need to be with his harrowingly beautiful voice.

"You look different," he said, giggling. "It was easier to ignore it all under the lighting and whatnot, but now that you've changed, it's quite a sight. Like someone replaced your head."

I hadn't had a chance to wash my face, and it was astonishing how unrecognizable I was with seventeen layers of shellac. People always say I look so much better with makeup, and I usually only tolerate the barest minimum. Tom never liked it, though, when the label made me gussy up. He said it was like looking at an alien. I guess you get used to seeing someone look like shit all the time, when they show up all veneer and falsies, it's sort of hard to parse out who they are.

"Well, if you'd give me a few minutes, I could go get it off, but I might need a chisel," I said, running my fingers down my now greasy and slightly bumpy cheek. I knew I'd end up with one hell of a breakout.

"James is still seething." Tom leaned back to put his hands behind his head. "You're going to have to talk to him, you know. Not right now, but at some point in the not too distant future."

"He's being an asshole," I said. "He doesn't deserve conversation at this point."

"Of course he is. But, think about it this way—he's just experiencing his own drama. I mean, he's the only one among our present and departed members who hasn't had an explosion of drama in the last few years. Even the Sara stuff's been at a minimum. I just figure it's his turn."

"He was a bitter bastard to me. Did he tell you?" I asked. "What he said?"

Tom sighed. "He did. He's sorry for saying it like that, of course. But it doesn't change the way he feels, y'know?"

"For the record, I didn't sleep with Jesse."

"For the record, James just feels marginalized. And jealous."

"There are zero things to be jealous about. I am a recovering alcoholic and a failed mother."

"You think I don't understand where you're coming from?" Tom looked hurt, his brows crinkling between those moonlit blue eyes. I remembered kissing him there a thousand times, once. Tracing his eyelashes, his eyebrows. Dim memories, but no less powerful. "I understand. But James, he's a pillar of chivalry and nobility. He's never messed up like we have, and he feels like he's being punished for it. "

"Seriously, Tom. Look at my life. I'd happily trade him my baggage for his."

He gave me a sad smile. "Your talent, Kate. He's jealous of your *talent*, not your life. Of all the things you can do that he can't. The article was like all his worst fears spilled out because...it's like you said to me before. This will come to an end. And he doesn't think he'll come out of it well—you'll be the one with the career after, and he'll just fade away. You've got the attention. He's just a footnote."

"That's stupid." It wasn't stupid; it was damned insightful. But hell if I was going to give that to Tom.

"Think about it this way. October Revival was run-of-the-mill until you started writing songs together."

"You were never run-of-the-mill, Tom. The first night I heard you sing..."

"Maybe we're greater than the sum of our parts, sure. I believe we were put together for a reason; I think God wanted us to find each other, whether or not you think it's utter bullshit, I don't care," he said. There was defensiveness there. A fire. I would be lying if I said I didn't think it was a bit sexy.

I mentally hit myself in the head. Stop. Thinking. About. Tom. That. Way. Kate.

"It's not like that, Tom. I don't just write songs for *anyone*...I mean…I write songs for *you* to sing and for us to play. It's not like they're even mine. They belong to October Revival."

"You might tell yourself that, and maybe it was true for a few albums. But Cakes—I've sung your words more than anyone else. This album, it's different. It's full of *you*. Full of fractures and splinters and memories. You've grown. Even through all you've been through. And James knows it, and it frightens him."

"Why the hell would he be scared?" And since when did he get so fucking poetic?

"Because he hasn't grown. It's still harder than it's ever been for him."

I didn't know what to say, so I sat down next to Tom and hugged him. It was more than a hug. We just sat there for quite some time, nestled together, saying nothing. It was remarkably comfortable and not remotely sexual, and honestly a relief. That hug said more than I could ever tell him about how I felt, how I would always feel. I didn't think he heard my lyrics. He was always so aloof about them, focused more on the words and pronunciation than the whole meaning. But I realized he got it, he really did. The messages had been received, for what good it did us.

My phone went off and broke the mood. James again. I showed the text to Tom.

James: Cakes, we need to talk. I was an asshole.

"Before you start, I wanted to run something by you," he said. "I've been taking guitar lessons, d'you know?"

"No, I didn't," I said, already feeling embarrassed for him.

"I know it's silly, but I'd never show this to anyone else. It's a bit religious, and really just a fragment, but I thought…"

"Sure. Sure, Tom." I couldn't think of anything else to say. You can't tell your five year old you don't want to see their cartwheel, do you? Well, maybe you do if you're a fucking jerk. He had the same love-struck look as a kid learning how to race across the monkey bars for the first time, and God knows I can never say no to Tom.

The song was heartbreakingly earnest. You could tell Tom was still getting used to the guitar chords, but he'd clearly practiced for quite a while. Not surprisingly his voice obliterated everything else. The melody he'd written was simple and sweet and catchy, definitely in line with the sort of Christian music I'd grown up listening to, the all-pervasive "praise and worship" style so popular in the late nineties.

The lyrics were something out of Corinthians, if memory serves right, and he'd sort of made it a half love song about a girl and then talking about loving God instead. Regardless of my personal opinions on religion, I was moved by the fact he had taken the time to create something. The old Tom, the one we'd chased down in LA twice and found him shooting up in back alleys, would never do something like that. He didn't have time to create anything because he was suffering from a sort of internal combustion of energy and strength, fueled by his never-ending search for fulfillment in drugs and alcohol.

I realized, listening to him, just how much had changed in the last few months with the band's dynamic due to his beating his addictions. I mean, whether God had anything to do with it, for the first time, he was living his life without searching for another fix around every corner. And stranger even, this person sitting in the hotel room with me—in spite of the fact we'd shared every intimacy once—was like meeting an old friend. The real Tom, the one James knew from before they hit it big, who was a little shy and a little awkward and hadn't quite grown into his body yet.

"So, what do you think?" he asked when it was done.

I was so lost in thought I almost forgot to clap, so I did so.

"I didn't know you were learning guitar," I said, trying to go around the subject a little. It's not that the song was bad. I just wasn't sure how to address the Savior in the Room.

"It's not good, is it?" He was crestfallen.

"No, no. Tom, that's not it. It's good. I'm just surprised. And I have…"

"Issues with religion?" he finished for me.

I nodded lamely.

"I know it feels that way, and I've really tried, y'know, to stay out of it because I know—at least in part—of how hard it was for you growing up. Kurt filled me in. Rather colorfully. With some comic book handouts and a trip through the dark bowels of the Internet. But I promise you, I'm not like those people you grew up with. I've got a sense of peace, now. Like I can focus on moments instead of chasing highs. Because the high's not as good as this feeling of serenity."

Ah, yes. The twelve steps talking. I shrugged. I doubted he had any idea what it was like to live with the daughter you had at thirteen being raised by your mother as your sister, and an adulterous father who preached abstinence from the pulpit, and a church community that demanded retribution from women who showed signs of their sins, but never the dudes. I could have filled his ear. But I let it slide. He was being nice. I could try and meet him halfway.

"But the song's half about you," he finished. "I mean, you're the only woman I genuinely felt as if I'd fallen in love with. And…" Tom was having a difficult time explaining what he meant, but it didn't do anything to mitigate the huge lump rising in my throat. "I'm not sure what really happened with us. I know it's over, and I'm at peace with it…It's just, I think for a long time I was searching for the feeling I had when we were first together. When things were good. The way when I thought about you, everything was limned in light. And now, with the Lord, I feel like I have that, but on a more permanent level. On a deeper, more spiritual place."

***

**James:** You know I didn't mean any of that.
**Kate:** You sounded committed.
**James:** I'm tired. This is all tiring. I just felt edged out.
**Kate:** Tom pleaded your case. I'm sorry you feel that way. But I didn't know what to do.
**James:** I've got a rough mix from the last session if you want to meet me. We can listen together.
**Kate:** You got me. Where are you at?

---

"THAT'S WHAT HE SAID?"

James and I were talking again. We hadn't had a fight in almost a year, and looking back, I think it was just part of the whole process as we got closer to touring and the endless grind of working. He didn't apologize, exactly, but he said he was being an ass and he needed to get over himself if we were going to have a successful run of it. He was putting his ego before the band, etc., ad nauseam. Before you call me a total and complete moron for forgiving him, you've got to understand it's part of band dynamics. We have to allow some room for hate in the band, and for expressing it from time to time. Otherwise, it'd all boil over, and we'd never get anything done.

"Yes. He said he loved Jesus like he used to love me. Or something. I don't know. It hurts my brain to think about it."

"How'd you feel about it?"

We were eating ridiculously expensive food at a swanky London restaurant, and neither of us were dressed well enough. But they let it slide. Being a quasi-rock star has its benefits sometimes. I will admit to a slight ulterior motive. I'd agreed to meet him at this particular location because I knew the likelihood of him exploding in anger or frustration would be at a minimum. James is well behaved in public. He's had to be, considering how long he's had to put up with Tom.

I wasn't sure what James meant with his question. "How do I feel about what?"

"Tom's *your* muse, love," he said. "I mean, I know that. He probably has some idea, even if he is a daft goose most of the time. Has he ever been so forward with you before?"

"It's over, we're over, it's not like I expect anything to change."

"I don't mean that. I don't know. Maybe I'm just talking out of my arse because I feel like such a fucking idiot for being terrible to you earlier."

"It's okay. The article is slanted. I talked to Jesse, but he said it's the way his editor wanted the story to go."

"You deserve it." James took my hand from across the table. In another lifetime, I'd have been downing the wine, and I might not have remembered how tender and honest he was, but with just some ginger ale and about three buttered rolls in my stomach, it was all very clear.

"I don't know about that…"

"I'm proud of you, Cakes. I spent half the day in the studio listening to the finalized tracks, and it's like I could hear you growing up. Not to say our stuff before wasn't good, because it was. No doubt. But there's something amazing about listening to where we are right now. It's like…we're all on the other end of the tunnel. Tom and his Jesus stuff, you and your recovery, me without Sara. Dee's drums are slick and exciting."

Smiling felt good. James was hard to please, and I'd never heard him speak so glowingly about an album. Usually he had more gripes than fingers and had to be placated somehow. But this time, he was genuinely happy, and it always made me giddy.

"Well, we better be on top of our game. Between the upcoming shows, the tour kickoff, and the release, it's going to be an uphill battle."

He squeezed my hand and let go. "We'll do it together."

"God, when did you get so corny, James?"

He laughed, and our meal came. It was a good night.

# CHAPTER TWENTY

THERE HAD BEEN a ton of debate as to where we'd host the kickoff show, and plenty of speculation. I think we were all a little worried no one would really care, but Dusty gave us this cute little lecture about how all our drama and negative press had actually done quite a number on bolstering general interest. Dee agreed, as our resident social media maven, and she supported Dusty's claims. Apparently our following numbers had skyrocketed, and thousands of supportive messages had been sent my and Tom's way. Like I've said, the internet is not my thing. I know that makes me a practical dinosaur, but I think it comes down to the fact I get insanely uncomfortable when I'm being scrutinized. Kurt was great at it, and Dee, thankfully, has a knack for it. She hasn't even needed any intervention like Kurt had. She seems to know what to say when, and our fans love it.

Fans. Yes. They were the biggest consideration. In the end, management decided the best bet was the Roundhouse in London, which made sense. It was one of the first big venues we'd had, opening for Keane in 2004. It had a solid rock history and a good capacity without being overboard. It's not like we were playing stadiums. I mean, that was part of the whole idea behind *Something Else*. We were playing more shows, but smaller shows, keeping most venues under the 5K mark. We didn't even have many openers, which was an interesting approach.

It had been James's idea, initially, and even though it was likely we'd make less from the tour, I was on board. Touring is tiring. I mean, it's awesome on a hundred levels too. But huge show after huge show, especially in some of our hot zones like Brazil and the UK, just takes it out of you. That's why Tom usually is on high through the whole thing and I drink myself into silliness every night. Except it wasn't really an option this time around. James, the teetotaler and general organizer of the group, likely just wanted something he could control better. It was the first time we were going on tour with a dry bus (save for weed).

Even though touring has never been my favorite thing, for obvious reasons, I was excited to play live again. The new material was sounding really good, and Dee was fitting in perfectly, giving her own unique flavor to the older stuff. Our bassist for the first show was Azir Connor, a really solid musician, but, unfortunately, unable to stay with us for the duration of the tour. For that we had Kelsy Hanner, an American session musician who'd just finished a bunch of studio work and was itching to get on the road.

"You and your bass players," James said as we left the practice space the studio provided the night before the Roundhouse show.

We were walking the rainy winter streets, and in spite of the copious holiday decorations draped over every possible surface, it still felt cold and lonely out there. Especially leaving the warm comfort of a well-rehearsed set.

"What's that supposed to mean?" I asked.

James laughed into his scarf, elbowing me. "You think you're a gentle instructor, but really you're a pop music dictator."

"Am not. You ass."

"Did you see Azir's face? Love, you treat him like he's six."

"He was being sloppy."

I had to defend myself, but I knew James was right. The problem with Azir was he wasn't Sara and he wasn't Kurt, and as much as I hated to admit it, I missed both of them tremendously. Neither of them required much in the way of schooling when it came to getting the music right. As it was, constantly hearing the wrong notes from the current bassist made focusing on my own playing really difficult.

I had sort of snapped at one point and told him I'd just sample the right bass line and play it on the synthesizer if he couldn't get himself together. I may have been a little bit of an asshole. It happens.

"Come on, Kate, he's only had a week to learn all this stuff."

"I don't want to suck tomorrow."

"We're not going to suck tomorrow. You're just not used to playing with a bassist you don't have a psychic connection to. Even Kurt on his worst, most restrained days, was tons better than Azir. But it's not his fault."

I stuck out my tongue at James, and he shoved me playfully again, then put me in a headlock and ruffled my hair. I never felt more like a little sister in my life.

"Well, did you try to reach out to the Miraculous Ginger again?" he asked.

I hadn't. "I think he made it pretty clear he wasn't able to change his life to suit us."

"You'd be surprised what dangling the fruit could do," he said with a wink. "I'd say it's worth it. If he can't, he can't. But we've got two weeks before everything explodes and, if you're not having the idea of playing schoolmarm to Kelsy and whoever else we might end up with, you ought to try."

---

So two things happened. First, I got a text from Jesse informing me he was going to be covering the Roundhouse for a blog piece, and he was hoping to talk to us a bit backstage. I wanted to still be angry at him, and I had a feeling James wasn't going to be thrilled, but even Dusty insisted it's something we ought to do. "It's not like he just writes for *Rolling Stone*," she pointed out. We didn't want to tarnish our already questionable reputation. And she reiterated that James had to play nice.

Then I got a voicemail from Jon.

"Kate. Not sure if it's too late and all. But things have cleared out here. Could possibly be a part of the band if needed. Anyway. I can be in London next week—meet for coffee?"

I set it up and didn't tell anyone else in the band. We had enough going on, and I didn't want to bring any false hope into the equation. I didn't have much confidence about the Roundhouse show and didn't feel we were anywhere near as good as I wanted us to be. I felt like I had something to prove after all the bad press I'd brought upon the band. This was our big rebirth, our own revival, a return to our roots, digging deeper into what makes us musicians and songwriters and people. James's work was astonishing; Tom had never sounded better. And even after losing Kurt and gaining Dee, I felt like we had something amazing to give to the world.

And maybe it was amazing for some people. But that night was not amazing for me.

Jesse didn't show up. He canceled. All I got was a terse text: "Got re-assigned. Will check in at a later date. Sorry, Kate. Talk soon?"

I let his text get to me way too much, thinking it reflected on the band as a whole and my music and everything. I don't usually get nervous, I mean not so nervous that anyone can tell—but waiting in the green room made me so anxious I had to get up and throw up. It didn't make me feel better. On the contrary, before getting on stage, I was sweating through my makeup, and I couldn't find a fucking toothbrush. I wanted a drink. Ten drinks. I couldn't remember my last sober performance.

I knew it wasn't going to work with Azir. James called me a dictator, but I think I was so hard on him because I knew precisely that this moment was going to come.

All I could say is thank the skies and heavens and gods of five thousand civilizations no one was recording us live. Not legally, anyway.

Tom was pristine. Everyone was talking about him afterward, and they should have been. He was the most amazing part of the band. And not to shoulder all the blame myself, James sucked almost as much as I did. We opened up with "Marietta" and "Call the Car," which were the final two tracks on *Something Else,* then went straight into "Lost and Loving"—more up-tempo than the original. And really, it was fine until we started going into "Eleven Melodies" and I started thinking about Kurt and, simultaneously, Azir played the wrong note like…fifteen times in a fucking row. I wanted to go over to him and hit him or take the bass from him and show him the goddamned runs myself.

I got angry. I don't play well when I'm angry. My nerves got all mixed up with the anger, and it turned into a big bowl of fear soup in my stomach.

James flubbed the solo in "Crowds," and I forgot to sing backup vocals for half of "Game of Love"—and really, by the time we were done, I was so pissed off I just left after the half-hearted encore. Which, really, I didn't even want to do in the first place.

Once again: life sucks when you've mitigated all feeling and emotion with liquor and then you don't anymore. I didn't have anywhere to go if I wasn't drinking. And no amount of anti-depressants could help me through the horror of knowing I failed at this show.

I felt like shit. I saw the look in James's face and was sure he felt the same way; his nostrils were flaring as we made our way back to the green room and I just kept walking outside. Even when he called after me, I flailed my arms like a child and growled at him to stay away. I'm allowed a tantrum every now and again, which was immature even for me.

I found a little alcove behind the chain fence in back and buried my head in my hands like some poor, chided little girl, and cried. Again.

For years I thought I'd only cried when I was angry. But I realized that when I was drinking, I basically boozed it up instead of letting myself feel sad. Or boozed up while feeling sad. See: nearly dying a few months back. It's effective while it's happening, but stopping the progression of a rising BAC is not something I'm good at.

And you know what? It felt strangely cathartic when I was done crying. The night had not gone well. We were off to an inauspicious start. We'd failed, and I'd felt it. But I hadn't numbed it away, I'd let it just happen. No one came to rescue me. The cold drizzle did enough to wake me up and remind me I'm not the only one in the band with problems, nor the only one who fucked up the chords and forgot to sing.

"Shit, Cakes, we thought we lost you," James said, all smiles, when I made it back inside.

The greenroom was buzzing, and people were laughing and smoking cigarettes and drinking various beverages. Lots of people I didn't know had made their way—someone was interviewing Tom and laughing, Dee was showing a local reporter, some kid who looked younger than Rhee, her sticks.

"Needed a breather. That was…" I started.

"Amazing. Did you feel it?" he asked, squeezing my shoulder.

"No…I didn't really feel it."

"Maybe you just didn't notice before. We're always a little rough around the edges, but it was magnificent. I haven't felt that plugged in in a long time."

Didn't notice. Code word for: you were usually drunk. He laughed, practically giddy. "I mean, Jesus, it's been so long since we played to a crowd that tuned in—and they were just such a part of it. You should read the tweets!"

"I don't do tweets," I said, confused.

People asked me a lot of questions, and I did my best to sound coherent. But clearly, reading the soundbites came afterward, I wasn't particularly with it at that point. It's not surprising one journalist supposed I was drinking again. I wasn't. I was just confused because, apparently, everyone loved the show except for me.

Okay, not everyone. Most of the reviews were positive but not glowing. They used words like "promising" and "refreshing" and "return to their roots," which was encouraging. Someone even singled me out saying my songwriting had "matured beyond the bounds of what we thought October Revival was capable of" and that we were "growing up into something more fully realized, past lovelorn heartsick pop." Dee was praised universally, and Tom heralded as one of the greatest comebacks in recent memory.

I guess it could have been worse, right?

---

We were leaving London in a week, and I was trying to get everything in order at the hotel, when my phone rang. It was Jesse. He was here.

Shit. Fuck. Goddamnit.

I was supposed to be mad at him, but before I knew it, I had agreed to meet him downstairs. But it had to be short. Jon was in town in the afternoon, and I wasn't going to fuck it up this time.

I did some work on my makeup; I tidied up my hair. I grabbed my maroon leather jacket and a plaid scarf and headed downstairs, checking my ghastly glow in the elevator mirror. It was going to have to do. I rehearsed what I'd say to him in my head, promised myself I wouldn't look at him straight in the eyes because *damn*.

Then I saw a familiar face when I hit the lobby: James was there too, which was both encouraging and disappointing. I knew talking about anything other than October Revival was going to be impossible with James around. But then, James had been sidelined before, so maybe, just maybe, this was for the best.

So. We gave Jesse the interview he was looking for.

---

**"Reviving October Revival"**

The Metropolitan seems a little unusual for October Revival, but it makes sense. In recent months, they've reclaimed some of their bad girl/bad boy status, banding together in spite of personal and professional challenges to produce a new record, which is due to hit stores just in time for Christmas. By all accounts, it's their best in years. So the clean, modern English decor suits their newfound focus. Not to mention they spent the majority of the summer recording in nearby Kent.

When I meet up with James Vayne and Kate Styx, it doesn't feel like I'm meeting with three-time Billboard UK Top Ten rock stars. Vayne is comfortable in a tweed jacket and t-shirt, stubbly but presentable. Styx dresses in an understated, grownup Goth kind of way, with just a splash of color added by her red scarf. They look rested. They joke with one another over coffee and have the rapport you'd expect of a songwriting duo of almost a decade.

"It's good to be playing out again," Styx says. She's a lot quieter off stage than one would imagine, her voice a bit rough from the night before. "I guess that's just what we're all feeling. It's been a while."

Vayne agrees but elaborates. "I think what people are seeing now is that we're sort of coming through a dark place, a tough place. Here, it's familiar. London feels more like home." He laughs and glances at Styx. "For most of us, anyway."

Styx, born in the American South, lets her drawl out a little. "I like London. It's charming." The sarcasm is on thick, as with most of Styx's sentences. But she softens a little when she looks out the window. "But I agree. Being back here, especially after finishing off the record in the country, helped remind us of why it is we do what we do."

Since starting their fourth studio album, the band has seen quite a few incarnations. Their original bassist, Sara Plummer, left the band halfway through the second album and was replaced by Styx's close friend Kurt Bastian. Bastian left before the band retreated to Kent to finish the new album.

Currently, the group is touring with a handful of session musicians to fill the gap. But it hasn't been perfect.

"It's nothing personal against any of the chaps we've worked with. They're all solid. We're just used to something a little more intimate. I joke with Kate, but it's like she's got a psychic connection with the rhythm section—it makes sense, y'know?

Keyboards sort of link them to me, and me to Tom. She's always been sort of their Master and Commander," Vayne explains.

When asked if they have considered any new permanent bassists, Styx is coy. "We have someone in mind. We'll see if it works out."

"We don't want to rush things. But ideally, we want someone for the tour, at least part of it. At this point we're cutting it a little close, but stranger things have happened."

Perhaps no one has received more praise for October Revival's current buzz than Tom Chesley, the lead singer and childhood friend of Vayne.

"He's in a good place," Vayne said. "He's really been taking a lot of time out to learn about himself as a vocalist, and you can hear that in the tracks. He's healthy. He's happy."

Chesley has gone sober in recent months. Known for his stints with the police, visits to rehab, and two overdoses, it's clear both Vayne and Styx are relieved at the turn of events.

But Chesley isn't the only one fighting his demons. Styx fought a public battle with alcoholism and, for the first time in the band's history, racked up her own headlines.

When asked how she's doing, she shrugs it off. Notoriously private about her life, Styx just states: "I feel good. And I feel confident in our music. You can't ask for much more than that."

# CHAPTER TWENTY-ONE

JON WANTED to meet me at a "normal" place, whatever that meant, so I did my best incognito attempt and met him at the Barrowboy & Banker, one of those quintessentially British pubs in the Fuller's family. I once used to frequent them more often. I mean, it's the English normal, right? Good beer, sure, and none that I could (but wanted) to drink. I ordered a fizzy water and pie and waited for him. He was an hour late, but he'd at least had the courtesy to text me to let me know.

It was a good view from the table, those huge windows looking out to the street and amazingly high ceilings. I guess the place was once a bank, hence the unusual architecture. But I always thought it was amazing, despite not exactly being an art or architecture buff. All the warm wood and the light. It's a nice place.

I ordered a second pie because I'd skipped breakfast and felt justified in doing so, this time one of their seasonals. While I wasn't thrilled about spending the holidays away from the States—it being one of the only times in the year where I usually spend some time with Rhee or take time out in New York—there was something quaint about the food and festivities lingering on every corner and, apparently, in every bar menu. It's like the origin point of all our watered-down, boxed-up American traditions.

When Jon walked in, I couldn't miss him. Being so tall and flame-haired meant he'd stick out in a huge crowd.

I waved to him, and he made his way over to the booth I was in. He looked a bit haggard compared to the last time I saw him, but he was smiling more, which I took to be a good sign.

"You missed quite a show," I told him, sliding a poster from the Roundhouse gig toward him. I'd saved one, thinking he might enjoy it.

He unfurled it, shaking his head. "I heard about it. Wished I could have made it."

"So you've had a change of heart?" I asked. "I mean, we're heading out next week. You're cutting it kind of close, don't you think?"

"I'm sorry, Kate. Really. This has all felt so fucked up. From the beginning. I don't want you thinking I'm flaky or anything."

"Hell, Jon. It's a big decision. If anything, I respect you for taking your time to think about it. We were all blown away by the session at the Oast, you know. But everyone understands if there's too much for you back in Bristol."

"Well, not anymore, there isn't," he said.

He held up his left hand and wiggled his fingers. I hadn't noticed a wedding ring before, but I hadn't been interested in anything beyond his bass playing. A bit shallow of me, I realize but the truth.

"Didn't know what your situation was," I said. "I'm not usually one to pry. I mean, man, your playing. That's what I'm after. But I'm sorry to hear, still."

"You ever been married?" he asked, apparently unfamiliar with my bio.

I laughed and attempted not to sound bitter. "No. I've never been one for long-term, stable relationships. Come to think of it, I think a year might be my world record."

"Ah, never fucking get married." He rubbed the bridge of his nose. "That's what I couldn't…that's what was holding me back. I mean, I married her right after school. Her father had a job for me at the shipyard. It's like, the second I was out of school, I had everything lined up for me. Other people were making decisions for me and working at the Thekla was my only escape. And even that wasn't so great."

"So you're telling me you left your wife to be in the band?" I asked.

"Well. Not at first. She was the one who told me to go meet you and play at the Oast. She said it was a chance I couldn't pass up. I called her, that night after our jam session, and she just exploded. Went crazy at me. I couldn't deal with it all right, so I took some time out. You don't have a bassist now, do you?"

"No one permanent. I've had…some issues with our current lineup."

"The set was sloppy," he said.

Man, my heart was so full of joy. Jon totally understood. But I wanted to make sure he was going into this with a level head. He'd basically told me he'd given up everything in his previous life to play for us, and honestly, I wasn't sure how much longer October Revival had in this world.

I didn't want to put it to him like that, either, because that would be majorly shitty of me. Just because I'd achieved the dream and become numb to it, didn't mean it was my place to tear it down for someone on the precipice of their own dreams.

I tried not to smile too much. "Well. Yes. It's been a little challenging getting the right groove. Dee's really good, but she needs a little reigning in. Usually our bassists would be good at something like that, but our rotating lineup hasn't really given us an option."

"I want to do it."

"Of course you do."

"I'm not sure what I need to do though. I feel like a wanker for being so out of it with you, but I was in the middle of some right terrible shit with the wife. The ex-wife, soon. I just didn't think I could get out."

"There's always a way out. Just sometimes it isn't pretty."

"She's very angry. But I think, in the end, she got it."

"Got what, exactly?"

"That she couldn't prevent me from this. That my whole life I'd practically been owned by her family. I honestly don't think she even loved me anymore; she just had this perverted sense of ownership."

I had a feeling we would see more of this woman at one point or another, but I'd have to let it slide while we got things together. We had a tour to start and a week until the first single dropped. And due to being on the outs with James, we really hadn't spent a lot of time finalizing the tour bus details for the Continental Europe and American branches of the tour.

Then came Christmas.

Jon was welcomed with relief. After James's discussion earlier about my pickiness and ruthlessness with bassists, it was good to know I could have someone to depend on musically. Despite his insistence to the contrary, Jon was still dealing with the details of divorce and spent a little longer than we'd all have liked on the phone. But he'd obviously been doing his homework (I'd sent him home with some rough cuts of the album before we left the Oast). After a week of performing, we sounded better than we ever had. Sara was a decent bassist, and Kurt was a practical virtuoso. But neither really had their hearts in it, and I think, corny as it sounds, it makes all the difference in the world.

The first single, "Call the Car" did pretty well. None of us expected to have the same kind of success we did with our first album, so as long as people were buying tickets and excited. Jon was fielding tons of questions from fans and from the London press, and he was remarkably good about it. Not embarrassed in the least. So far, the only issue I'd seen with Jon was him clearly flirting with Dee. A man out of a long, bitter relationship was a gamble, and even though he was a good nine years older or so, I think she welcomed it.

Our big tour kicked off just after New Year, but we had a few London gigs and a few others in the area. Christmas, it was decided, would be spent with James's family, the Venkatesans. I was initially confused, figuring Hindus didn't really celebrate Christmas, but James explained his family was oddly affectionate when it came to English holidays and always threw parties. Apparently, it coincided with some winter solstice festival that included a statue of Ganesha or something, and James was keen to share with us the weird, hybrid, elephant/Christmas tree combination. Tom bowed out, explaining he wanted to be in church for the festivities and that he'd promised his father he'd come by. Dee was also going home, and Jon needed deal with a few things in Bristol for a few days.

So that left me with the entire Venkatesan clan. James's parents are second-generation Indians, and his mother's father was a British General, though she was raised Hindu and grew up in the culture. Early on in our careers, James and I decided to take new names because his was a mouthful, and mine sounded like a sorority girl. I had met his mother, way back in the day, but I don't remember much of it. She'd come down from Hounslow to see us play at the 02 arena and come-back state. I was probably drunk, so I have no idea what kind of impression I left.

"So…" James said as we pulled into the driveway. Since James was actually making money, his parents had—with his help—bought a semi-detached, six-bedroom Tudor. But they'd stayed in Hounslow which, essentially, was right next to Heathrow. Not a quiet place, to say the least. When James was younger, he talked about the Concords flying overhead all night long, before they were grounded.

"That sounds ominous."

He cleared his throat and checked his face in the mirror. "Do you, ah, do you remember the last time you met my mum?"

I felt nervous. Immediately. Overwhelmingly guilty for something I couldn't remember. A familiar and dreaded feeling.

"You probably wouldn't be surprised to know I don't remember much, other than I think she was wearing green sari," I said.

"It was blue."

"Right."

"Anyway. My mother…is traditional. The last time she saw us, she was certain I would be marrying you, which, even though that makes her a walking contradiction, she highly disapproved of."

I squinted at him, feeling my stomach squirm. I felt like I'd done a very good job of repressing any feelings toward him at all. I took Kurt's advice. I suppressed it. I buried it under a thousand rationalized excuses. It's amazing how well that worked for so long. Until he started talking about marriage and his parents, and I saw just how silly and potentially mortifying the visit could be. Up until the day before, we'd anticipated at least Tom coming with us, but he'd delayed his regrets until the last possible moment. He was oddly worried he would offend James since he'd known his parents pretty well.

"Disapproved…" I had a feeling I really didn't want to hear.

"Well. And you know. With the news in the press. Dad's very, uh, aware of the goings on with the group. He's even got a Google Alert out for our names, even if it fills his inbox like crazy. That's what happens when you can't travel anywhere without your oxygen."

"So, they already didn't like me before I almost died of alcohol poisoning."

"Right. But the good news is they highly approve of your, you know, turning things around. If you play some music for them, they may just forgive you entirely."

"Play music for them?" I wasn't sure what he had in mind. I never liked the idea of parlor concerts, let alone for James's parents.

He gave me puppy eyes. Then he smiled. I relented, provisionally.

"If they ask, I'll play something I haven't played yet. I don't want to be the October Revival monkey."

"Oh, come on, Kate. This is just my parents were talking about, not some record critics. They're not like Tom's folks; they don't listen to everything we write. It's more of a status thing with them." He opened the car door and said, "And thanks. This means a lot."

"If you say so."

He looked at me fondly. "Happy Christmas, Kate. I'm glad you're here."

I'M NOT sure what I was expecting, but it certainly wasn't the house we walked into. I could see where James got his tendency to collect cute little things because almost every surface was covered in tchotchkes. It was a hybrid between English cottage style and an

Indian restaurant. The house smelled absolutely divine, and there was something like a Christmas tree on top of the fireplace. But I moved a little closer and realized it was a bright orange elephant figurine draped with lights. Before I had time to ask any questions, James's family descended.

One of the things James forgot to mention was that it wasn't just his parents waiting for us, it was a collection of aunts and uncles and cousins. Some apparently had even flown in from India. I never felt so conspicuously strange. I had to explain to six people on my way from the living room to the kitchen that I wasn't his girlfriend or his wife. I also heard James speak in Tamil for the first time. Which was impressive. His voice was totally different when he spoke it; it was gentler. There is something very touching about the way he spoke with his mother and father, and I had to respect him for it. My particular family life was in shambles, and I had no hope of ever resurrecting it.

I wish I could say I've remembered everyone's names, but really it was all beyond me. Despite my apprehension, I really felt welcomed. Maybe James was a little bit worried my reputation would precede me, but nobody asked me awkward questions or alluded to the fact that I was "getting better." It was about celebration and good food and friendship. I really couldn't have asked for more.

And James was really loved. Truly loved. I'd spent so much time with him on the road, and often head-down in my own issues, I never stopped to notice. His parents looked at him with this mixture of pride and affection that brought a lump to my throat. His aunts showed me pictures of him as a kid; his uncles relayed stories about little James standing up to bullies in primary school. They didn't quite understand his lifestyle, but they embraced him as an artist and as a person.

Hotheaded, stubborn James, the James Vayne who was known for his brooding and perfectionism and laser sharp critique, just soaked it all in. He smiled. He kissed his mom on the cheek. He danced with his aunts. He looked at pictures of his cousins. And he absolutely doted on his father. Helped him around in his chair, spoke with him in Tamil and in English, laughed with him. All to the rhythm of Mr. V's oxygen machine, in and out like the heartbeat in the house. It wasn't a perfect family, but it was a perfect moment. And I had the feeling he'd had a lot of perfect moments with his family.

What a lucky bastard.

When it came time to perform, I was surprisingly excited. They had this upright piano in the living room and it still smelled like Pledge, so clearly there was an expectation before I even arrived. I wasn't sure I wanted to do the singing, but James was very encouraging. He gave me a sweet smile and told me it wouldn't just be a gift to hear me sing for his family but for him as well.

I sang a song called "Open Up," which was something I'd worked on when I was in rehab. No one had heard it, not even Jesse. It was one of the songs I had been working on during off times when we were at the Oast. The sound of the song is really nothing like the rest of the October Revival catalog. I guess, at the heart of it, it's a ballad. But it has nothing to do with falling in love, and everything to do with getting past being a closed person.

When I was done, James had tears in his eyes.

And when we drove home later, he was very reflective.

"You're going to make one hell of a solo album someday, Kate."

"Where'd that come from?" I asked.

He laughed, as if I was the silliest girl in the entire universe. "You know what I mean. That casual concert in there, it was the best music that's ever been played in the house."

I tried to brush him off, but I knew what he was saying. What I played wasn't part of the band, it wasn't part of *us*. It was another thing entirely, something I'd been working on the whole time, even though I wasn't thinking about it. I think part of it just had to do with self-preservation. Like I told Tom before, we weren't going to be around forever. Maybe we'd just take a break; maybe we'd come back to it later. But even though it felt like things were going better and better these days, I couldn't stop worrying in the back of my mind that big things were going to change. And that if I was going to survive those changes, I had to start doing things differently.

And I couldn't keep writing about Tom. And I couldn't keep drinking. And I couldn't keep James tied to my sinking ship, either.

"You know," he said. "You hide behind this guise of pop music. It's really easy for us, as a band, to just shovel out more of what people are used to. And I think sometimes, as songwriters, we're both guilty of it. I have to admit, I'm really not that deep. I love playing music. Hell, Kate, I love playing music with you. But sometimes I look at you and I just see that you're going far beyond where we are right now. It almost hurts me to know I'm taking all of your time."

"James," I said. "You sound so gloom and doom."

He sniffed, this was hard for him. "I just want you to know I'm not blind. If you ever get to the point where you feel like you've got to move on, I'll probably get furious initially, but I'll understand. I don't want to be the one holding you back."

I laughed derisively. "Holding me back? James, you're the one that got me into this in the first place. If you hadn't heard me play that night, if you hadn't talked to me…"

"Don't you see?" He put on the radio, signaling the end of our conversation. "It's not just about tonight, Kate. It's not some revelation. The moment I heard you, I knew it then, too. You are your own thing. You've got to let that show one of these days."

# CHAPTER TWENTY-TWO

Hey, Jesse.
Been feeling kind of strange lately. Since the holidays. Thinking about
my mom, thinking about everything with Rhee and the upcoming
tour. I don't think I've managed through the holidays without
drinking since I was about seventeen. I'm not sure I know what to do
without it.
No rush to reply. Just…wanted to get it out there. To someone who
gets it.
Love, Kate

Kate:
Busy as all hell here. Sorry for the brevity. Just remember that it
doesn't go away, but in some ways, it gets easier. I had my regression a
few months ago. It happens. Just know you're not alone.
Love, Jesse

JUST BEFORE THE TOUR, things got really shitty. I could feel it in the air,
like on a molecular level. I don't remember exactly how it happened
or what was the trigger. You can see things were going pretty well.
Tom and I did this great interview for the *New York Times*, we were

really on top of the world—James was working with Dusty on last-minute details, Dee was engaging the fanbase, Jon was practicing fanatically and getting better every day. We felt high on the verge of success.

See, Tom and I got a very stupid idea. We decided to go out. To celebrate. With the old crew in London: Dougie and Maeve, Charlie, Mikey, Anna. The crew who, to put it mildly, had turned Tom into a junkie and me into a barely functioning alcoholic. Maybe in the back of our minds we thought we'd grown up enough to cope with it. A half of year of triumph felt like an eternity to two addicts like us.

I know neither of us ordered the first glass. Someone recognized us and sent it over. The club was loud and full of people we knew, and in that week between Christmas and New Year, it sort of felt like it was our own personal purgatory. We were both so tired of fighting it. We didn't have to say it, but both of us felt like we were owed a celebration. One night to let go again, to give it up to the demons.

Listen, I don't hold with Tom's religion. You've got that part down by now, I'm sure. But if anything is demonic, it's addiction. It's the way it edges in through the good, strong, rational thoughts and twists them, makes you feel entitled and owed and important and, most dangerously, strong enough to deal with one more drink. Just one more...

Just one more drink. Then, just one more kiss. Just one more.

That night was a blur of lights and bodies and music and liquor. I didn't enjoy a single drink, but I kept drinking them thinking, eventually, I'd feel happier. That, at a point, it would fill up the pit of despair in my stomach—the knowledge that the band wouldn't last, the fact that Rhee hadn't called me for Christmas, the fact that I felt so alone in the universe and insignificant, the fact that James was ready to let me go if I wanted. If I could have enough fun, it would all go away. Because I deserved it. I could stop any time. I was completely in control.

So when I woke up in the hotel room with Tom's arm draped across my chest, and the reality of what happened started descending upon me, I really did think for one minute about killing myself. While he snored, I figured it was a good time to just take the jump and get the fuck out of this existence. I didn't want to have to face the rest of the band. Not before the tour. Not before I'd had so much success with sobriety. Not in the face of all the good wishes and get wells and personal trumpeted triumphs.

And the fact I'd taken Tom down with me? Jesus Christ. I don't think I've ever hated myself as much as I did in that moment.

Kate Styx: human garbage.

I tried to move, but I felt Tom's arm tighten around my waist.

There weren't any tears. I just couldn't breathe.

"It's okay, Kate." Tom pulled my head toward his chest as I shook with anger, the adrenaline in my body threatening to propel me out the nearest window or off the ledge.

"It's so not okay," I said, muffled. "I am such an asshole."

"We are both assholes."

I pulled away to get a better look at him. Even though the shades were drawn, I could tell he looked pretty shitty. He had circles under his eyes; his lips were chapped. He appeared exhausted. Pale. Strung out on something. I'd been here before. I knew it so well it was like slipping into a terrible pair of ratty slippers.

Naked and shivering, I pulled the blankets up over my shoulders.

"No, no, no, no," I said to the sheets. "No…no no…"

Tom didn't reply. He was breathing shallowly, regularly at least. I pinched my arms under the blankets, hoping there was some small chance I was, maybe, dreaming.

But no. No dreaming. I heard my phone ringing across the room.

"You're eventually going to have to come out of there," he said, nudging me with his thigh. "We do have a show tonight."

"I'm so sorry I did this to you," I muttered.

"Did this to me?" he laughed. It wasn't a happy laugh but a derisive one. "Kate, I hate to explain this to you, but it's not like I wasn't complicit—"

"I fucking know it doesn't…that's not the point…" It was getting too hot to hide under the sheets, so I pulled them around me and went across the bed from him.

Tom grabbed my toes, and I quickly put them back under the bedsheets.

"D'you think this is the first time I've made a mistake since… everything?" he asked.

I did. I did honestly think that, since finding Jesus Christ as his personal Lord and Savior and everything, he'd managed to live a perfect, blameless life. That he'd not erred at all. In fact, considering how I'd barely managed to keep my shit together, I was pretty convinced I was the only one with serious problems.

He grabbed me and pulled me over next to him, then held out his arm so I could see it. There were track marks. Nothing new, but not exactly vanished either. Not super recent, but…close enough.

My heart broke for him. I saw my fingers were shaking as I traced the lines near the crook of his arm, biting down on my lip so hard I tasted blood.

He kept talking, answering the question I wanted to ask.

"Right before we left Nashville. A few weeks before. I got the idea to come here after that…"

"Was I… when I…"

"Two weeks after you entered rehab," he said, still holding me close. He'd wrapped his arms around me and was resting his chin on my shoulder.

I swallowed hard.

"I found you in your apartment in Nashville." His perfect voice broke for a second. "You know, years went by, and you were always the one to find me…like that. When I saw you so…helpless, so wrapped up in your addiction, it was really hard. I didn't know what to say to you after. I didn't…I just felt so guilty. So selfish. I couldn't handle it."

"Why didn't you tell me?" I asked. It was better that I couldn't see his face. I might have tried to kiss him.

He sighed in my ear. It tickled. "I was ashamed. Angry. Embarrassed. It hasn't happened since, but I bounced back. I can recover from this, with His help. The spirit is willing, the flesh is weak, as it goes. Thankfully, last night it was nothing *illegal*. And I'm sorry…I shouldn't have invited the chaps along...I'm not perfect. Part of me knew if we walked into the bar, this would happen. Hoped it would happen. Kate, when we were together...there were times I felt like I was, at last, home. I just wanted to feel that way again..."

What was he getting at? I didn't know. I didn't want to know. "I feel terrible."

"Me too."

I took a deep breath. I didn't try to get out of his embrace. It felt too good. Strangely platonic. Comforting. Welcome. I hadn't slept with anyone in months. Seriously, months. Despite James's accusations, Jesse and I were just flirty friends. But being with Tom was more than a little confusing for me.

"Listen, Tom," I said. "I just...I forgive you."

I hadn't expected to say that. I had expected to say something selfish, about what we were supposed to do. What that night meant for us. What we would tell people. Except, I realized, where I stood really had very little to do with *me*. It had to do with the fact that Tom and I, if left to our devices, would probably destroy each other. And the only way to prevent that from happening was to truly, honestly let him go.

"Kate, you don't have to..."

"No, listen. It's not just for the saintly." I kept going. "I forgive you for your bad choices. For keeping me up at night for years, pining and wishing I was with you—and for breaking my heart. I forgive you for last night, and a hundred other nights I don't remember. And I forgive you for finding Jesus, even if I can't..."

He didn't argue with me. He squeezed me tighter.

Then we made love. My phone rang, the room phone rang, but we ignored it. We weren't drunk or stoned or angry. We were sad. We were saying goodbye. Finally. Our skin spoke the words we couldn't say. In hushed whispers and cries, we marked the moment, at last, where we would part. I'd put up so many walls after his infidelity, and I'd hated him and hated myself so long because of it.

To be totally candid, which I'm trying hard to do, I don't exactly remember what caused our breakup. It sort of happened over a two month period. He cheated on me, I got really angry and drunk, we got back together for a few weeks, and I told him I was done. I seem to recall talking to James about it a lot during that time, and he seemed to think we were burning each other out, Tom and me. I have a vague recollection of an evening where I came to visit his flat—this was before we left New York for Nashville—and he wanted me to play him some of the songs I'd been working on. They were horrible.

I think he said something like, "If you don't break up with him, this will be the end of us," and he happily pointed out Tom hadn't really been faithful at all, in spite of the fact I was lead to believe so. It just wasn't in his nature at that point. I tried to argue myself out of it, but James had proof. Too much proof. And eventually I just told Tom I couldn't do both—I couldn't be his girlfriend and be in the band and, ultimately, the band was too important. And I was aware I needed to stop partying so hard. Though it took a while for it to actually happen.

He didn't fight me, and I think that's what broke my heart. But tangled with him in the hotel room, both of us finding comfort in our physical goodbyes, I knew he regretted it, our growing apart. He'd probably always regret it, and he was aware there was no going back.

We both startled at voices outside.

Someone knocked, but before we could get to the door, the passcard went in and a handful of hotel security and James came through the archway into the bedroom.

The room was strewn with beer cans and smelled like weed and sex and sweat. It's like, for a second, I was James taking it all in and not myself in the bed. The shame was enough to bathe my body red, splotchy patches of embarrassment.

"Aw, fuck," James said. His teeth were bared, he was so angry. "I thought you... Jesus Christ, what the fuck is wrong with the two of you?"

"Do you want it alphabetical or numerical?" I asked.

Then he kicked over a table and left.


**Kate:** It's not how you think, J.
**Kate:** Come on.
**Kate:** Talk to me.

**James:** Fuck you, Kate.
**Kate:** Hear me out.
**James:** No.
**Kate:** We messed up.
**James:** Mild way of putting it. Y'know there were pictures taken of you two. It's all over the fucking internet.
**Kate:** We shouldn't have gone out. I feel like shit, okay? I'm sorry.
**James:** I wish the two of you a happy life.
**Kate:** It's not like that. We're not together.
**James:** I honestly don't know what to say to you, Kate. I'm so disappointed on so many levels I'm going to implode from anger.
**Kate:** I slipped up. Again. I know, I need to do better. James, please.
**James:** G'night, Kate.

---

**Kate:** You up?
**Jesse:** Hey there.
**Kate:** I suck.
**Jesse:** I saw.
**Kate:** Ugh. I was hoping not.
**Jesse:** It happens.
**Kate:** I can explain…
**Jesse:** I know. Will have to chat later.

# CHAPTER TWENTY-THREE

LEAVE it to Dusty to fix everything. With only a week left until the tour started, the band was in shambles. Tom was avoiding me, which made sense, but he was mostly holed up with his holy friends. James was systematically ignoring me. The new guys were just a little edgier than usual since I'm pretty sure they thought we were going to break up before we even set foot on stage for real.

She booked us an honest-to-goodness conference room. With swiveling black leather chairs and a big phone in the middle and everything. A screen. She lured me there on the pretense she was going to have me talk to a stylist, and despite Jesse's attempts to bolster my self-esteem, I fell for it. Turns out it was an intervention between James and Tom and me. Dee and Jon weren't there.

I hate being the last person in a room, especially with a guilty conscience. Everyone looked at me, and I sat down in one of the chairs as far as possible from anyone else.

"First of all, I just want to say I thought you were all over this shit." Dusty sat down in a flurry of fur and sparkles. "I almost believed it was true, October Revival was all grown up and ready to put their drama in the back drawer. But then I remembered what industry I work in and knew it was just too good to be true."

It may have been the first time I'd ever seen Dusty without her sunglasses. Her eyes were icy blue, even. And she'd aged. I mean, clearly, she'd had stuff done. She's not the kind of woman to abide by drooping jowls or a saggy neck. But she looked tired under the thick makeup on her face.

I stared at my fingernails. I'd painted them blue two days ago, but they were chipping already.

"Now, in one sense, it's good to know you can still catch the eye of the tabloid media," she said, waving her hands in the air. "People are still interested in your inability to behave like adults. Not that I particularly care. I don't give a shit what you do on your off-time, and I never have. But when your antics involve putting the entire tour on hold, that's when I get pissed off. We already had to cancel the show two nights ago, and I am not pleased."

James snorted; Tom tried to apologize.

Dusty stood up and flicked her fingers in the air. Four minutes, exactly.

"You're going to be in here until you've talked it out. I'll be in the lobby," she proclaimed, heading for the door.

"What's this, a fucking time out?" James asked.

Holding the door open, Dusty said, "You're acting like children, so yes." Before shutting the door, she added, "Call me when you're done."

Sometimes I forget just how good of a manager she is. We couldn't be any more different, and her whole act is totally beyond me, but she does a hell of a better job doing her business than I do.

We were quiet for about fifteen minutes, all playing on our phones. I tried to get a hold of Jesse, then thought twice about it. He probably figured I slept with Tom. I mean, it was clear from the pictures we'd been making out most of the night. And I don't blame him for wanting to distance himself from my perpetual train wreck of a life.

I felt like I wanted to go drink again, to feel it this time. Maybe if I tried again, and went more slowly, I'd enjoy it. But as it stood, I'd had two cups of coffee and was still only slightly more animate than a corpse.

Tom caught my eye across the table, shook his head, and rolled his eyes. I mouthed, "I'm sorry," and he shrugged me off, then blew me a kiss.

That's when James just started talking.

"I thought you were both like...dead in there," he said, speaking more to the table than us. "You didn't answer your phones. I'd been tipped off from Dee as to where you'd both been, and who you'd been hanging out with."

"It's not like it hasn't happened before," I muttered in response, immediately regretting it.

James laughed bitterly in my direction, still not making eye contact. "Ah, that's your excuse now, is it? Well, forgive, darling, but I was under the impression you were *rehabilitated*. That we'd given you enough time to sort things out. And the business of the two of you was over. But from the *TMZ* reports, I was under a rather false assumption."

"It *is* over," I said firmly. Tom gave me an understanding nod. "We made a mistake. You can't say you don't get it, because you and Sara hooked up plenty of times after you were 'over.'"

"Yeah, but we weren't alcoholics and drug addicts," James snapped. "We picked up the fucking phone when fucking people fucking called!"

Tom got it more than I did. He stood up and sat next to James, putting his hand on his friend's shoulder. "Listen, mate. We didn't mean to scare you. We both made some awful errors in judgment."

"What a sweet way of putting it," James said as he shrugged the hand off.

"It won't happen again," I grumbled toward James's general direction. "At least not the hooking up part. We...I know you won't believe us, but it won't."

"Right," James said. "Same old song, darling dear. Same old song."

"And I'm trying really hard," Tom said, putting the hand back on James's shoulder, reaching into their past friendship. "Can you at least acknowledge that both Kate and I have come quite far in the last few months? It's not been anything like before. This is one time among dozens of opportunities."

He didn't mention his backsliding in Nashville, and I was glad. But Tom did give me a look saying as much—he was likely never going to tell James. Sometimes it's better to lie a little to protect the ones we love.

James took a deep breath, and I mustered a smile, even though I felt like running away. I can't even start to tell you how embarrassed I felt. Somehow sleeping with Tom was worse than the drinking thing. I mean, come on, I think James expected me to fall off the wagon at some point. I had hardly spent any of our friendship together sober, and despite half-hearted attempts to cool my liquor-fueled jets over the years, I'd never really taken sobriety seriously. As we marched away from my time in rehab, he was probably waiting for the call.

But both of us, together, and clearly not very much with it. I wouldn't have wanted to have been him in that moment. I felt like a childish teenager and as if James were my disappointed dad. I'd had enough disappointed dads.

Eventually James relented. His anger, as always, just couldn't hold out long enough. And, like the rest of us, he was excited about touring, even if it did come with its own set of concerns and worries. Touring really used to be a code word for "road party" back in the day. This time we made every effort to turn the tour bus into a happy, fun, exciting place, where we could play music and games and watch movies.

But I couldn't help thinking about how it used to be. I'm not sure if I was honestly missing it or just disturbed by the weird sensory memories. There's a reason I started writing this down when I did because I, frankly, don't remember huge chunks of the first few years we were together. The last tour I spent the majority of the time sleeping off hangovers or getting drunk, and Tom was typically rocking amphetamines by night and any variety of opiates by day (when he was awake, which wasn't often).

We had plenty of fans willing to sleep with us, and while I've made a point to show how much James stayed out of the general using of the group, this is never an area he failed to take advantage of. Not even when he was with Sara. I mean, there's a reason they fought a lot, and much of it had to do with the fact his eye strayed quite often. He always knew the quickest route to pissing her off royally was sleeping with a random chick he had no intention of following up with. It got to her feminist sensitivities, but not so much she wouldn't do the same to him in the bat of an eyelash.

At least that's one thing I didn't miss on tour.

Anyway, touring sober was boring by day but exciting by night. It was hard for me and hard for Tom, but we dealt with it separately, checking in on each other now and again. The exciting part was we had a good lineup at last, with virtually no drama to speak of. We set up little phone reminders to go off at intervals. He set his off to give him Bible verses with some app, and that was fine with me. I was starting to hate him less for finding Jesus and found myself being a big girl about the whole thing and simply being glad he was alive and continually improving himself.

Our little setback wasn't as damning as I thought it'd be. In fact, Tom and I were closer, and not just because we'd had sex for the first time in two years. If anything, the intimacy somehow gave us permission to move past not hooking up anymore. I certainly don't feel like it was a sin to do what we did, and he never acted as if it was. More than anything, that night was a resolution for both of us, an attempt to put a very jagged puzzle together before we embarked on something much larger than the two of us. Which sounds hokey now that I look at it on paper, and of course, there were days when I still entertained the notion of getting back together with him. But for now, he wasn't trying to convert me, and I wasn't trying to prevent him from drawing closer to his God. Which was a big start.

The album was received the way most of our music has been, sort of middling, always looking for something we weren't trying to do. Music critics like to write their own opinions into your liner notes, measure you up against the sounds they wish they'd heard in their heads. Of course, it's impossible to measure up. Someone complained we relied too much on Tom's voice, another said some of the lyrics had become watered-down clichés and wondered how much collaboration we'd had (a personal shot at me, perhaps?). But overall, our fans, though not quite as plentiful as they once were, still bought the album and came to the shows, they filled up our social media feeds and professed their love.

I like our fans, but I'm not good with them. Not like Tom or Dee, or Kurt was. Maybe that has to do with the fact they never had to put their work on the line. I mean, sure, Tom is an artist—what he does with his voice is amazing, and I'm not saying he never had his share of nerves about putting an album out. But he didn't write the words. People aren't tattooing things he made up on their bodies, or saying their vows to them, or writing rabid letters claiming we stole their ideas. I don't know. Tom plays the audience. He's with them. He gives them hi-fives. He winks and struts and laughs and gets bouquets of flowers. Not that I never have—because it's not the case at all—but he gets the spotlight. And that's fucking peachy to me.

Anyway, in a nutshell, Europe was a blur. I mean, you've got to imagine it. It's work. It's not happy fun play time. It's an exhausting schedule, in and out of cities so quickly it's almost impossible to enjoy anything. We spent time either on a bus or on a plane, whatever saved the most money in the long run. We played four or five shows a week —sometimes more. There was no time for sightseeing, no chance to sample the local cuisine. Sometimes we're lucky, and we're near a market or food trucks or something else exciting, but more often than not, it's just the same old thing, just another language. I promised Tom that I'd take a break soon and actually see Europe someday, and he agreed.

But every step of the way, I was gritting my teeth, willing myself not to party. Not to drink. Not to fall down that hole again. A few nights it came so close I sat in front of the wet bar sobbing in my room until James came to get me and called the concierge to remove everything. At some point, there's no longer a wet bar to worry about.

Our personal drama neutralized for the moment, Dee and Jon were happy to be along for the ride. James retreated into his own head space, spending at least seven hours a day in his "egg" as we called it— nestled in the back corner of the bus with his huge, noise-canceling headphones, furiously texting away. I'd have been worried if that was unusual for him, but to my dim recollection, it's how he'd spent the majority of the last few tours too. At that point, I think it was just to get us out of the way; this time it was to find his own place.

Instead of drinking or using, Tom played video games. He played insane amounts of space creature shit, and swords and armor shit, and when he wasn't, he was finding a church or holding a prayer meeting. I didn't have many chances to talk to him because he always seemed to be finding an escape, leaving the bus, going for a drive. I know why he was doing it, so I didn't want to intrude too much. We checked in now and again, like I said, but when he started only showing up for shows, I began to get concerned.

I confronted him about it when we were in Paris. Yes, it's the city of love. You guessed it—in the back of my delusional brain I had some disgusting romantic notions that, still maybe somewhere, we could salvage hope. Even though I knew the only way of that happening probably included another baptism on my part and "giving" myself to Jesus. Again. I almost laughed at the idea of it, since I'd been baptized three times already (once at birth, once at twelve, and once after I'd had Rhee).

The Paris show was exciting and terrifying. "Call the Car" had made it to number three in the UK, and the album was still in the top ten and, according to Dusty, potentially going higher. I suggested to Tom, in one of those brief moments when I found him, that we should take a walk. At first he looked at me kind of blankly, like he used to when I roused him from a drugged out stupor. Then he shrugged and agreed.

We didn't go anywhere clichéd: no Eiffel Tower, no Champs-Élysées. Instead we just meandered around through old cafe-lined streets and shivered into our jackets, readjusting our scarves, and shoving our hands deeper and deeper into our pockets. The picture of moody hipster musicians in their thirties.

I knew it would be difficult for him, but the group touring with us since Budapest, Marching Mad, was very much like an earlier incarnation of October Revival. Lots of craziness. I'm not sure they were doing anything hardcore—not like Tom in his heyday—but sleep and rest and taking it easy were not in their repertoire. It was their first big tour stretch, and they were going to rock and roll it up to the nth degree. Not like I blamed them. I mean, hell, I'd done the same thing. But I could tell, when they looked at us, they saw us aging before them, worrying that someday they'd be just as fading and pathetic.

"How are you holding up?" I asked after we'd covered the basics (performances, rumors, that sort of thing). It was starting to rain a bit.

Tom glanced at me, thoughtful again. "It's hard," he said, squinting down the street. He didn't want to look at me for long, apparently. "I didn't think it'd be this hard, to tell you the truth. I keep thinking…"

"We fucked it all up?" I finished for him.

"Pretty much. Yeah."

I tried to remember if we'd talked about this sort of thing before, like really sat down and shared our demons. We'd both let them take us to the brink of death, but we'd never really talked about what that meant and how it made us closer, in a terrible way. Sure, you can count the morning in the afterglow, but beyond the "how are you doings," it really hadn't gone much deeper.

Thinking of Kurt and missing the hell out of him, I suggested coffee. We had to be on stage in three hours, so we had a decent window of time and the venue wasn't far away. We found a quiet corner in a little cafe and huddled over our steaming coffees, considering each other like shy kids.

"It's like…the memories are everywhere, aren't they?" I asked, hoping to goad him into more discussion. We both needed it. "I mean, it's not like I remember the last two tours with any clarity…"

"We sound better. I know we do. But it's as if there's this strange version of me I can still see, doing all these terrible things." He laughed. "And it's not like just a shadow. I was that bloke, just a few weeks ago. What an awful thing to have to think about all the time."

"It wasn't all terrible," I reminded him. I reached across the table to take his hand. It was so cold to the touch. "I mean, just don't let your friends tell you everything about who you used to be was terrible. Yes, you made some bad choices. But you don't have to stop celebrating what makes you…you. I was stupid enough to love that horrible bloke once."

"So wise, Katherine, my dear," he said, smiling a little.

"Seriously."

He sighed, studying our twined hands. "It's hard. It's…I mean, I want to be able to let go. To let God take care of it, to make me new. You understand more than anyone, I think, even though you're not…exactly practicing."

That was a mild way of putting it.

"I know what you mean, at least," I said.

"I thought I could shrug it off, what happened. I thought somehow, confronting my demons meant I'd be more clearly aware. Not that you're a demon, I didn't mean—"

"No offense taken… I've been called worse."

Tom almost laughed. "I just…do the shadows ever go away?" he asked. "Ah, shit. You're the last person I should ask, considering what you've gone through."

"We're a pair," I said. "But in answer to your question, I don't think so. I don't think we can ever rid ourselves of the shadows. We just have to learn to live with them. Eventually, maybe—hopefully—they just become part of the furniture after a while. You're not struggling to stay in the light every damned day like some strung-out vampire. You wake up one morning and, for the first time, you don't think about it."

"And if I fail again?"

"You can always start again. But, and I can speak from experience, it'll be harder. Every time it's like starting from level one all over again in Super Mario Brothers. No extra lives. No save state." That was, perhaps, the best metaphor I could have ever given him. "You were wrong—we were wrong—in thinking we could just let what happened fade away."

He perked up a bit, his eyes getting a mischievous glint to them. Forget it was also his "I'm horny and I'm about to jump you" look. It was still endearing. I had to battle a thousand memories and haunted strains of songs I'd written about him, pining away like some lovesick teenager. I hated how long I'd taken to let him know how I felt and hated even more that we'd never manage to get together. Not really. Not in a way that matters. Just in a broken-down mockery of a relationship.

Ours was not a love of the ages, that's for sure. I was at my worst when I was with him, and likewise for him. And yet there were a few moments, during those dark days, when I believe we were truly in love. I have to believe it now. I didn't use to. Another really fucked up thing I'm going to say is that I'm glad I slept with him one last time because in a really demented way, it finally proved I meant something to him. That even dead drunk—without actual hard drugs in his system—he wanted me. Tom Chesley wanted to sleep with *me*. If I had a bow or a ribbon to put on my lapel to prove it, I can't say I wouldn't wear it.

We walked slowly back to the venue, his arm around me.

"There is something I noticed," he said as we rounded the corner and the breeze picked up. "About your songwriting. I mean, I know I'm not exactly Mozart when it comes to composition, but you're changing too."

"I am?" I asked.

"Well, for one thing, none of the songs you've been writing are about me."

I laughed. "Not directly."

"Well, it's the first album you're not writing love songs to me, cleverly hidden—or hate songs. They're about bigger things. Better things."

I felt embarrassed to be so transparent but grateful he'd been able to see through my creative guise.

"You know," I said. "Three years ago…that's what I wanted. More than you in bed or you as a boyfriend or whatever. I just wanted you to notice."

He leaned over and kissed my forehead. "We all noticed. You're—what's it that James calls you?—the fulcrum. That's it. You're the very center, the sun. We're just the planets in gravitational pull."

"You're totally mixing your metaphors."

"Which is why I don't write much, of course. I'm just the pretty voice."

I squeezed his waist and felt, for probably the first time since we'd broken up, that we understood each other. Whatever had passed between us as lovers had changed; we'd managed the near impossible: we'd become friends.

# CHAPTER TWENTY-FOUR

We PLAYED sixteen more shows and shuffled off to the States for the first time in half a year. Despite making the trip more or less every few years for almost the last decade, coming back always feels so disorienting. Everything is just so big here in the States. The streets are so wide, the suburbs so sprawling. I always get this turned around feeling when I get into New York, and it's even worse when I find myself in Atlanta or another of the big, new cities. Sure, Paris and Frankfurt and London are big. But they're old. Even when you're on the ground level, it feels old, hedged in. New York feels endless.

Getting into the car at LaGuardia, I saw three missed phone calls. From Rhee.

Immediately I started worrying and chided myself for doing so. No, I'm not her mother. Not technically. She doesn't call me often. Sometimes just to say hi, but the calls never last long. She called me on New Year's Day after I called her; she remembered my birthday and left me a very sweet singing message I never returned because I'm that shitty of a person. But as soon as I saw the three missed calls, I worried that Dad was dead. It wouldn't be much of a surprise. He's not a young guy, and stranger things had happened. I figured it was just a matter of time. Mom might not have been the most stellar individual in the world, but she did take care of him. She was forever a doting wife, even when he fucked around behind her back for years. She's the kind of wife that always had his lunch ready, who ironed his pocket handkerchiefs, who read the same books he did just to have something to talk about.

Yeah, she was way too good for him.

Anyway, by the time I was in the car, some rambling SUV Dusty had arranged for us, I tried texting. James and Jon were in the car with me, and I didn't feel like talking personal family drama around them if I could help it. But when Rhee replied to my text by calling me back before I could reply to her again, I didn't have a whole lot of a choice but to answer. I didn't need more clues to know she seriously needed me.

"Rhee, what's up?" I asked, feeling a knot in the center of my chest. I didn't know what I thought about the possibility of Dad dying. He was almost in his seventies. He was fit, sure, but he wasn't exactly a candidate for heart patient of the year. If I recall, he'd had a heart issue a few years back, and from what I could remember, he didn't really give a shit about cardiac rehabilitation or eating right, instead insisting God would take him in His time.

"Can...can you come home?" Rhee asked. Her voice was thick from crying, her nose stuffy.

"What's happened?" I asked. I braced myself.

James immediately looked up from his phone, concerned. Jon was listening to his iPod and staring out the window, a little bug-eyed. We'd planned to give our English country bumpkin a real tour of the city, but he was already quite overwhelmed. James promised they'd start by touring some of the almost decent English pubs.

I shook my head at James.

Rhee continued. "I'm...I just need you here. It's not...it's me. I need you. Not anyone else."

Not anyone else.

"I'm..."

"I know…you're in the middle of things…and the tour…"

I took a deep breath, not really knowing what to say or what the proper protocol was. This was a conversation she should have been having with my mother Claire and not me. But Claire was dead. So I had to do what I thought she'd say.

"Rhee, I'll be there if you need me to be," I said, though the words felt rehearsed, hollow. We had a show in two days. We hadn't had a break. I was exhausted and jet lagged and still putting my head together after everything. Still worried about myself, worried about Tom…

"No, it's okay…you don't have to…"

"Rhee. Listen. Just tell me what's going on."

I could hear her straining to speak through her tears before she sobbed: "I think I'm pregnant."

---

I WAS able to get a flight to Atlanta that evening, and I only told James the details. I'm not really sure why I told him and no one else. I guess, when it came down to it, I wanted his approval. And I could tell he understood, even if he was still a bit on the sulky side. He didn't have a twenty-year-old kid. But he had family he treasured, and he was loved and treasured back. Not all of us could say the same.

I promised everyone I could make it back for the show, even if I had to go right back to Georgia—we had two days.

The whole trip I couldn't stop creating scenarios in my head of what exactly had happened to Rhee. Was it rape? Just the thought alone made my hair stand on end and brought out an insane maternal reflex I thought was still dormant. I worried more than anything about that, really, despite the fact I knew it was unlikely. I mean, I kept telling myself that. Surely it couldn't be rape—but what if it was? Did she have a boyfriend? If she did, she never mentioned it to me. Not that we talked often. How did Rhee get old enough to have sex in the first place?

For the first time in my life, I had to act like someone's *mother*. I could see no way my dad would have been of any help to her, at least not in any measurable way. The last thing I wanted was to take away the choice she had—granted, she wasn't thirteen like I was—but she was still young enough that having a baby right now would drastically change everything in her life. I know the arguments he'd make, and while I found it really challenging to think about abortion—something I'd never imagined other than in a medieval sense (I recall wondering if I gave myself salmonella or something if I'd spontaneously miscarry and end my misery or, horribly, taking my own life) —I knew it would be impossible to even consider with Dad around. To him, all life was sacred. And Rhee was living proof. Through my misery, he'd been given a second chance with a child. And *voilà*. As if he needed any other argument.

Rhee went to school at Emory, so finding her was as easy as going through Jackson Hartsfield and renting a car and driving to her. I never liked navigating Atlanta on my own, loathing the garble of streets and horrific public transportation and endless, unrelenting traffic. I couldn't just show up in a taxi. The last thing she needed, I figured, was her too busy, rock star, emotionally distant biological mother showing up in a stretch limo in front of her friends. Or whatever the situation called for.

I texted her, and she told me she'd meet me outside her apartment, which I'd paid for and was significantly nicer than the dorms. She was never really party girl material, and in spite of the school's good name, she found herself uncomfortable with the atmosphere her freshman year. So she and one of her friends had gotten the apartment (with my help, since Dad was never going to let such special treatment fly). I'm not even sure he's aware of the arrangement since he never even sees the college bills (those come to me). I guess that's the one thing I'm proud of. I am not Rhee's mother, at least not in the important ways, but I could help where it made sense. I wasn't smart enough to get scholarships—and even though she knew I'd pay (I'd told her so when we sold our first album, and damned if I didn't put the money aside for her) she still got a mostly free ride because she's so fucking smart. Still, she didn't have to worry about books or rent or "fun money" or anything. Truthfully? I paid off my own student loans two years after we'd broken it big. The money is still there just in case she goes doctor even though I could have used Rhee's money on some stupid shit. See? Sometimes I'm actually a redeemable human being.

I spotted her where she said she'd be and noticed she was wearing sunglasses and shivering into her jacket. I pulled up, she got in, and for the first fifteen minutes of driving around in no particular direction, she didn't say anything.

In all honesty, it felt more like fifteen hours, and I kept thinking of things to say and then not saying them. She was twenty, not thirteen. I had to keep reminding myself of that because the whole situation had just dragged up so much stuff I'd buried for a long time. I decided she had to make the first move, she had to say something. But when she didn't, and didn't…and still didn't, I had to say something. I was getting itchy all over.

"Do you want to get something to eat?" I asked.

"Not hungry," she said.

So, knowing that driving around aimlessly wasn't going to work, I turned on the radio, tuned it to a classical station, and pulled over by a park. I shouldn't be driving and emotional, and I had no idea how else the discussion could turn. But she was already crying, so clearly, I'd broken the ice enough.

"Have you talked to Dad?" I asked.

She shook her head. I thought briefly that I should take her hands or something—which is what mothers do, right?—but hers were firmly embedded in the crooks of her elbows while she stared ahead through her glasses, tears running down her cheeks and plopping on her leather jacket.

"You have health insurance through the school?" I asked. Yeah, there you go. Cool thing. Bring up abortion right away! Living up to my fallen reputation, I suppose. I cringed inwardly, just imagining what Dad would have to say if he were a fly on the wall.

She nodded.

I drummed my numb fingers on the steering wheel. "I know you're just trying to process all of this, and…I don't know. You can talk to me. I'm here."

Rhee wouldn't look at me. So I kept looking at her. I noticed her clothes were somewhat more bohemian than they used to be. Her hair was layered, her jacket faux leather with fringe. I recognized her, but she'd shed a lot of much of the co-ed cuteness she'd had; I wasn't sure if it was a show or if she genuinely was moving on, or if somehow Mom's death had freed her, or depressed her, or what. The bare truth of the matter is I barely knew Rhee as a woman, and I only had a vague idea of her as a child. I wasn't just a shitty biological mom; I was a shitty fake sister.

"I just can't believe this happened," she finally said. Rhee looked up at me took off her sunglasses to wipe her mascara-smudged eyes again. She'd apparently made the effort to put on makeup and cried it mostly away.

"You have options," I said. Again with the being lame. I didn't want it to sound like I was only thinking of her terminating the pregnancy, but it totally came out like that. I was just so afraid she'd been brought up like I was that she'd have no idea it was a possibility.

"Of course I have options. I know I fucking have options. Why the hell do you think I asked you to come here?" she shouted at me and kicked the glove compartment. I almost made a snarky comment about this being a luxury rental, but I kept my mouth shut and let her blow off steam.

She wasn't done yet.

"Do you think I could possibly call our father? 'Oh, hi, Dad. Yeah. I fucked a guy. And he got me pregnant, and now I want an abortion.' I mean—Kate, seriously? There is literally not a single person in the family who could understand and you…you…"

"He has talked to you about birth control, right? Or at least through school…"

"I must have skipped a day. I don't know how it happened," she sobbed. "Mom got me a prescription when I was sixteen, as a precaution."

Mom did what now?

I cleared my throat to gain a little time and recover from the shock. I tried again. "I suck at this stuff, Rhee, but, at very least, I have an idea of what you're going through. Sort of."

"Sort of? Sort of? I'm a freaking generational curse."

"No, no you're not. It happens. To lots of girls. I'll do whatever I can to help you through this. I just don't know what you want from me," I said, trying to tell the truth as best I could. "I hardly know you, but I know enough I'm a huge disappointment."

"Sometimes," she admitted. "But you came. Even though I never thought you would."

Ouch.

"I did. Now…what can I do?" I asked. I could hear the note of pleading in my own voice and I realized, in spite of my general confusion and sadness over the situation, I was all she had.

Rhee took a deep breath and spoke more steadily. "I'd like you to tell me about my dad."

Unexpected. This was a subject we hadn't broached, and I really didn't see how it had anything to do with her problems at the moment. It was also not something I wanted to talk about, but given the situation, I didn't want to be even more of an asshole about it. If she asked me to alphabetize the entire Emory library, I'd have done it in that moment because, more than anything, I felt absolutely guilty and responsible for what had happened to her.

"Your dad," I said, struggling to find the right words. "Well. Let's see. He'd be about forty now. I was thirteen. He was eighteen. Nineteen maybe. I can't remember if he stayed back a year."

Rhee blinked at me like a confused owl brought into the light. Apparently, this was all news to her.

"What…what did Dad tell you about your dad? Maybe we should start there," I asked her before continuing.

She looked a little embarrassed. "That he was some bad man, some cruel man, who took advantage of you. It wasn't…"

"Rape? No. I mean, not technically. He was cute, athletic. Book smart, but not exactly a Rhodes Scholar. He was into metal. He told me I was beautiful and that he wanted to marry me. He was…"

"He was what?"

I cleared my throat. "He was in a *band*."

The irony was a little thick for the both of us. So I continued, "I don't think he's still in a band, to be clear. I mean, if he is, I've never run into him. I don't even think he even knew what happened. My parents freaked out—I was about five months along when I figured out I was pregnant, and they whisked me out of Athens quicker than God smiting the Sodomites out of existence."

"You never told me about him."

"Rhee. I was thirteen. I was terrified."

"Didn't you love him?" she asked.

She wasn't talking about Jason. She was talking about whoever the father of her child was. But she made the mistake of thinking I was capable of behaving in the same way as her when I was so young.

"I don't mean to sound callous, but it doesn't really matter. It's not about how much I loved him, which, I promise, wasn't much considering he never found me, and I'm not terribly hard to find."

"You changed your name," Rhee said, gesturing wildly at me like I was some freak out of nature, some horrific abomination of shame. "You're all. Different."

Rhee had a point.

"Anyway. His name is Jason Miller. I'm sure there's hundreds of other Jason Millers, but he grew up outside of Athens, Georgia. He went to Oconee High. I have absolutely no idea what his life is like, even if he happens to be alive or not. His dad always threatened to put him into the Army, so maybe he ended up going that route after everything. I don't know."

"Does he even know about me?" Rhee asked.

"Did you think he did?"

"Kinda. Sorta."

"Unless Dad told him, I don't think so. I was too scared and ashamed to tell him. We didn't have email back then. If he ever looked me up, or cared for me, I don't know. The last thing I remember talking to him just after Thanksgiving about him wanting to see other people—two days later, I started throwing up every morning like clockwork."

"You seriously haven't spoken to him since?" she asked.

"Seriously. You know what Mom and Dad…how they are. Mom promised she'd take care of you and no one would ever know. And, I guess, no one did for a long time. But apparently Mom wasn't terribly thorough."

"She didn't expect to die, or to have me rooting through her shit. So, if I never found proof, you never would have told me."

I said nothing because I didn't have any clue as to what the right answer to that one was. Sometimes you live inside a lie so long you forget it's masquerading for the truth. I probably would have waited until we were old to tell her. I dunno. Until I had kids of my own, or she did, or something.

Rhee sighed and stared at her hands again. "You're right. I'm not you. I'm not thirteen. This is my problem."

I took a deep breath. "I'm here to help. However you need."

Her eyes met mine, like a mirror reflection. "I have an appointment in two hours, Kate. At the clinic. I made up my mind, no matter what happens. I just needed to know…"

She started sobbing, and I put my arms around her, and we wept together in the car as the windows fogged up.

---

THIS PARTICULAR ABORTION clinic was best described in terms of what it was not. It was not comfortable. It was not inviting. It was not a regular doctor's office. It was not filled with people who met your gaze or gave you well wishes or start up short conversations. It was not filled with old people, sick people, babies, or any of the typical fare you see. It did not have a television or much in the way of magazines.

But it did have some praying protesters outside. So there's that.

Everything was running late, which made the waiting in hermetic hell even more intolerable. When we were finally called into the counseling room, I was shaking with nerves. And why the hell did I even have a right to be nervous?

We sat down across from a short woman in her mid-fifties with short, spiky gray hair. She had warm brown eyes, I remember, behind thick glasses, and peered at us with a look between pity and understanding.

"I'm Dr. Clevens," she identified herself, rhyming her name with Stevens. "You're Rihannon Marshall, correct? And this—"

"This is my mom." She said it without looking up at Dr. Clevens. I noticed an expression on the doctor's face I'd never seen before, that of someone calculating the years between us with quick math and coming up a little short. But she didn't say anything ugly or judgmental, she just started going through Rhee's file.

I also felt like I'd just stepped off a cliff.

I was someone's *mom*.

While I mentally processed that, Rhee asked questions. Lots and lots of questions. I learned things I didn't know about Rhee. She'd become sexually active at sixteen; she'd had three sexual partners. She had not had the HPV shot; she had three tattoos.

Dr. Clevens listened and took notes, nodding her head every now and again. She didn't ask me anything, really, other than to state my legal name and relationship and whether I had health insurance. I just told her whatever Rhee decided, I'd take care of her. Expenses weren't an issue.

We moved to an examination room. They drew vials of blood, made her pee in a cup, and did some other general tests on Rhee while she sat shivering in her robe. She looked so small, so afraid. I saw her as a little girl at that moment, during one Christmas, crawling into my bed. She was three. I was sixteen. She told me she loved me and that I made her feel safe. I sang her a song. "All My Loving" by the Beatles.

We were informed they would be back in a few minutes.

She sniffled, but I didn't see tears. Her hands were shaking.

"You okay?" I asked. It was our first moment alone since the waiting room.

"You said you didn't have a choice," she said.

"Rhee...I was thirteen."

"But if you did."

"Rhee."

"I mean it, Kate. If you were given the choice. If someone told you that you didn't have to have a baby, would you have gone along with it?"

"Jesus Christ, Rhee. I can't answer a question like that. I didn't even know what a condom was—I'd had my period for like a year. I hardly knew what happened to me."

"But when you found out. Why weren't you...I mean...you didn't *want* me."

"I didn't know it was *you*, but no. Of course I didn't want a baby. I'd never even been to a prom or a bonfire or a homecoming. I'd just stopped listening to The New Kids on the Block and had no proper musical tastes. My first thought was that I'd have to raise you, and that I wouldn't have a life."

"But Mom gave you a way out."

"It was not easy. It was *hell*. Do you think for a minute that she ever let me forget just exactly what a huge sacrifice she made for me? That she ever stopped giving me that look over her glasses, that I'd been the one to kick Jesus to the curb and run away? Rhee, she cut me out like some fucking sore. I was invisible."

"You did run away." Rhee looked at me intently with a stare that wasn't from my side of the family. "Repeatedly."

I sighed. She was right, of course. I'd been running since she was born. Before then, if I was honest. "If I'd known what an abortion was, I'd have probably thought Jesus would strike me down dead if he found out about it. Which of course he would, being all-knowing and everything. I read about it later, when you were a kid, and heard the phrase on some television show."

"But if Mom had taken you to a place like this. If you knew about it."

"I'd have made a shitty mother, Rhee. I didn't get an abortion, but...sometimes it's almost like I did. Aside from birthing you, I had no hand in bringing you up. We all lived a lie so long most of us believed it. I'm here for you, now. I've made a big mess of things. But I wasn't given a choice. Back then, I was just terrified and sure I was going to burn in hell forever. Things have changed. If I'd been your age, it would have been a harder decision."

"I don't want a kid," she said and buried her face in her hands. "But I don't want to run away from this, either. I knew better. I was stupid."

"No. You were human. Big difference." Her surprising insight brought tears to my eyes.

The doctor came in, holding a chart. "Let's take a look," she said, waving in the nurse and her ultrasound device. Rhee gave me a panicked look, but I squeezed her shoulder. We could do this.

There was a great deal of looking around, the smell of the ultrasound goo bringing back a dozen unwanted memories of my teen years. A few interesting vocalizations from the doctor as she placed and replaced the ultrasound wand.

"Well, it looks like what you have is a chemical pregnancy," the doctor said. "Sometimes that happens. It's a kind of false positive, an early miscarriage. Very common, and it shows up as a positive pregnancy test, but within days, you should bleed, and you'll be back on track soon."

The world spun, tilted. I was not going to be a grandmother in my thirties. And my daughter wasn't going to have an abortion. I didn't know what to think about any of it, but I held her hand as she asked a series of well-thought-out questions and consented to a new birth control prescription. The one Mom had got her had lapsed while Rhee had been in college. I'm not sure what would be worse if Dad ever found out, the birth control or the near termination. But I felt the child in the situation.

<hr>

WE PLAYED three gigs on the East Coast, and a week later Rhee called to tell me that she'd started bleeding, just like the doctor had told her. She was a mess. I arranged for her to take a semester off from school and invited her to come stay with us on the bus through the winter and spring. Internally, I wanted to come up with some sort of reason for her not to—say that the boys wouldn't take to her or she was too young or whatever. But she was twenty years old, and she'd never been out of Georgia. Not to mention she was right; I'd been running away forever. It was time to settle down. Or, at least, the rock-and-roll equivalent.

She turned down my offer, though. She wanted some time to herself. I could give her that, too.

# CHAPTER TWENTY-FIVE

The tour lumbered along. I didn't remember ever feeling so tired after gigs, and I wasn't sure if it was just that I was getting older or that I had just swigged to get past all the fatigue since time out of mind. I guess it's hard after a point to tell the difference between a hangover and exhaustion.

I could see I wasn't the only one. James was withdrawn, to say the least. It confused me. I'd have thought he, being the relative saint among us, would be the happiest with the new changes. But he was distant and wouldn't open up to me when I asked him what was going on. Tom thought it had something to do with the new lineup, that he was having trouble somehow getting on with Jon and Dee. But I knew; James has always been a consummate musician. If I had to guess, I'd have to say he just didn't feel confident in his own performances. He was always hardest on himself.

I wondered if that's just how he always was on tour. It was hard to remember considering I was never the most lucid in the past. There were a thousand things I passed over in favor of drinking, so I tried not to let it bother me.

In Cleveland, I met up with Jesse again.

Rhee had just texted me to let me know she was hoping to come out the following week as we dipped down into Texas for a few shows, then up the West Coast. I was looking forward to it beyond belief as the Midwest winter was really starting to get to me. Even ensconced in our warm bus, it was miserable. I was meandering around the bus, trying to get a better signal on my phone (my texts to her kept failing) when I heard someone call my name.

Jesse waved to me from across the street behind the club, one of the many Houses of Blues we'd found ourselves in.

"The first time I caught October Revival," he said, stuffing his hands deep down into his pockets and leaning forward. He appeared to be freezing. "I think it was filled to capacity. And it was a much bigger venue."

"Nice to see you too," I said playfully, hitting his shoulder with the back of my hand. "You sure know how to bolster a girl's confidence."

He grinned a little impishly. "You guys sounded awful though. Tom was wasted. You forgot half your vocals during 'One Way Home'—but you know what? It was still fantastic."

"Well. I'll try to screw it up a little more tonight. Maybe you'll have, I don't know, fond memories."

"Nah, I like you tons better now. You even sound like a proper band. I mean, no offense to Sara and to Kurt, but Jon is really something special. And Dee is solid. Really solid."

"I'm glad I have an impartial third party to make judgments. I still feel like I sound like shit every night."

He laughed at me like I was the dumbest girl in the world. Except also, somehow, charming.

"Listen. I came here to see you tonight, but I also wanted to invite you to my place tomorrow, if you're still going to be around—and judging by your schedule, you should be."

"Your place? You live in Cleveland? On purpose?"

Jesse shook his head. "Well, I'm from Kansas. So, Cleveland is practically New York City to me. Or it used to be. I've always liked it here. But anyway. I've got some friends I'd like you to meet."

"This feels weird," I said right away and regretted it. I'm constantly an ass around people. And the chances rise exponentially around men

I find attractive. Even though Jesse was nothing like my usual fare, he made me feel kind of dumb in the brain, in a nice way. "I mean. What sort of friends?"

"Music friends," he responded, innocently. "Listen, if you're busy or you don't want to come, that's fine. But it's not like a date. It's just friends. Though, if you conceded to a date, I'd like that, but something tells me you're not so keen."

I didn't know what to say so I muttered something about not being relationship material.

"Well. Just out of curiosity. When was the last time you had a normal relationship?" he asked, leaning close enough so I could smell his cologne, which I didn't want to like.

"Um. Never," I said, without hesitating. "My longest relationship was with Tom, and it lasted three hundred and twenty-four days. Not that I was counting."

"And since?"

I pursed my lips. My sex life since Tom had been random, at first, then nonexistent after the whole nearly dying from drinking thing. It was a little too personal for a cold Cleveland night, considering I had a show in a few hours.

"Jesse, I don't really know what to make of this."

"Neither do I," he admitted. "I just had to see you. What about you? What does it feel like?"

"I'll write you a song about it," I told him, with no idea why I said it. "And maybe I'll come visit you. Tomorrow."

He handed me his business card with the address scrawled on the back in enviably neat handwriting. He had come prepared.

"Either way," Jesse said, "I'm looking forward to the gig. It's always good to catch October Revival in the act."

I leaned over and kissed him on the cheek and staggered through the ice back to the House of Blues under the stare of Dee and James who were hanging out by the tour bus.

That night was amazing. Hands down the best show we'd had in years. I mean, nothing after was as good, or at least it never felt that way. Maybe it was just my brain buzzing on thoughts of Jesse. Which was possible. But even as we got off stage after the last encore, James was grinning from ear to ear, chattering about how it felt like a bolt of lightning rock. One of his turns of phrase, but totally something I understood.

Sometimes when you're caught in a musical high, it's like you hit some transcendent place of rock holiness, some incomprehensible Nirvana. You stop thinking about the chords and the notes and the sound guy and the acoustics—you suddenly become the music and the song, and it's like it's moving through you rather than coming from you. Tantric music. Something like that. I do a really shitty job of explaining things—James or Kurt could do it better—but it's all I got. Perfection. Epiphany. There we go. That's why I do it. For moments like that. If I close my eyes, I can still live in that moment now. Like a Faberge egg of blissful melodies.

JESSE'S HOUSE WAS IMPRESSIVE. I hadn't expected that. I guess I figured that he must suffer from the same inability to be a grownup due to drinking like I did. But instead I found the house alight, sending a golden glow out onto the snow and beckoning me to come inside. Seriously, it was like the house from *Home Alone*—quintessential Americana, festooned in the remnants of the New Year. It made Cleveland feel considerably less bleak.

I saw quite a few people moving around inside and many cars far nicer than my rental vehicle. I wondered who else would have come out here on purpose.

When I got to the door, a little kid answered, and I knew right away it was one of Jesse's. I remembered he said he had two, but he hadn't specified. This little girl had a shock of red curls that made her look younger than she was, but I could tell by her leggings and mock-grownup makeup that she was somewhere around eleven or so. He'd have had to been pretty young to have her, I figured, putting his age a few less than my own. I vaguely remembered him telling me he'd gotten married right out of high school, so I guess it made sense.

"Hi," she said and stepped back. "DAD!" She shouted it and started bouncing backward, grinning. "Kate Styx is here! KATE STYX IS HERE!" She shook her freckled fists in the air until Jesse emerged from the area I presumed was the kitchen. Seriously, the house was like the one in *Home Alone*. Rambling. Painfully American in design and taste. A brick monstrosity.

Jesse was wearing a tweed jacket over a plaid shirt and Chinos, looking like some poster boy for Polo. I had jeans and a blazer and still had my sunglasses on for God knows why. At least I'd showered and taken a sparkly scarf, but I still looked more like a department store Christmas tree after the season than a rock star.

"Ah, haha." Jesse watched his still jumping daughter. "Kate, welcome. Elaine is excited. She likes your music."

"Likes?" Elaine gasped as if she'd been betrayed by her father. "Dad!" She looked at me, halting her constant fidgeting. "I'm in love with Tom Chesley. And I want to play keyboard just like you."

I was aware of the awkward silence and grateful that Jesse grabbed my hands and started leading me away toward the sound of voices and tinkling glasses. Part of me was actually relieved to smell the tinge of liquor in the room as we entered the kitchen because I felt like people weren't, for once, accommodating me and my—our, I remembered—problem. Jesse was further out on his recovery than I was, but it didn't make it easier for him, I didn't think.

"You might want to say thank you," he whispered. I looked over my shoulder and obliged, watching Elaine's face brighten like sunshine through rainclouds.

"Sorry," I muttered. "Here, wait…"

I had put together some of my demos and a little song that I'd written the night before. Before second-thoughts took over, I pressed a flash drive into his hands. He'd heard the beginnings of a few of the songs in rehab; I figured he could listen to what became of those seeds.

He looked shocked at first, but then he asked, "Is this…?"

"For your ears only," I said with a wink.

He tried to say something more, and maybe even tried to kiss me, but I stepped away and gestured in the direction of the party. "Don't want to start any gossip now, do we?"

No one was in the kitchen, save a handful of people who appeared like they were there preparing the food rather than partaking, and he offered me a variety of soda. I accepted some Diet Coke and followed him out to the large room adjacent to the kitchen. I guess it was a three-season porch or something, but he'd set up heaters and lit up the backyard. The result was a sort of winter wonderland thing going on. The trees around the house bent down over it, so walking into the porch was a little like walking into the woods.

"What's the event?" I asked him, scanning the crowd for faces I might know and coming up empty-handed.

Faces turned toward me, and he whispered, "My thirtieth birthday."

I was going to say something about our age disparity—which wasn't enough to really matter other than making me feel vaguely proud of myself for attracting his interest—when I saw her.

"Just some old friends… colleagues… I used to have Christmas parties, but now that Stacie has the girls…"

Marla North was standing by the window, balancing a glass in one hand and talking animatedly to a guy with a mustache like a porn star. Her eyes flicked to mine for a second, and I felt my gut twist. My legs must have gone rigid because Jesse whispered some calming words to me and helped me down the two stairs.

"You…uh…"

"Marla falls into the old friend category," he said, not needing much of an explanation. "She's one of the first interviews I ever did. I'd never heard her music. But we hit it on. It wasn't long after…"

I did the quick math. "After her son…"

Marla North's only child, Aidan Moore, had died in a car accident about six years earlier. He was in his early twenties. Aidan was a model, and it was highly suspect he'd been part of a heroin deal gone wrong. Marla took another five years to write an album after. That's the one I listened to on endless loop when I was in rehab.

He nodded and started introducing me to people as a way to snap me out of my daze.

A few folks looked at me, surprised. People try to keep the things they hear from affecting their faces, but unless you're a really good actor, you let it slip. I'm sure two-thirds of the people there only had a vague idea of who I was—plenty of them were producers and reporters I'd heard of but had never seen in person. There were some impressive singer/songwriters there, too, and some local musicians.

I pretended to be cool and not act like some freaking stalker, but I couldn't stop looking for where Marla was sitting or standing or noting who she was talking to. I'd never have run into her in normal music circles—we aren't on the same label and don't even play remotely similar music. But it didn't change how much she meant to me. I never have picked up the piano if it wasn't for her. Her music, quite literally, kept me from killing myself after Rhee was born and prevented me from losing my mind when I was in rehab.

And she was standing a few feet away from me talking about snake charmers in India, the Mississippi twang in her accent still charmingly apparent. She never was one to talk much in interviews or during shows, so I hadn't realized how strong it was.

And the next minute Jesse was calling her over, and I was staring at her face to face, and Marla North told me she liked my music, and I almost fell over. Damn, but I wished Sara was standing there. She'd texted me a picture of her and Tori Amos not long after she left the band, a big fuck you one-upmanship attempt. I liked Tori, but she was no Marla.

"Jesse tells me you used to listen to my music," Marla said, her voice sweet and low. She put out a hand to touch my arm, her nails painted black, catching the light. I'd thought she was wearing all black, but as she came closer, I noticed it was deep green, like the eye of a peacock, iridescent all over. She was draped in shawls and lace, so it was hard to tell where she started and her outfit ended, but she looked good. Older than I'd seen in footage and pictures but still beautiful. Her dark hair was long as ever, pulled back and in a snood studded with pearls. Only Marla could pull off a snood and still rock harder than anyone.

I don't remember what I said, but a few sentences in, someone called her away and I slipped over toward Jesse.

"I hate you," I said to him. He laughed and excused himself when Elaine asked something, and for the first time in the night, I was really alone.

I'm happy to report I didn't do too badly, in case you're wondering. I was even nice to people. I had some good conversations, and they weren't all about music. I'd been catching up with television on Netflix during the tour, and I even had some insightful things to say about actors and show and movies and stuff. I was almost a decade out of the loop but not hopeless.

People were kind. They asked about the next album, most often, and I gave vague answers that we were working on something to follow up after the tour. But I realized, quite suddenly, I hadn't been thinking about the next album. That James and I hadn't talked about it at all. We hadn't jammed. We hadn't started plotting like we always did. I knew in that moment it was the source of his anger, his distance.

We were cracking, like Kurt said. The fissures already there. Well, shit.

I was returning from the bathroom when I met Marla in the kitchen. She was chatting with one of the cooks about the canapes, and she beckoned me over when I tried to slip by.

"What say we talk by the fire?" she asked.

Nodding dumbly, I followed.

The living room was pristine, set with oriental rugs and window treatments and well-appointed stuff on mantels. Overwhelmingly charming and clean. The dark leather couches squeaked under me as I tried to get comfortable. I didn't have anything to drink, so I stuffed my hands in my coat.

Marla went to the fire and poked it with the tongs, the flames deepening her wrinkles and giving her the appearance of some merry witch. It fit her whole image. But it was still weird for me.

"So how are you doing?" she asked me, taking a seat in the wing-back chair by the fire. The room still smelled like Christmas trees, and I found myself reminded of good Christmases as a kid. There were a few good memories there, even if they were few and far between.

"I'm okay," I said, not wanting to lie.

"I've only heard good things about the tour."

"It's…good…" I said, not sure what to make of her hearing things about my band. "Not the kind of attendance we used to get, but it's… good to be playing."

Marla smiled knowingly, closing her eyes for a second like she was taking in the sun. When she opened her eyes again, she confided, "It's where the strength to keep going comes from, you know. Knowing what you do moves people. So many times I've contemplated stopping. After Aidan. During the divorce. But eventually someone comes through, someone who believes in me more than I do… That voice on the phone, or in a letter, or just on social media, these days." She laughed.

I knew what she meant to some extent. But her situation was undeniably different. She didn't have Tom and James to lean on. It was just her. I didn't know how she'd managed it, year after year, with a two-decade career like she had. Granted, she never played stadiums, exactly, but it didn't mean her touring was any less taxing or difficult. Not to mention the need to always make something better than before.

"You were…really important to me…are really…" I said, tripping over my own lame attempts. "That sounds stupid. I'm sorry. I just…"

"Jesse told me a little," Marla said, casually. "He thinks a great deal of you, too, in case his piece in *Rolling Stone* wasn't a massive clue."

"That didn't go over too well with the rest of the band…"

"Well, fuck them, Kate. As far as I'm concerned, you've played wallflower for too long. Now, I've heard your music. I've heard your voice in the background. You can sing, dear. I'm just not sure why you choose not to."

"Because Tom Chesley is in my band," I said, not meaning to sound sarcastic. "Seriously. Have you heard him?"

"Of course! He's a stunning performer. But you don't have to give up your band to carve out your own corner."

I shrugged.

"Don't shrug at me," Marla said with a laugh but only to disarm the seriousness in her tone. She sobered very quickly. "You can't work out your demons if they're dancing there on stage with you, Kate. You've got to face them on your own terms. With your own weapons. With your own voice."

**Kurt:** Marla North seriously told you to STFU.
**Kate:** Pretty much.
**Kurt:** Still. You must be freaking out.
**Kate:** A little. I still don't really believe it happened.
**Kurt:** Did you take a picture?
**Kate:** Yeah, because that would have been the coolest thing I could have possibly done in the face of my idol.
**Kurt:** What else did she say?
**Kate:** She wants a demo of music. My music. She has a label.
**Kurt:** Are you going to do it?
**Kate:** I don't know. I don't think it would go over well.
**Kurt:** With you or with the demons?

# CHAPTER TWENTY-SIX

"WE WANT you to do another leg of the tour in the US—in the spring," Dusty directed in a conference call. "It's not that the first one wasn't great because it was. But maybe you need to cast the net a little wider. Go into the secondary markets where people might not be able to access you typically. It's just another fifteen gigs, but I think it'll make an impact."

We agreed, and when the laptop went dark, we stared at each other across the table on the tour bus. No one said anything. Fifteen shows wasn't a huge number, that wasn't the alarming factor. The alarming factor was that the label, in business speak, was disappointed in our showing. True, we hadn't sold out every single concert, but on the whole, they'd been received really well. The idea of doing some second-string suburban crawl wasn't thrilling.

James was chewing his nails; Tom was picking his ear. Dee was drumming to an invisible song on her knees, and Jon was avoiding eye contact by playing with his iPhone.

"Maybe...we..." Dee thought out loud, "umm...should add some new material to the mix? Just make it a little more exciting for the average fan."

I felt eyes on me, and I shook my head. "I've got stuff...but..."

I didn't mean to say the but part, and now even Jon was looking at me.

"But what?" Tom asked.

"It's not…uh…" I was not doing well.

James got up from the table, rolling his eyes. "She means it's not for us. It's not material for October Revival."

"Dude. I'm allowed," I insisted. "You gave me fucking permission. Not that I needed it."

James and I hardly fought these days, especially not in front of everyone. We'd had our spats over the years, but most of his ire had been saved for Kurt and Sara and Tom. Apparently I was on his radar now, which I sort of figured. Since his momentary kindnesses around Christmas, he'd been so distant and sulky I had no hope he'd come to me with anything less than fury.

As it was, I couldn't call it fury. Anger. Frustration. But more than anything, it was disappointment.

I felt it too.

"This isn't the time to be writing little ditties for your future solo project," he said. "If the label isn't happy with this tour, they're not going to up the next album."

"We haven't even talked about the next album, James," I offered.

"That's because you've been off with your sodding drama, and Tom's been off with his bloody Jesus, and everyone else is just so fucking thrilled to be breathing our air it really doesn't matter, now does it?" James snapped.

I winced and looked across to Dee who appeared a little bemused but unruffled. Jon, on the other hand, flushed a few shades.

"Get some air, James." Tom pointed to the door. We were parked somewhere in California, ready for the last three tours—in San Diego, Burbank, and San Francisco respectively.

"Stuff it, Tom," James said and left anyway.

When we heard the door hiss shut, Tom sighed and leaned back in his chair, putting his hands behind his head. "Well, that may actually be a record. I can't recall the last tour we had that he didn't fall apart at least two shows into it."

"We're better. Musically," I pointed out. "But he's not shepherding a drunk and a junkie around and sorting out the unconscious bodies, now is he?"

Dee frowned. "I can't say, since I wasn't there and all, but maybe he's feeling...a bit lost at sea, y'know? It sounds like what you're saying is that he used to have to take care of you both, and now he doesn't, and with the label pushing back..."

From the mouths of babes. Tom and I both stood up to go talk to James at the same time. I nodded and followed him out.

WE FOUND James sitting on the curb smoking a clove cigarette. Okay, something was exceptionally wrong if he was *smoking*. I wondered if I'd make it out alive.

"Well," he said, "you don't have to come out here. I'll apologize. We can go back to normal, like we always do."

"Normal?" I asked. "When the hell have we ever been normal?"

He almost laughed, and Tom sat down next to him. We could hear some of the roadies talking on the other end and smell the familiar scent of their cheap pot. Now that they weren't mooching off of us—I had promised Tom I wouldn't even bring that on the bus—they were left to their own devices.

Tom shoved James. "We should talk about the next album, mate."

"Should we?" James replied, very quickly. "Because to be quite honest, guys...I don't know. I just..."

And he started to cry, just like that. The label's lack of confidence in us had been the straw to break the camel's back. James just lost it, right there, like I'd never seen him do. Through all the crazy drama going back years, he'd been the one to keep his shit together; he'd been strong for us and met with the studio execs when we were too strung out or drunk or missing. And we hadn't ever thanked him for it.

Even as we sat there next to him, we didn't know what to say. Tom looked at me, and I knew he was thinking the same as me.

"You've done good, man." I looped my arm through his. "You've worked hard at this. Harder than either of us."

"It isn't fair," Tom said. "What we did. What we've done. But we're just so bloody used to you running the show that..."

James shook his head, tried to say something, and just made a choking noise I knew as him desperately trying to get his cool together.

We waited for him, Tom and me. I don't think either of us wanted to put words or thoughts into the air for fear of taking all the oxygen out of the conversation. James didn't say it explicitly, but we could feel it; for the last few years, it had always been about us. Sure, he'd had his moments of glory, but overall, he'd been the one shoved to the sidelines more because he'd simply behaved. You never read about James trashing hotel rooms or knocking up co-eds or being found in a gutter half-dead. I remembered how angry he'd gotten over the *Rolling Stone* piece a few months back that Jesse did, and it made a lot of sense now, thinking how he had reacted. No one had ever done a piece on him, and he'd done everything right. Or wrong. I don't know. The rules of rock and roll defy logic, and in his case, I think he was penalized for being too responsible and un-fucked up.

It was surprisingly chilly for California, and I wished I'd brought a sweater. But maybe the chills weren't just because of the weather. Maybe I knew what was happening. It's like one of those movie montages, y'know? I could hear Kurt telling me the band was cracking, things were falling apart. My heart was beating fast, and I couldn't catch my breath. Flashes of me in rehab. Flashes of us arguing. Then on stage, then in bed with Tom...

"I just need a break," James said, finally, as if the idea had just dawned on him. "I'm sorry...I'm just out of it. I can't sleep. I can't eat. I feel like a ghost."

Tom and I exchanged glances. He pursed his lips, holding back his own tears.

Neither of us said no. Neither of us put together an argument.

"We'll do whatever you need, mate," Tom assured him.

"You don't need to be sorry," I said. "I'm the one. We're the ones who should be sorry."

"No, it's not that… It's gone. The joy I had. The drive. The passion. And I'm worried I'm never going to get it back if I don't step away for a while."

We hugged him, from both sides, huddled on the curb. From the inside of the bus I could hear Jon practicing "Lost and Loving," and I finally started to cry too.

# CHAPTER TWENTY-SEVEN

You'd think that the rest of the tour would have been horrible, that we wouldn't have been able to perform. But it wasn't bad at all. In fact, I'd say James was happier and funnier and better than he'd been in a long time. I could see the relief in his face. We'd set him free from something that had been eating at him for nearly a decade, and he was finally seeing something at the horizon beyond more studio time and more touring and more babysitting.

It's funny. Sure, Tom and I have had our setbacks since, but we both beat our biggest demons. Once we were okay on our own, once we didn't need James to be our conscience and our manager and our wrangler, it's like he had the time to examine himself and see all the work he needed to do to be happy. Sure, he wasn't going to find it in Jesus or a renewal of self-worth, but his journey was just starting. In a way, I envied him.

The word we used was hiatus. In that way, Kurt was wrong. It's not like October Revival never got together again. We knew we'd record more albums, we'd collaborate, we'd keeping talking and working together. But each of us had to strike out on our own. Dee and Jon were in demand and had plenty of gigs if they wanted, but both promised to make themselves available if need be. I wasn't going to hold them to it. Sure, we'd "discovered" them. In Dee's case, it was just a matter of time. In Jon's case, this was just the beginning of his musical career. If he wanted it.

I bought a house. In spite of all our traveling over the last year, I found the one place I kept thinking about was Nashville. James was planning on returning there, too, after he spent some time in India visiting his father's family and then touring Japan. He wanted to travel and to experience things outside of his life with October Revival.

Since the end of the tour, he hadn't called me, but we'd had plenty of text exchanges.

---

**James:** And there's another bit I forgot to mention.
**Kate:** Oh?
**James:** Yes, there's a girl. I mean a woman. I'd like you to meet her. Her name is not Sara.
**Kate:** LOL. Good. Otherwise I might have to drag myself over there and punch you in the face.
**James:** Though Sara did call me a few weeks ago. I blocked her number.
**Kate:** Wise move.
**James:** Anyway. She's someone I met through Dusty, believe it or not. She's a studio tech for Marvelous Studios, and we have tons to talk about. I'm really enjoying spending time with her.
**Kate:** Good stuff. When you're ready to scare her off, I'd love to have dinner with you both.
**James:** You ought to bring that Kansas chap of yours.
**Kate:** We're not dating, doofus.
**James:** You are in utter denial. But don't forget to invite me to the wedding.
**Kate:** HAR HAR

---

AT FIRST, it was really eerie living alone in the house. Though as spring passed and the streets came alive with flowers and birds and woke up from the long, brown winter, I started to enjoy it. I found myself perusing antique shops and flea markets and actually picking up eccentric art to put on my walls and in the entryway. I'd never taken the time to care before, and surprisingly, I found it very satisfying. I'd spend weeks finding the right place for this statue or that sculpture, and before I knew it, I was setting up rooms with themes and inspirations.

I even made myself a little studio in one of the spare rooms, working with Jeff and Ian from our studio to put it together. It didn't have to be perfect, but I wanted a retreat in the middle of my house, a meta escape. To the best of my memory, I made it like the room Tom had built for me at the Oast, the same blues and beiges. I ordered some paintings online from a local Lamberhurst painter and hung them in there too. I wanted to bring as much of it to me as possible. I still dreamed of walking in the fields and climbing up to the castle.

I spent most of my days playing music, by myself. Occasionally I met with session musicians when I was trying to work on something beyond my own skill set, but mostly I just enjoyed the time.

James sent me random pictures and texts and even postcards. Tom called at six o'clock every Sunday evening, and we usually talked for an hour or so. He was working with a Christian group in the UK called Summer's Grace, singing a few tracks for them, and really enjoying his time. He hadn't had any setbacks. He was planning a trip home to see his parents in the summer.

Jon went back to Bristol. I didn't hear from him for almost two months, but he wrote me to let me know he had started a local group, and they were planning to send their demos out and wanted to know if I had any business suggestions. Of course he was still available if we needed him, but he wanted something "genuinely" himself for a while. I could understand that, late-bloomer as he was.

And Dee played lots of music. She was often in Nashville with Starflower Matinee, the country-rock fusion band I'd introduced to her. All girls about her age, but decidedly Southern. She loved it, and they thought her Britishisms were hilarious. She was planning to go on tour with them in the fall if we were all still on hiatus. But I didn't hold my breath. I didn't want to hold her back.

It was almost Easter when Rhee called.

"Hey, Kate…"

It turns out she wanted to come live with me for a while. She'd gone back home and had told Dad—something I wouldn't have done in a million years. He was furious at first, but she said once he got over his desire to hunt me down and kill me, he came to accept what had happened. I still didn't know what I felt about it. I had helped her have the choice I hadn't had…but if I had, I wouldn't have known her at all. Sure, she was just a fledgling person, but she was growing and changing, and I was finding that more and more essential to my own understanding of myself and life and everything after.

"I'm thinking of transferring schools, and majors, and…well, just taking some time off," she said over the phone. Her nose sounded stuffy. "Do you still have that apartment in Nashville?" I'd told her I'd moved back, but I hadn't given her many of the details for fear I sounded like I was dumping my own life issues on her. I knew she needed space.

So Rhee moved in. I had two bedrooms for her to choose from, and she chose the one I'd decked out in lemony yellow and green. It overlooked the street and had one of those built-in benches in the window. I mean, it was a room meant for a little girl. I knew she wasn't a little girl, but in some ways having her live with me felt that way. Sure, we're a little more than a decade apart. But our life experiences are hugely different. I felt old. Motherly. Sage. It was nice compared to my usual opinion.

I wrote more music, occasionally sent songs to Jesse. He served as my general critique partner, helping me hone out my own sound apart from October Revival. We developed our own language during the process and grew close. I'd never let in anyone else into my writing process that closely, and it felt more intimate than anything

I'd shared with James who was, as he admitted, in awe of my writing and composing and was great at improving upon things without directly changing them. It's hard to explain.

Jesse showed up for Easter, explaining he didn't have the holiday with his kids and wanted to see me.

He arrived early one April morning just as Rhee and I were sitting down to our morning coffee ritual. She was playing some new music from her iPod, and I was trying to prevent my snarky comments from dampening her enjoyment (we rotated morning playlists to keep the peace).

I introduced them a little awkwardly and quickly showed Jesse to his room.

While Rhee and I waited for him, she tried not to smile. We heard him coming down the stairs, and she whispered, "You did not tell me he was *cute*."

I waved her off, embarrassed.

We sat in the parlor—to my knowledge, I'd never used it as a proper parlor, as we usually settled ourselves in the living room where the TV was. I put a log into the fireplace and made more coffee, and Rhee busied herself in the kitchen promising we'd have scones in a half hour.

"Scones and coffee," Jesse said. "Reminds me of Lamberhurst."

"She's in a cooking zone right now," I explained. "She's between majors. Thinking of going to culinary school or something. But I won't complain, even if my jeans do."

I realized how stupid that sounded but just sipped more coffee instead of explaining it away. See? I can learn things.

"You look amazing, Kate." He was seated across from me, leaning forward with his elbows on his knees, dressed in a plaid button-down and loafers and jeans so new they looked like a pair of dress pants. I don't think casual is in that man's vocabulary.

"Thanks," I said. "I've been walking. Funny. Exercise is kind of nice, especially when it's so pretty outside."

"And this place is something else. I...had no idea you had an entire house. I was thinking apartment, but when I saw the address on my GPS was in an actual neighborhood. Didn't you tell me once you'd rather die than live in a house?"

I laughed. "Well, it was weird at first. I'm not Holly Homemaker. But I've made it my own, I think. I like it."

"I never pegged you for a Mid-century girl."

"Mid-what?" I asked.

He laughed. "The style you've picked for most of your furniture. It's Mid-century style. Eames. Saarinen. Those folks. In the sixties, they were at the forefront of furniture design, and I've always thought it was the last hurrah before furniture really hit the skids. Beautiful wood. Clean lines."

I examined at the coffee table. I'd just liked the way it looked. "Well. I hate swirls and flowers and whirly things," I said, knowing none of the terms of the design I didn't like but figuring I'd make a go of it anyway. "So this seemed to work. Glad you like it."

"I've been thinking of redecorating the house in Cleveland, but I don't know."

"You didn't decorate?" I asked, and immediately realized how silly the question was. Of course, it had been the house he'd shared with his wife.

He gave me a sad smile. "I was keeping it just the way Julie left it. For posterity. For stability. For the kids. I guess I thought if the house was the same when they came to visit me, they'd want to come more. But it turns out, I'm a pretty boring dad."

"They love you," I said. I'd seen it firsthand. But his kids were quickly departing that period in their lives where they'd adore their father. Soon he'd have teens.

"Elaine has her first boyfriend. I'm horrified. And she doesn't want to come visit me in Cleveland. So I'm thinking I might be selling the house soon. It's not a big mortgage, but then again, it's a house I tend to avoid. It's weird to have a place that feels haunted by people that are still alive."

"I'm sorry," I said. I was glad for the relative blank slate of my house. There weren't many memories in it yet. "Maybe that's why I avoided houses for so long. The only houses I remembered living in were horrible. But this place feels different."

"I like Nashville," he said. "I can see why you came back. The music is everywhere…"

I nodded, looking out the window at the tulip magnolia bobbing in the wind. "Which is what I like. It's all music, all the time. It's what people expect you do. And it isn't overwhelming like LA or New York. Though I've got to say, I do miss it sometimes…"

Rhee came in with a plate of fluffy oat scones, beaming with pride. "Kate's been letting me take care of grocery shopping," she declared. "You should have seen the kitchen when I got here. It was one step away from a college dorm."

We talked about Rhee and her culinary plans, and she told Jesse she was thinking of getting her own apartment in the city once things got underway. I didn't want her to go, but I didn't tell her that in as many words. Sometimes, at night, I'd freeze up thinking about being in an empty house again.

I was working on my second scone when Jesse started talking about music again.

"So, I have something to confess," he said to me, looking guilty.

Rhee started texting someone and excused herself. I reminded her about our dinner plans, and she said she planned to do some shopping in the afternoon for something to wear. It was surreally normal.

"Confessions," I said. "Sounds grave."

"Well," he laughed. "I haven't been honest with you."

I almost choked on my scone, feeling like he was going to hit me with something awful. Okay, we weren't dating. But that didn't mean I hadn't thought about it. I had little dream sequences that involved spending lots of time with him and maybe included a wedding. Maybe.

"Nothing…catastrophic, I don't think," he said, coming to sit next to me.

"Okay…"

"So. Your songs. I sent some to Marla."

"You *what?*" I asked. I knew my face was beet red; I could feel my heart whooshing in my ears.

"She begged me practically. You never sent her anything."

"It wasn't ready."

"If it was up to you, it never would be."

"Touché… But still!"

"She wants to produce your solo album. She's got her own label. She'd love to sing backup…"

He said some other things, but I couldn't concentrate on his words. When I recovered enough to string words together, I found myself making a ton of excuses.

"Jesse, why are you doing this for me?"

"Because I can't stop thinking about you, Kate. I told you that. I know my life's a mess, but I think we have a shot. But even if you don't think we do…"

"I didn't say that."

This elicited a wry smile. "Even if you don't," he repeated, "the *music* is important. It's the best part of you. And your demo… Jesus, Kate. You've got to make time for it. You've got to know I'm not shitting you when I say it left me covered in goosebumps from head to toe."

I bit my lips trying to keep from a smug smile. I wasn't sure what made me giddier, that he was still interested in me or that he loved my music. Maybe it was both.

But I would never let that kind of thought escape my mouth. So I delayed. "I just feel like there's so much dangling. So much left to process…before I do this…"

"So write it down." Jesse took my hands, squeezed my fingers. "Sit back and write it down. Get it out. On paper. Stop letting it echo around in your head like bad reverb."

"I don't want to write a fucking memoir," I said. "I'm not that kind of person."

"So write it for someone else. Write it for me. For Rhee."

"I don't even know where to start," I argued.

Jesse smiled and reached into his breast pocket. There was a small notepad there, old-fashioned as he was, and a pen. He scribbled something down and then showed it to me.

The words read: "Chapter One: Tom Chesley gets saved."

**THE END**

# ACKNOWLEDGMENTS

This book would not be possible without music. I am forever indebted to my parents, who survived the 60s and 70s and came through not only with amazing stories of their own lives as musicians, but the music that went with them. My sister and I grew up in a house filled with music, access to any instrument we needed, and love and singing and joy in the process.

Thank you as well to the many musicians I've had the pleasure of playing with throughout the course of my life. I painted hints of some of you in the members of October Revival. I'm also grateful for the studio sessions at Derek Studios in Dalton, MA, and the first-hand experience of watching songs take shape and become pieces of art. I'm thankful for the rehearsals and recitals and trips to the record store. And for Dynamite Music in Northampton where I was cleverly steered toward The Beatles' *Rubber Soul* at just the right time in my life. And, of course, for Nick Hornby's *High Fidelity* and *About a Boy*, which showed me that fiction and rock music don't have to be mutually exclusive.

I am also indebted to The Beatles, Fleetwood Mac, Keane, Mumford and Sons, and the Civil Wars, for serving as real-life influences for October Revival's relationships and sound. Rock music is stuffed full of love and passion, to say nothing of its connections to gospel, faith, and magic.

To John Hartness who took a chance on this manuscript and asked, upon reading it, "Where the hell did this come from?"

And lastly, to my first readers, Karen, Dorothy, and Michael. It took a while to see this come together, but you agreed this story needed to be told. Thanks for believing in me, in Kate, and in October Revival.

October Revival – Catalog

- *Strife Round the Bend (2005)*
- *Blindside (2007)*
- *Lester Hotel (2008)*
- *Something Else (2010)*

Original members of October Revival, ca. 2005

- Tom Chesley, lead vocals, tambourine
- James Vayne, lead guitar, vocals
- Kate Styx, keyboard, vocals
- Sara Plummer, bass, vocals
- Paul Crowse, drums, percussion

# ABOUT THE AUTHOR

Natania Barron was born singing, so her parents tell her. The #1 song on the day she was born was "Bette Davis Eyes" by Kim Carnes.

Natania's love of music began in the womb; her parents and godparents were in a band called Serenade in the 70s, and so her childhood was filled with music, particularly punctuated with the deep harmonies of the Beatles, Fleetwood Mac, and Crosby, Stills, Nash, and Young. It was inevitable that she carry on the family tradition, and so she began playing guitar at the age of eleven and her dad helped her figure out almost every song on Counting Crow's *August and Everything After*. She soon started her own band with her sister, Llana, performing for their grandparents and at school functions. She also played in her family band, John and the Lord's Sandals, throughout high school and has no shame because her folks are rock stars, and her dad's guitar solos are a legend. Other groups in that era included Box of Cosmos, Riptide, Penfold, and many others consisting of essentially the same group of musicians who couldn't settle on a name.

In the ensuing years, Natania has continued to play music in between writing gigs. Her current lineup includes a guitar named Gemma, a concert ukulele named Astrid, a concertina named Ruby, and a keyboard that doesn't have a name. When she's not trying to figure out how to play Tori Amos songs on the guitar, she's a speculative fiction writer, a global marketing director, a mom, and one very lucky daughter.

Her desert island albums are: The Beatles, *Rubber Soul;* Neko Case, *Middle Cyclone;* Lorde, *Pure Heroine*; Gillian Welch, *Time (the Revelator);* Crosby, Stills, Nash, and Young, *Deja Vu;* Florence + the Machine, *How Big, How Blue, How Beautiful;* Tracy Chapman, *Tracy Chapman;* They Might Be Giants, *John Henry;* Led Zeppelin, *II*; Keane, *Perfect Symmetry;* Travis, *The Invisible Band*; Sia, *This is Acting*; Janelle Monae, *Dirty Computer*

"Music self-played is happiness self-made." - They Might Be Giants